RACHILDE was the pen name of Marguerite Vallette-Eymery (1860–1953), one of the most important writers of the Decadent Movement. Her most famous work includes the novels *Monsieur Vénus* (1884), *La Marquise de Sade* (1887), and *La Jongleuse* (1900). She also wrote a 1928 monograph on gender identity, *Pourquoi je ne suis pas féministe* (*"Why I am not a Feminist"*).

BRIAN STABLEFORD's scholarly work includes *New Atlantis: A Narrative History of Scientific Romance* (Wildside Press, 2016), *The Plurality of Imaginary Worlds: The Evolution of French roman scientifique* (Black Coat Press, 2017) and *Tales of Enchantment and Disenchantment: A History of Faerie* (Black Coat Press, 2019). He has translated more than three hundred volumes from the French, mostly in the genres of *roman scientifique*, *contes de fées* and Romantic and Symbolist fiction. His recent fiction includes the visionary science fiction novel *The Revelations of Time and Space* (2020) and its sequel *After the Revelation* (2021); the last in his long series of "Tales of the Genetic Revolution," *The Elusive Shadows* (2020); and the comedy fantasy *Meat on the Bone* (2021), all published by Snuggly Books.

RACHILDE

THE PRINCESS
OF DARKNESS

TRANSLATED AND WITH AN INTRODUCTION BY
BRIAN STABLEFORD

THIS IS A SNUGGLY BOOK

ISBN: 978-1-64525-125-5

CONTENTS

INTRODUCTION

L A PRINCESSE DES TÉNÈBRES, here translated as *The Princess of Darkness*, was originally published by Calmann-Lévy in 1896. The manuscript had been submitted with the signature "Jean de Chilra," but a printer's error resulted in the title page bearing the name Jean de Chibra. The confusion was increased when Jean Lorrain, the author's voluntary publicist, published a critique of the novel in his regular column in *Le Journal*,[1] attributing it to "Jean de Childra", bungling what he knew to have been intended to be an anagrammatic pseudonym, the author's more usual signature being "Rachilde." One of the author's close friends, Alfred Jarry, pointed out Lorrain's error in a piece of his own, but to little avail. The correction has, however, some slight significance in suggesting that Jarry must have discussed the novel with its author while it was in progress. Presumably, he also discussed his own work with her, perhaps in her weekly salon, then held in the offices of the *Mercure de France*; she and her husband, Alfred Vallette (1858-1835) had hosted

---

1 "Les Princesses des Ténèbres" 19 April 1896; tr. as "Princesses of Darkness" in the similarly-titled Snuggly Books collection.

a private performance of his play *Ubu roi*, a year in advance of its sensational première in December 1896. It is probably not a coincidence that, of all Rachilde's novels, *La Princess des ténèbres* is the one in which she extrapolated the Symbolism to which she was deeply committed furthest into the surreal (or, in Jarry's own terminology, the pataphysical). The novel was swiftly reprinted with her more familiar signature, but that did not save it from the relative obscurity into which it was soon relegated, perhaps because many of its readers found its symbolism indecipherable or uncomfortable.

The author's real name was Marguerite Eymery (1860-1953), which she often embellished with a *particule*, although she compounded the confusion in 1889 when she married Vallette, and was known thereafter formally as Madame Vallette and informally, but more frequently as Rachilde, a signature she had invented for her first publications in her teens. She retained that pseudonym in the great majority of her literary works and in her capacity as Vallette's associate when he became the editor of the *Mercure de France* in 1890. For the next forty years she was the periodical's co-editor, and she did as much to shape and guide it, and the publishing imprint associated with it, as her husband, although she kept a relatively low profile, perhaps in deliberate compensation for the notoriety that she had gone out of her way to cultivate in the decade before the marriage, when her salon had become one of the principal crucibles of the "Decadent" offshoot of the Symbolist Movement.

Vallette was one of the most conspicuously respectable and staid members of that small community, but prior to her marriage Rachilde had flaunted her disdain for convention, becoming for a while one of the Parisian "amazons" who made a fetish out of dressing in male attire. She caused a sensation when she published her novel *Monsieur Vénus* (1884), which was prosecuted as pornography in Belgium, where it was initially published, resulting in a conviction and a sentence of two years' imprisonment imposed *in absentia.* The scandal also resulted in her temporary banishment from the most important of the other salons she attended regularly, that hosted by "Georges de Peyrebrune," the most prominent female novelist in Paris, who had attempted to adopt her as a protégée, perhaps in the hope of serving as a more salutary influence than Jean Lorrain, whose laudatory newspaper article nicknaming Rachilde "Madame Salamandre" helped boost her initial success and that of *Monsieur Vénus.*

Georges de Peyrebrune—who called herself Mathilde de Peyrebrune in private life, although the patronymic was invented—probably thought, when Rachilde got married to Vallette and settled down, that she had succeeded in exerting that salutary influence in her protégée, having anticipated the reform in a novelette presented as a psychoanalytical character study, "Une Décadente"[1] (1886; tr. as "A Decadent Woman"), but the account given in the novelette of the psychology of the heroine's reformation does not seem to fit Rachilde at all, who succeeded in maintaining the apparent perversity of her own character despite toning it down somewhat in her life and work. The heroine

---

1 In the *Revue Bleue* (20-27 March).

of *La Princesse des ténèbres* undergoes a psychological metamorphosis of her own, partly occasioned by marriage, but it has nothing in common with the one imagined by Peyrebrune. It does not reflect Rachilde's transformation either, but the novel contains many echoes of her own self-examination; the author frequently referred to herself as a paradoxical character with lycanthropic tendencies and she was later to write another novel, *Le Meneur des louves* [The She-wolf Leader] (1905) exploring that symbolic analogy even more melodramatically.

"Une Décadente" was not the only commentary on Rachilde's personal philosophy and behavior disguised as fiction in the period of her greatest notoriety; in 1887 a short novel entitled *La Vierge-réclame* [The Advertised Virgin] signed "G. d'Estoc" was issued, advertised as the first volume of a (fictitious) series of *Les Gloires malsaines* [Unhealthy Glories], which is a slanderous caricature of Rachilde's biography and work penned by one of her fellow amazons, who had formerly been a good friend. "Estoc" apparently felt that certain aspects of the heroine of *Monsieur Vénus* were an insult to her, and took a savage delight in asserting that Rachilde's claims to virginity, publicized by Maurice Barrès in his introduction to *Monsieur Vénus*, were false, although much publicity had been given to the relentless pursuit mounted against her for a year by the notorious rake Catulle Mendès, apparently without success (although Mendès claimed that he was the victim of her infatuation rather than *vice versa*). Some of her other male friends, including Jean Lorrain, with whom she attended costumed balls, and Maurice Barrés, were

10

reputedly homosexual, and posed no threat to her perverse reputation.

The truth of such matters was impossible to determine in the *fin de siècle* and remains impossible now, further confused rather than clarified by the profusion and inconsistency of Rachilde's autobiographical writings and continual plundering of her own ideas in her fiction. There is no shortage of commentary on her life and work but it is entirely based on unreliable sources, much of it consisting of rumor heavily polluted by fantasy. Jean Lorrain took delight in portraying her as sex-obsessed and sexually perverted, and her fiction sometimes went to considerable lengths to lend sly support to that allegation, but her work also features many characters who, like the central character of *La Princesse des ténèbres*, have a pathological horror of sex, psychologically transformed into hallucinatory fantasies that cry out for analysis as symptoms of neurosis or psychosis. Like many Symbolists, Rachilde was intensely and understandably interested in contemporary developments in proto-psychoanalysis, publicized in the late 1880s by weekly public lectures given the clinical asylums of Paris by such luminaries as Benjamin Ball and provided with sensational publicity by Max Nordau's *Entartung* (1892-3; tr. into English as *Degeneration*), written in Paris by a German, whose conclusion that all writers were insane, and that French Symbolists were the most insane of all, was perhaps not entirely engendered by scientific objectivity.

Rachilde was not unsympathetic to that judgment, and was quite content to analyze *Monsieur Vénus* as "the most marvelous product of hysteria arrived at the paroxysm of chastity in vicious milieu"—a capsule description even more appropriate to *La Princesse des ténèbres*, although the "hysteria" experienced by Madeleine is more complex, and arguably more interesting than anything experienced by the heroine of the earlier novel. Whether or not she was actually a virgin when she wrote *Monsieur Vénus*, as she and Maurice Barrès claimed, she certainly was not by the time she wrote *La Princesse des ténèbres*. She had borne a child, named Gabrielle, on 25 October 1889 some months after her marriage, but she seems to have had little contact with her thereafter and reference sources mostly maintain a stubborn silence in her regard, although Geneanet records that Gabrielle Vallette married in 1911 and did not die until 1984.

What relevance Rachilde's own marriage and motherhood had to the marriage and near-motherhood of Madeleine in *La Princesse des ténèbres* is purely a matter for speculation, but it is difficult to imagine that Alfred Vallette and (eventually) Gabrielle read the novel with any great pleasure, although Rachilde's parents, by whom she felt neglected and whom she accused of abuse, probably took even less pleasure in reading the cruel representations of Madeleine's father and Aunt Julia. She was, of course, perfectly entitled to assure them that the work was manifestly fictitious and to point out that its characterization of its protagonist is also far from flattering, but every author knows that her nearest and dearest are always inclined to find representations of themselves in her work, rightly or wrongly, and to take offence. In essence, *La Princesse des ténèbres* is a neo-Gothic novel featuring a haunted house and a family curse, in which the fact that the "apparitions" have materialistic explanations does not make them any less menacing, or the narrative any less doom-laden.

Jean Lorrain points out in his analysis of the text, that the content of Madeleine's hallucinations owe a good deal to one of the great works of French scholarly fantasy, an essay by the Romantic historian Jules Michelet called *La Sorcière* (1862; tr. as *Witchcraft and Sorcery*), which adopted the assumption that many of the victims of the late Medieval witch-trials really were "witches" who had made a tacit or explicit symbolic pact with the devil—but asserted that the psychology of their "Satanism" was entirely virtuous and heroic, in an age of fervent Church tyranny whose fanatical adherents were enthusiastic to torture and burn those they accused of being their enemies. Lorrain found in Madeleine a new model of the witch as *femme fatale*, linking her to a number of other contemporary literary representations and hailing her as a potential role-model for future portraits:

"Princesses of darkness . . . Jules Bois or Michelet said somewhere that the long amorous soliloquy of woman with herself created the devil. The devil is woman's own desire having taken form, her alerted sensuality awakening her and charming her; the evil influence of the beyond is her own troubled and mysterious soul offered to her soul in a mirror, and the princess of darkness springs forth spontaneously, like an accursed flower, into a realm created by her: hysteria—that frightening paroxysm of instincts and sexuality, a disconcerting deformation of femininity itself, in which the obsessed victim struggles, simultaneously sovereign and victim of the most delirious and baleful visions."

That judgment echoes the text so precisely that Rachilde could have offered it herself—and might have done so, in conversation with Lorrain. Even so, Lorrain's subsequent identification of Madeleine as a *femme fatale* comparable to several other contemporary literary images is not entirely correct. If Madeleine is a *femme fatale* at all, in regard to Edmond Sellier, the fault is far more his than hers, and she suffers for it far more than he does—a much more accurate reflection of the sexual politics of the day than the vast majority of *femme fatale* stories (mostly penned, of course, by male authors). The most original and interesting aspect of the story is not its analysis of the hypothetical psychology of a "witch" but its representation of "the demon," Hunter—or, more accurately, the not-completely-split personality of the handsome Hunter and his dog Silence.[1] That stubbornly-enigmatic characterization was strikingly original in 1896 and remained almost unique thereafter, although the clear influence of the novel can be seen in two other novels written a generation later: Hélène Picard's *Sabbat* (1923) and Sylvia Townsend Warner's *Lolly Willowes; or The Loving Huntsman* (1926). Neither is identical in the particular quality of its sympathetic Satanism, but both have a similar genetics, even though the latter is a tongue-in-cheek feminist comedy of manners which strives to make its deliberate perversity as amiable as possible.

---

1 Rachilde's relocation to Paris in 1880 or thereabouts from the Dordogne was reportedly financed by her father selling his pack of hunting hounds.

It is significant that Hélène Picard was a lifelong "neurasthenic" who was encouraged to write *Sabbat* by her close friend Colette, who had been befriended at the beginning of her career by Rachilde. Colette persuaded Picard to write it in the hope that the exercise might prove therapeutic, much as Colette's own writing of the Claudine novels, at the behest of her then-husband Henri Gauthier-Villars (alias Willy) had helped to ameliorate her own "hysteria". *Sabbat* was published by J. Ferenczi, who was Rachilde's principal publisher in the 1920s. Picard's Satan and Warner's "loving huntsman" are just as enigmatic as Rachilde's Hunter, but their character is softened somewhat and the lies of which they are the father tend more to the white than the black, while Hunter remains as stubbornly resistant to brighter dye as Aunt Julia's poisonous wall-hangings. All analogues of Satan are treacherous by definition, but as a model of the *homme fatale*, Hunter is gifted with a very special and elaborate perversity, just as his author was as a model of fatal feminism. He remains, therefore, an ultimate archetype of which later carbon copies are faded or adulterated. The same could be said of his creator and her calculatedly perverse brand of feminism—a philosophy and a crusade that she refused to endorse, publishing a long essay explaining and justifying her refusal.

La Princesse des ténèbres is not one of Rachilde's best-known novels, and it remains very hard to find today, but it is certainly one of her best and is one of the finest novels to emerge from the French Symbolist Movement of the *fin-de-siècle* in its heyday. Its Symbolism is not easy to decode, at least in its fine detail—the role of

Silence is particularly resistant to easy interpretation—but that is deliberate, and arguably essential to the exercise. The novel is certainly a striking and daring work, because rather than in spite of the fact that some of its motifs are calculated to alienate readers as well as to challenge them, although any connoisseur of perversity is bound to savor it and to think it precious—even those who are not fortunate enough to be female and creatively neurotic.

This translation was made from the copy owned by the London Library, which I first read many years ago, although I refrained from translating it at the time, not expecting to live long enough for it to fall into the public domain. The task was still undone when I resigned my membership in the Library, having been forced by ill-health to relocate to Swansea. I am very grateful to Daniel Corrick, who obtained a one-day pass to the library in order to have the text scanned, and to Brendan Connell for undertaking to keep the translation in cold storage until April 2023.

—Brian Stableford, November 2021

THE PRINCESS
OF DARKNESS

I

THE flame of the lamp, tormented by an air current, flickered singularly, and Madeleine had to get up in order to go and close the door; but she did not have the courage to close the window, because the odors of freshly-cut hay were arriving from outside. She only noticed, as she went past that window, that the wooden bar where the casements joined—a very old-fashioned system—formed a cross with the nearest branch of a tree, and, in the very center, at the imprecise point of intersection of the arms of the shadow cross, an enormous moon was resplendent, ringed by a light halo.

The deserted countryside retained the slightly bleak appearance that it usually had. The garden, bordered by a little walled terrace and frail hazel trees reminiscent of poor torn curtains, extended its strip of bushy box funereally, conserving the same physiognomy of a provincial cemetery. The road still unfurled its shroud of bright dust, spectrally white, and its poplars still had the rigid bearing of tall fleeing monks. Always rising menacingly, the stony hill was crowned with somber rocks. Yes, the hill was truly disquieting . . . it gave an impression of bitter desolation, unconsoled by the perfume of the meadows.

Madeleine attended to her lamp, which was sputtering as it lowered. She sat down again next to the crude massive table and extended a dazzling white cloth with a tranquil gesture, which she folded over. She liked to work thus in the evening, far from them, and sometimes, in order better to persuade herself that she was alone in the world, she shot the bolts. On the sparkling cloth was a pair of scissors whose blades shone with red and blue gleams alternately, according to whether they were reflecting the light of the lamp or the moonlight. Without taking account of her movements, the young woman looked behind her from time to time, then plied her needle more rapidly. Capricious flickers of phosphorescence then illuminated the immaculate cloth.

A church bell was sounding the hour feebly in the distance. The lamp suddenly went out, after a last gasp. It was necessary to take it to the window to let it exhale a bitter thread of smoke. Impatiently, Madeleine stuck her needle in a pin-cushion. Was it so late, then? it was much cooler now, and, bizarrely, a persistent draught lifted up her hair over her forehead, Desirous of hearing another chime, she became motionless, her hands abandoned on the cloth, flat on the pallor, staring at the same wisp of smoke that rose up toward the radiant moon, blossoming discreetly.

Everyone was asleep in the house: the heavy slumber of a paralyzed old woman no longer capable of movement. How dead and buried everything seemed! Madeleine could not get used to that profound rural silence. It seemed to her that the incessant rattle of vehicles, the noise of hasty beasts and the hum of nocturnal labors which endowed her dominating brain with a disdain for the tempest, thinking in spite of the thunder, that it had fallen silent, whereas in here, having fallen at twenty years of age into the repose of unhealthily brutalized people, she felt that she was already weakened, buried in a crypt, where it was necessary to talk in hushed voices, out of human respect, no longer seeking to understand too much and to amend oneself. A species of pessimistic philosophy drawn from memories that were perhaps unhealthy ordinarily sustained her and gave her the momentary smile of a mocking Parisienne; this evening, however, she felt ripe for violence of another order. Oh, how long, how tedious life was when nothing cheered up the day and no charming idea burned her in dream!

With a gesture that she did not perceive, her hands came together, her thumbs touching, while a convulsive frisson ran through her body. She wanted, feverishly, to change existence, to change in a second, before the "what's the point" and the reasoning of well-brought-up schoolgirls had plunged her back into the nothingness of stupid mediocrity. My God, the sheet would not be folded up again, that was all! She would not tidy up the linen eternally. She would suffer the sharp scolding of Aunt Julia, and she would be lectured again about the unnatural creature who believed that she had been born with millions and would marry a prince of the blood . . .

Well, so be it! A shrug of the young woman's shoulders responded to that thought of marriage. She stopped gazing at the moon in order to look at the tablecloth;

her gaze, hot with anger, was lost there as if in a bath of snow. Did she not have her diplomas? A woman possessed of a certain education is always someone. Only, among the inhabitants of this savage country, she divined that she was defeated in advance. She was invaded by a splenetic bad faith. It was not the elevation of views that set you apart, it was the arid summit, devoid of springs and fruit, with no discovery of gold and without precious plants, condemning you to live ignored, scratching the sand in order to pass the time.

Her parents had their occupations of limited beings, their gossip, their cooking, their dressing of all the residues of Paris with provincial sauce, and finally, their table—a silent laugh curled Madeleine's lips—oh, yes, the epileptic table, the famous waltzing table! And the reading of the local newspaper, and the comparisons of the different prices of poultry; here, a chicken cost next to nothing, but was so tough, with bruises on the skin, as if the birds had been beaten to death, whereas out there they were very tender, but tasteless. As for beef, it was necessary not to think of it: a kind of reddish veal whose juice melted into water as soon as it was on the skewer!

Madeleine raised her head. A large insect flew in madly, bumping noisily into the furniture, the kind of sinister hairy moth that raced everywhere during potato-gathering season, drunkenly, seemingly having seen phantoms. It fell on the cloth, where it made an equivocal stain. Its wings trailed, weighed down by chalky dust, and its head nodded with a jovial allure. It knew the "apples of the ground"—the ground that one scratched with such difficulties! Filthy *fumures* and ivory femurs.[1] It had sniffed everything with the tips of its short antennae, planted like horns, palpitating with a long internal snigger. Its caterpillar, once sumptuously hairy, had only produced a mixture of neutral tones, drawn from mud and fused by a funereal seal. Could it be happy in its mortuary livery? It strode over the cloth in a circle, seeking the lamp that it had perceived from afar from its home. But the lamp was already extinct, a sacred flame in which it had hoped to roast its abdomen, to finish one and for all! It stopped before Madeleine, crackled, shook with crazy laughter, feeling with the pale digits of its brown antennae, and then departed again on its furious and paunchy round, still quivering with macabre gaiety.

Momentarily, Madeleine searched for an object with which to crush it; examining it more closely, she was seized by pity; she caressed its poor stigmatized wings with her index finger, and showed it mercy because it was frightful. The moth flew away, straight toward the moon.

Pressing her hands on the tablecloth again, the young woman, without being able to explain her sudden enthusiasm, said aloud: "How fortunate they are, the dead!"

A second church bell rang, closer to the house, and the vibration of the bronze resounded on the windows, sliding into the depths of her ears. That one was the bell of the hospice of young mutes, which was adjacent to their house on the north side. Madeleine decided to make her bed. She went to part the cretonne curtains

---

1 The pun cannot survive translation; *fumure* means manure. "Apples of the ground" [*pommes de la terre*] are, of course, potatoes.

closing her alcove, removed her green silk coverlet—an old aristocratic coverlet, so said their landlady—and gave an angry tap to the bolster as if to lodge it permanently in the hollow of her nape. She drank a glass of pure water while saluting the moon with an ironic toast: "Your task is finished this evening!" She got ready to forget another stupid day in order to recommence one even more stupid, doubtless the issue of a banal dream—for out here, where people did not dream anything remarkable, the brain was completely entangled.

Madeleine did not say a prayer. She sketched a vague sign of the cross, pronouncing neither the name of God nor that of the Virgin. She signed herself, therefore, and immediately felt a chill—the particular chill that comes in odorous gusts from newly mown meadows, the chill of the breath of all the ingenuous grass felled beneath the blade, dripping their sap. Would it be prudent to leave her window open, as she had acquired the habit of doing in fine weather? But the strange freshness spread by the death-throes of verdure . . .

Madeleine's bedroom was on the ground floor. The garden's only enclosure on the side of the road was the terrace, and the road belonged to any passer-by. No, it was not prudent. She wanted to close the window; the two battens resisted; she could not succeed, and was amazed. Why did the battens not close naturally, as they did in daylight? Why, above all, was it so cold on a night in June? Anguish seized her. To sleep so far away from any possible help was truly unreasonable. The view over the garden? That was a joke! Oh, it was cheerful, that garden, with its bare flower-beds, its narrow and desolate cemetery box.

A sudden rage made her torment the sash-bolts of the battens, breaking one of the little cloudy panes and grazing her fingers, Finally, she gave up and withdrew slowly, backwards, now dreading that on turning round she might see the door open upon the obscure gulf of the corridor. She stayed still, her back against a chair, her teeth clenched. Fear fell over her like a cold shower, that inexplicable chill coming from so far away in long damp gusts. Evenings are never reassuring in these ancient provincial dwellings. She had read that and laughed at it. Come on, did the fear exist? Was she losing her head—she, a skeptic, a Parisienne, very strong in philosophy? No, that couldn't be!

She sensed the presence of someone in the garden. She knew that; there was a focal point in the middle of her open casement, which she followed with her eyes. There had to be a person there . . . oh, that word, *person* . . . who had come from the road into the garden, having passed over the wall, and was probably leaning on the window-sill in order to climb through. All that might be invented by her terror, but all of that could be true. Nothing that she imagined was incapable of realization. She lowered her eyelids and told herself not to look, not to think about it any longer, trying to calm her heart, which was leaping and quivering, as the flame of the lamp had leapt and quivered, and the wings of the crazy moth. Life was lacking around her; nothing was sufficiently alive any more to help her to breathe!

How many minutes went by between her resolution not to look any longer and her imperious desire to see again? She did not count them. In a muted manner, however, a third chime of the bell reached her, a quiet half-chime; there was a simple impact in her heart, a confused buzzing in her ears. The sound appeared to emerge from her breast rather than arriving from outside. She raised her eyes, her eyes lit up and her hands extended; *there was, in fact, someone there, looking at her.*

In the moonlight, obliquely illuminating a fine white mist reminiscent of troubled water, she distinguished the silhouette of a man. That man moved his arm in a decisive gesture.

"Ah!" he said, almost in a whisper. "The house is inhabited!"

She heard the remark, faintly, and she believed, as for the sound of the third chime, that the sound of the voice emerged from herself, so much did she shiver with its vibrations. She chased away all superstitious ideas in order to respond valiantly: "Yes, the house is inhabited. There are my father, my aunt and the neighbors; I can call them if I wish."

The man smiled. In the white mist he had a livid face in which the bloody, beardless lips were especially noticeable. In a childish voice that was tremulous and not at all appropriate, she added: "It's very late for a stroll, Monsieur!"

"Does my dog frighten you?" he asked, still smiling. He was no longer moving, looking at her in an insulting fashion, upright and tall in the fog that fluidified objects, like a tree, a spontaneous bloom of mysterious darkness.

Madeleine discovered a dog behind the intruder, an unreassuring dog, very thin, tall on its paws, with a square muzzle and pointed ears: a shiny black dog with short hair, seemingly all wet.

She could no longer be afraid either of the dog or the man, for she found herself in a state of absolute unconsciousness. She desired above all to hear herself speak, to proffer syllables, sounds of some sort, in order to break the oppressive charm that the two apparitions emitted.

Yes, all that was quite simple, but that nocturnal stroller had no need to envelop himself in fog! Why did his felt hat—a very ordinary hat, in sum—not terminate clearly, and why did his legs, his body, take root like that before her window, while the torso, the upper part of his body, swayed, as if independent of the rest?

Mechanically, she said: "What do you want?"

"Good," murmured the man. "I have come because I thought someone was calling me. You made me a sign while I was on the road."

He darted a sharp stare toward her and removed his hat with a slow and graceful gesture. She thought that he must be very young, her own age, or very nearly. He had a broad brow, brilliant eyes, a flexible neck like the neck of a woman, and so long that the idea occurred to her of a bird bearing a head that was too heavy,

"You're in a closed garden," she said, in an aggressive tone. "You leapt over the wall!"

Coldly, he replied: "There is no closed garden. I have not leapt over the wall."

He swung his hat phlegmatically: the kind of Tyrolean hat that certain elegant travelers adopt, to which he had not neglected to attach the traditional eagle-feather, elongated in the mist with the disconcerting appearance of a knife-blade. Was the passer-by local? No. Madeleine did not remember that strange appearance of solemn impertinence.

If he goes any further, she thought, *I'll call for help. It would be ridiculous, but too bad!*

"Oh! I'll go away," said the young man, responding to her mental reflection.

"Go away," she exclaimed, discovering a sudden sensation of terror. "No one called you. Do you hear, Monsieur!"

He stepped back.

"You're wrong to be annoyed, Mademoiselle," he said, gravely, after having kept his gaze fixed upon her momentarily. "*I had come back to see the house.*"

He replaced his hat with an automatic movement and turned his back; the dog seemed to undulate in the same direction as its master. Both headed for the wooden gate separating the garden from the meadows, the odorous sea of which bathed the foot of the rocky hill. Bewildered, Madeleine felt both of them *emerging from her flesh*, and abruptly, not calculating the folly of her step, she passed through the window, jumped into the flower-beds and ran, crying out.

The dog stopped and turned round, its eyes ferocious.

"That beast is going to bite me!" she said to herself, horrified.

"Eh! No, he won't bite you!" declared a voice whose mocking tone burst directly against her ear.

And although the moon was hidden, and although the fog was metamorphosing things, she was convinced that it was *him, the man,* too distant to make himself audible so distinctly. He must have opened the gate, knowing the primitive secret of the lock, a little key introduced into a chain hidden in the brambles, and he plunged into the hayricks. His silhouette disappeared gradually along the path leading to the rocks. Now three hundred meters away, how could he have spoken to her in a whisper?

Out of breath, bathed in a cold sweat, Madeleine leaned on the trunk of a linden tree, facing the gate. The sound of a mill-wheel and steaming cascades was buzzing within her, and her arms writhed; there was a light foam on her mouth,

Why had the dog stayed behind, watching her with malevolent eyes? Why, suddenly, had the animal executed a series of somersaults and disappeared *upwards* instead of fleeing normally along the path? Unless one wanted to admit that the dog, in order to rejoin the man, had, with a formidable leap, attained the hill whose crumbing stones its master was scaling at a brisk pace.

Then Madeleine conceived fear—a great fear! She felt the irremediable fear that kills or overturns reason blossoming within her. For a long time, no doubt, she had been carrying that muted evil, brooding in her lonely young woman's entrails like a fire smoldering beneath pink ashes. It seemed to her that a torch, issued from the earth, was blazing in her skirts, burning her body, a torrential fusion of lava rising within her all the way to the heart, a powerful meteor, a fireball rendered furious by an electric whip, launching from her breast to her throat, strangling her, choking her and finally splashing her, with frightful howls.

The ground hollowed out; the tree disappeared; she was cast down, forced to walk on all fours, as if thunderstruck, a bitch baying at death!

II

MONSIEUR JACQUES DESLANDES got up early, and was particularly early that following day, because he had slept badly, discovering his brain burning with the confused memory of nightmares. The nights of the full moon are always baleful; dogs howl; shy sinners prowl the meadows with lanterns, domestic animals agitate while dreaming aloud, and huge acrostic rats are heard in the grain-lofts of old houses. He drank his coffee, prepared by Aunt Julia on a corner of his desk, and then tried to get his bearings. They had no maid. Aunt Julia sufficed for the housework. Having also risen at dawn, she did not seem to be in a good mood when she encountered her brother coming out of his bedroom.

"What, there you are?" she hissed. "You get in my way every sainted morning. I've taken out my ashes and cleaned my kitchen! Why are you prowling the corridors like that?"

"I . . . don't know," murmured Jacques Deslandes, humiliated. He undid the corners of the handkerchief carefully knotted over his head, started to smooth it out and folded it up with the gestures of a methodical woman fearful of reprimands.

"You didn't hear anything?" he queried, timidly.

"Hear what?" growled Julia Bordes. "It's like a tomb here."

"The cocks were crowing in a terrible fashion!"

"A fine story! They crow every morning at sunrise. Another nice custom of your dirty province . . ."

They went down a few steps and penetrated into the kitchen.

"I'll wait for the postman with you," sighed Deslandes, lighting his pipe at the fire of the oven.

In the Deslandes house they were always waiting for the postman. It was the principal distraction. For hours, Jacques or Julia leaned on the window-sill overlooking the street, looking out for the unfortunate fellow, who, frightened by their grim expressions, often did not take the trouble to go that far.

Madame Bordes searched the whole length of the two deserted pavements with a sharp eye, saw him in the distance emerge from the post office in the square, chat for a minute with a wine-merchant, swallow a glass in passing, stopping, buckling and unbuckling his leather satchel. My God, so many needless words and stupid reflections before arriving at the last house in the town—"one of the most considerable," Aunt Julia affirmed. Finally, he passed over a periodical or a prospectus, items without importance, and Madame Bordes got annoyed.

"Come on! It's a joke, isn't it? You've lost my letters? I tell you that when we lived in Paris, we received dozens every day! Take care, my good man; if you fail in your service, we'll complain."

"They'll come tomorrow, Madame," replied the postman, pitifully. For the year that that she-devil had been living there he had made the same polite response and had not obtained a better greeting. She was his *bête noire*. For him, a simple man, smiling at the angels slightly because of numerous libations, he was afraid of Parisians as one generally fears all people well in with the government. One never knew whether a Parisian might have seen the minister, and he bowed, bending his back and clinging to the walls, full of deference, to Monsieur le Bibliothécaire and to the ladies, young and old, expelling his breath once he was out of their claws, sponging his brow, seeking to give himself courage. Anyway, so what? The most notable inhabitants of the town almost never received letters. What did these have against him? Unknown clowns, whose faces, after all, had nothing very impressive about them.

While looking out for the postman, who would not go past for three hours that day, Jacques Deslandes sang the eternal refrain: "How quickly one is forgotten, eh, my poor Julia?"

"Yes, yes! Exhaust the temperament," riposted the old lady sharply. "To be the secretary of a senator and to see you put your foot down without having the right to say two! They're nice, you're friends! One makes all the economies in the world here, and what good does it do? Oh, they've left us in the lurch!"

Every day they complained thus about the future chances of a further displacement. Not that they found it any worse than when they were in Paris, but those old maniacs, having grown old quietly in the noisy life of the capital, always thought they were on holiday and did not imagine that it could go on any longer. It was necessary for them to go away, to go back. Run aground there like wrecks, once the solemn moment of the shipwreck was past, they were no longer content to thank God; they stamped their feet in the feverish wait for a sail. People were occupied with them out there; they sensed it, or believed that they sensed it. No, everything had not been said! After their almost official position as secretary of a senator they ought to have descended to a place in finance—secretary to a banker, for example. The secretariat is a stream that always leads to a river. Some also led to the sea, but one could float there; Parisians are like corks!

Jacques Deslandes was fifty-eight years old, filled with little springs that made his poor machine move with difficulty, and only relaxed partly, always wiping his spectacles, always caressing his nose with two fingers like a hairpin; incorrect and improper, tormented by a harsh beard that he groomed stubbornly every morning while he forgot to comb his hair; convinced, moreover, that his appearance alone would procure him the traditional stroke of luck to which every mediocre individual aspires. Incapable of directing anything around him, he left his sister, a miserly creature, to hold his purse-strings. He proclaimed his rights loudly—for he had rights, that was incontestable, and he counted them on his fingers: a serious education, cousins by marriage who were magistrates, a daughter to marry, a sister whose defunct spouse had consumed her dowry, a wife who had died young of peritonitis . . . oh, one would see! He would write threatening letters; he knew how to turn out missives of that sort, having fabricated enough of them on behalf of others, and he had only to recommence . . . the other way around. On behalf of his senator he scarcely ever responded except to oppose refusals to solicitors; he tried, all the same, to show himself determined and menacing in his turn, by putting *urgent* on the envelopes.

In his shirt-sleeves, his trousers poorly attached to his braces, he walked around with an anxious expression, avoiding going here and there, making a thousand detours in order not to bump into chairs and utensils. Simultaneously very embarrassing and very embarrassed, he gazed tenderly at the saucepans, examined the dusters, touched the stove, got dirt or grease under his fingernails and then cleaned them with the tip of a needle. When he sat down at a desk, however, patting the stacks of paper that were confided to him with his meticulous hands, he became a grand figure; he could have been introduced with pleasure in the toga of a president of the assize court; and he was also benevolent, always anxious, knew useless things and was so inefficient . . . !

His sister, Madame Julia Bordes, resembled him enormously from the point of view of negligence in matinal grooming. Wisps of hair protruded like coppery darts over her wrinkled forehead; she wore a skirt of Havana silk, patched with squares of flannel; her camisole was parted, exhibiting flaccid breasts, and her skin changed its tone from one minute to the next, flamboyant punch when it was animated and bottle-green when she was meditative.

She stirred thick clouds of smoke from the ashes, agitating her sieve like a discus-thrower, Torrents of smoke rushed into the street or vanished gradually all the way to the ceiling-beams of the kitchen. At times she leaned over, raked forcefully, then withdrew a piece of coal the size of a haricot bean. Standing behind her, Deslandes sneezed, striving to see clearly.

"The postman isn't coming, I fear," he said, coughing.

Without ceasing to stir furiously, she replied: "No, of course, he's already lit up. He's found something to drink somewhere."

Deslandes reflected, parading his austere visage in the middle of the cloud, and paused to rub his eyes. His big nose and his little dark eyes, very close together, with a slight squint, his wide mouth like that of a stupid shark and his badly-trimmed side-whiskers gave him the appearance of an old creature of the sabbat, fantastic and pitiful.

Julia ceased sifting for a moment in order to withdraw the ashes from the fireplace.

"So," murmured Deslandes, "you didn't hear anything last night?"

"What?" grumbled Julia, adjusting her chemise.

"How do I know? Noises, cries—one might have thought that someone was weeping; it penetrated the walls."

"Stupidities, my poor old man; you're always imagining things."

"Has Madeleine come down?"

"Madeleine? Since when did she get up so early?" Julia held out her sieve in a tragic gesture. "In Paris it was because she couldn't see into the courtyard from her bedroom; here it's doubtless because she can see too much of the garden! Your daughter is a famous idler, you know."

"Oh, Julia, Julia, don't always repeat the same story. Try to settle things woman to woman, I beg you . . ."

Julia shook her arms and the ashes spread out.

"It's necessary for her to learn to work, to mix eggs, milk, meat and broth. She doesn't know how to make a sauce or clear a saucepan. There are petty households in which the work can be shared, people taking turns, but here . . . oh, you're lucky to have me, both of you. There are people who don't know how to make an omelet. When Madeleine is my age, you'll see . . . and I'll no longer be here to look after you . . ."

"Is she still not wanting to eat in the morning?" the father interrupted, scratching his nose furiously.

"I don't care whether she eats or not. If she wants chocolate she can make it herself. I've had enough of her whims. Did you see her face at dinner? She doesn't like cheese! Where does she get it from?"

With little jerky movements Julia made the embers in her sieve jump, so that even the lumps of coal crumbled. She put down the sieve in order to wipe her cheeks with a corner of her camisole and spread the ash over her skin, become green again; taking on a spectral majesty in the cloud. The poor man, accustomed to the acidic confidences of the morning, shook his head desolately.

"Wait, my love, wait! All this won't last forever. We'll have a little more wellbeing one day; we'll take a maid and she'll have her chocolate again."

36

"A maid?" Julia got carried away. "Oh, of course! No! I no longer want servants! You can become emperor, but we'll never have a maid. I've been treated once as an 'old witch,' that's enough for me."

In the indignation that the idea of the return of a domestic caused her, she knocked over her pile of cinders and had to bend down to pick them up.

"Oh, is there a fire in your house?" asked the postman, appearing at the window and holding out a modest newspaper.

The librarian hastened forward. "No, no, my good man. A little dust, that's all!" Vexed, deep down, that his sister had been surprised while sieving the ashes, he added in a gruff tone: "A fire! A fire! That's all it needs." And he closed the casement.

"It'll come tomorrow," stammered the bewildered postman.

"No letters again?" asked Julia.

"Beware of gossip," said Deslandes, bad-temperedly. "We're in the provinces, exposed to all kinds of malevolence. For four sous' worth of coal, damn it!"

He drew away rapidly, not wanting to risk any more.

At ten o'clock the librarian got dressed and made his way through the empty streets to his library, which was in the Museum itself, a former monastery whose cross had been conserved, and where the debris of Egyptian sculptures was gathered—a few deities half-woman and half scarab. Then Monsieur Deslandes began to chat about the good old days with their guardian—which is to say, started his principal labor. The large bookroom hardly ever received any visits; vague professors came on Sunday, and priests, because of the sanctity of the place, and from time to time a passing stranger, a commercial traveler who wandered through the various rooms, yawning with despair. The library, well-arranged and well-waxed, as somber as a tomb, was cheered up momentarily every morning by the customary banter exchanged between the guardian-concierge and Monsieur le Bibliothécaire.

"You have the face of a juvenile lead, my friend," Deslandes declared. Or: "Let's see, are these monks," one of them joked, "in your old convent of friars?" To which the other replied on a whim: "Oh, Monsieur, how can you say that? And me skirting my sixtieth year!" Or "Oh, these rascally plants, I believe they're going to seed." It was a matter of the monkshood growing in the barred windows of the poor edifice.

Once these various polite remarks were exchanged, everything returned to silence. Then Deslandes attended to stacks of paper, more out of habit than taste; he read, riffled though and ripped the rubber bands of scientific journals that fell there like stones into a well, piling up annoyingly, blocking up places, always babbling the same Latin words, always telling you about the same new discoveries and concluding with recipes of local distractions such as "how to introduce a melon into a carafe." From time to time his pen mechanically noted down details that did not interest him, without his hand guiding it to one place rather than another, like a peevish beak. He studied manuscripts corroded by damp without finding anything therein, internally astonished that sensate men could spend their lives reading such grimoires.

As soon as the warden wandered into his domain, either to water the monkshood or to communicate some important observation about the barometric pressure, he got up, hung up his blue apron—a solid apron giving the false impression of being made of leather—and followed him lamentably. He went through vaulted galleries that opened in ogives into a damp courtyard, repeating stupid phrases in order to hear himself talk to someone, but he spoke alone, because the guardian of the cloister had a horror of animated conversation; he responded "yes" or "no" or, for preference, "perhaps," leaving the other to perorate about his former social situation, only comprehending one thing, which was that a Monsieur could probably obtain a leave from a senator for his son, an only son serving in the navy.

Often, terrorized by the idea that that simulacrum of a living being might vanish, Deslandes abandoned him in the presence of Egyptian homunculi, even more taciturn by nature, proposing to him a complete cleaning of the display cases, even though neatness was not his obsession, and he started to dust, sweep and polish like a madman. Perhaps that was unworthy, his functions as librarian not obliging him to daub panes of glass with Spanish white, but he would get through to noon, then, with a good pretext for talking aloud. The worthy concierge held out his feather duster.

"There, Monsieur le Bibliothécaire! Do you see that bitch of a spider-web under the armpit of the Amenophis? I ask you how those beasts can fabricate such filthy things! They have no respect for anything! Since you're thinner, get on with it; I have my paunch, I'm too afraid of crushing the mummy."

And Deslandes, full of ardor, cleared away the spider-web; he jostled the mummy, saying that that would teach the damned contraptions!

One day, the warden, having become more familiar, wondered who the mummy was, and why noble people had been wrapped up in the olden days. Monsieur le Bibliothécaire ought to know, having so many old books by profession.

At hazard, Deslandes replied: "To prevent them from rotting, of course . . ."

"Yes, yes, I understand; they embalmed them first—but what about the binding, the bandages?"

"Well, I'll give you the short explanation, for if I employed technical terms, you wouldn't understand very clearly. They tied them up to prevent the soul getting out . . ."

"The soul! Well! the idea!"

"Yes. One of their beliefs. They wrapped up the monsieur, or the lady, while still warm, so as to conserve their vegetative life, so that they could live inside, like your monkshoods. They're bound up, aren't they, your plants, wrapped around the bars of their prison? We're wrapped up too! But it appears that, at all times, people have thought that it was better to live bound up than not to exist at all."

Respectfully, the concierge took off his violet velvet cap, looking at the mummy obliquely.

"Oh, Monsieur, death is a vile thing!"

The scientific explanation remained there. It would, in fact, have been difficult for Monsieur le Bibliothéhcaire to take in any further.

Midday chimed; Deslandes breathed out, polished his hat with a thrust of his sleeve, and fled.

On returning, scarcely had he crossed his doorstep than Monsieur Deslandes heard his sister yapping. Decidedly, nothing was going well on that nightmare morning. Out there is his library he had not even seen the shadow of the warden and had not even received the regular circular from the Society Against the Abuse of Tobacco. Now the women were arguing.

"Come, come, my love," he said, putting down his briefcase full of useless papers in a corner of the dining room. "What is it now? People can hear you in the street."

"It is," she said, "that Mademoiselle comes down from her bedroom just in time to find the table laid. She hasn't prepared the radishes, and she'll doubtless be seen eating them in a bunch, like the elephant at the zoo."

Madeleine was standing beside her chair, her back turned to the light. She was waiting for her father to arrive before sitting down. She said *bonjour* to him in a strangled voice and immediately collapsed, occupied in breaking her bread. Julia served, cursing between the kitchen and the table.

"Child," said the aggravated father, "I'm discontented, very discontented. Your aunt and I aren't idlers, why do you get up so late? In good weather like this! Birds singing, a blue, sunny sky. You'll ruin your health. You can no longer complain of lack of air, here."

Madeleine reached for the sat-cellar and bit into a radish unenthusiastically. She was blue, and her drawn features gave her the physiognomy of a convalescent;

barely-scarred scratches extended along her cheeks and her neck. There were tracks of fingernails on her wrists and her hands.

"What's that?" asked her father, touching her cheek.

"Oh, nothing," she replied, coldly. "A bramble in the garden . . ."

"You're pretty! My congratulations," mumbled Deslandes

Then, as his scoldings were never very terrible, he set about eating heartily.

Madeleine remained silent; she hardly ever talked in the presence of her father and her aunt. She retained the reserve of a stranger in their regard; they did not understand that haughty, umbrageous nature, which had the sudden revolts of a vicious animal. The lunch finished in a stormy atmosphere, furrowed from time to time by disagreeable reflections on the part of Aunt Julia, who habitually complained about the quality of provincial bread.

At dessert, before the three strawberries that his sister distributed, Deslandes relaxed slightly.

"We could call the doctor?"

"That's it!" exclaimed Madame Bordes, turning crimson. "Let's spend our sous with the sole objective of seeing her slapped with stupidities by a poor devil who doesn't understand the first thing. Anyway, in this hole one can't like looking after nervous demoiselles. A bone-setter for sprains, all well and good, but migraines and the caprices of spoiled children? A country doctor would make fun of us. Do you remember the face she pulled at the doctor you brought her when she twisted her ankle last winter? She had attacks of nerves because he'd tugged her ankle a little hard?"

"He seemed as meek as a sheep, though, that Edmond Sellier," murmured Deslandes, perplexed, "What do you think, child?"

"I'm not ill," replied Madeleine, getting up from the table abruptly.

"Not ill, not ill, with those rings around your eyes and those white cheeks. If you could even be made to unclench your teeth! Come on, I pass him every morning as I go past the post office, where he keeps his carriage. We exchange a little salute from a distance. I approach him, we enter into conversation, and without requiring the slightest visit, I ask his advice. What about that, my love?"

And he turned to his sister

"You're determined that people make fun of you!" replied the latter, while Madeleine went out, slamming the door.

Twisting a last morsel of bread, Deslandes raised his eyes despairingly. When he had finished, his two fingers crossed, he stroked his nose momentarily, while his sister began clearing the table.

"It isn't a physician that it's necessary to consult," declared Madame Bordes, lowering her voice and gripping his shoulder.

"Do you think, my love, that we have the right, given the expense?"

The old lady nodded her head affirmatively, in a solemn manner.

"Jacques," she said, "it is written: 'Knock, and the door will be opened to you . . .'"

III

THE brother and the sister went into the drawing room, both seeming mysteriously preoccupied. They closed the door again carefully and bolted it, desirous of isolating themselves in order to carry out that work of darkness. They both had a singular gleam in the depths of the gaze and frissons—like desires for forbidden fruit—in their fingertips. In that alone consisted the feast of their limited life, the little piece of heaven fallen on to their plate; they went there, without transition, for a stupidity as well as for something serious, quitting a spit that they left turning in the kitchen or a person in mortal danger.

That had come there from Paris, a land of all diabolical evils, via the intermediary of the influential senator. Occult soirées were held in the home of that individual, and the petrified Jacques Deslandes had seen a monumental table rise up there all the way to the ceiling. "Seen" was not the right word, for all the lamps went out at the vital moment, but the exclamations of the audience, the reflections in the corners a dull, inexplicable rap struck on the floor and the cries of enthusiasm that escaped from all breasts as soon as the light returned, troubled him so seriously that he resolved to make himself an initiate. Once master of the professional secret, although he had not obtained any result, he initiated his sister in his turn, and then—O eternal superiority of the visionary intellect of woman over that of a man!—Madame Julia Bordes, that scarcely primitive nature, dry and rebellious to sentimentalism, that narrow mind only haunted by the remorse of having allowed her late husband to dilapidate her meager dowry, that entirely sage widow, had metamorphosed into a remarkable spiritist.

The occasional table, which had not marched under the tremulous hands, too timorous or inexperienced, of Jacques Deslandes, was seized by an extraordinary Saint Vitus' dance under the red fists of Aunt Julia. It waltzed, leapt, swiveled, followed people like a dog, expressed bizarre mimes, thundered the most absurd orders, raged against certain of her brother's ideas, and distilled all the sister's venom through all the pores of its poor innocent wood.

Julia, devoid of devotion and devoid of imagination, suddenly became a ferment of extreme beliefs. She no longer spoke without mingling her speech with Biblical sentences, retained at hazard, with the dicta of popular superstition. The spiders of the morning and the parables of Christ were easily confused in the cauldron of those new ideas. Clawed by a need to preach at a critical age when feminine monomanias are complicated by neuroses, she embraced the affairs of mediumship as she might have embraced the affairs of the stock market, in a miserly and methodical fashion. She lent herself to the supernatural at high interest, invented, by a sublime effort of her mediocre brain, a usury of artificial paradises, of which cretins have as much need as geniuses.

In order to compensate herself for being ugly, ridiculous, poor, dirty, of square stature, with wine-lees patches on her face, and living at her brother's expense, she became a second-hand dealer in the wealth of Satan, made the devil descend into a porter's lodge, armed the exterminating angel with ladles, dressed the good God in a chasuble of mahogany, condensed in a ridiculous item of household furniture fit for a café trace: the occasional table! A religion made to her measure, having both servility and conjuring tricks. And anyway, it might all have been real, for the worst absurdities are the things that approach the truth most closely!

Jacques Deslandes believed he might die of unadmitted fright. It came back to him by night; he woke up all feverish, consulted his watch and found that it had stopped: magic!—an excellent Breguet, never varying, reset every evening very regularly! Photographs of aged cousins were found upside down in their frames, which had been seen the day before gravely right way up, in protective attitudes. Then, there was the lost cravat, the slippers walking from one side of the bed to the other, papers pinned to the bolster, bottles of ink poured into the soup—in sum, a sabbat in miniature, and their petty commerce of anxious people ornamented by unexpected catastrophes surging forth upon those who knew too much.

In the beginning, there had been difficulties. Jacques tried hard to rid himself of those ill-bred imps who shook his paltry misery brutally, but the attraction—the divine attraction—of mystery gradually reduced him to a role of rapt contemplation. He could not complain, since it was his stupid curiosity that had introduced the enemy into the house; he had installed it himself in the family hearth, making it a gift of the nice little table, bought for twelve francs twenty-five at a sale in the Rue Drouot, and he could no longer think of anyone dislodging it without ingratitude, for he owed very interesting evenings to it, and sometimes, at intervals, a cup of strengthened coffee generously granted to him by his sister during a late night.

After all, it was merely a matter of amusing himself with a cheap toy, and also outside nature. Reading the newspaper, begging letters and watching tiresome rehearsals of a senator's political performances, listening to the shrill cries of a housekeeper whose veins carried hot dishwater, seeing a sulky daughter waste away, and paying the baker's bills and the rent did not furnish an enormous quantity of wellbeing, and a human heart full to the brim of those various materials still has an empty space that one might as well abandon to vague dreams of the beyond. Catholicism is encumbered by its abuses of ceremonious practicality; it scarcely requires the skepticism of so-called Gallic wit with which every Parisian is armored as soon as he has fallen into the trap of baptism.

Now, that new religion of wood, transforming the sacred tree of Golgotha into an object both useful and portable, suited the amiable political secretary admirably, at the risk of a little mockery when he had been drinking. Furthermore, Jacques, genuinely progressive, had a high regard for creations of recent date which arrived, like electricity, from America. A religion rubbed with science, in which everything might be explained one day by the intrusion of animal magnetism, was polite, neat and clear. He found a little spiritual enthusiasm, not inconvenient, playing the part of diabolical fire in the turbulent manifestations of a young table in delirium, and he allowed a few fetishes to be broken and a few habits to be disturbed, and then rationalized it and educated himself. They limited themselves to the indispensable rituals. In thorny matters of life they consulted it.

The senator himself weighed the pros and cons, and claimed that it was necessary to mistrust female mediums, and that one of those she-devils had stolen his diamond-studded snuff-box on an evening of crazy calligraphy. However, he granted the necessity of the union of male and male fluids for any supernatural manifestation. In magic, black or white, women always obtained more marvelous results than men. How did they do it? A mystery, compounding the other. Doubtless their more resistant nervous force—like their long hairs, also very resistant, one of which, wound round a heavy object, could drag it for considerable distances.

"A woman," added that expert but prudent spiritist, "retains in her nervous system a spirit that is sometimes manifest, at the slightest imposition of hands, in external forms so extraordinary that modesty never permits us to suppose that a creature, generally well-educated and honest, can commit such absurdities of her own free will, if, on the other hand, we nourish certain doubts."

"Is it necessary, then, to suppose the demon?" the secretary questioned dolorously, moved by that turn of phrase.

"No! We shall suppose"—and the senator lifted the thumb and the index finger successively and shook his delicately nacred head—"firstly, a disordered sensibility provoked by continual frictions; secondly, a faculty of spontaneous beliefs nearing them to realize their vision spontaneously by means of an emission of normal fluids; thirdly, exterior phenomena, each of which correspond, in themselves, to a seventh sense still unknown to us but not unanalyzable."

And in order to analyze the seventh sense, the worthy senator, half-convinced by the force of women, partly deprived of their own means, frequented all the current spiritist séances where female mediums were encountered but no longer took away his snuff-box! From dissertation to dissertation and séance to séance Jacques Deslandes, who followed him religiously, also observed an impotence to produce anything supernatural or scientific by himself. The senator was right; it required a woman and a seventh sense, and he ended up adopting his sister's *Spirit* for want of anything better.

His sister's Spirit had a funny name; he was called Ludovic. Why? That was not his business, and then, a familiar spirit has to respond to a vocable that is simultaneously suggestive of an emperor and a domestic. When the latter manifested himself under the twelve-franc-twenty-five side-table, he burst forth like a fusillade, *toc, toc, toc!* There was no means of being mistaken; it was really Ludovic, and one immediately commenced to lose the notion of common sense. A few solemn phrases, a few sentences taken from the Bible, no religious theory. He traced *nos* and *yeses* half a foot long on a slate, passing via the hand of Madame Bordes, which became singularly more ponderous for that otherworldly work, or he struck them with his mahogany heel on the floor, *crack, crack!*

Often, seized with fury, in order to spare himself the annoyance of contradictions, he erased a whole slate, and broke the chalk with an abrupt gesture. When he addressed the brother he risked oaths, but he spoke to the sister in a bloated style full of metaphors suggestive of a hairdresser's apprentice. Gross errors of French peppered the whole and were only suspended by Ludovic's chalk in order to be disengaged from the noble prose of Napoléon I or Monsieur Thiers, individuals whom Jacques Deslandes took pleasure in evoking in the course of political discussions.

They did not understand it at all. Ludovic must be a malevolent spirit summoned by the senator, one of the "auxiliary principles of a woman's nerves," and yet, so clever, the auxiliary seigneur. How well he knew the strengths and weaknesses of Deslandes! How he was able to turn him upside-down with a precise remark! He only ordered possible things, occupied with minor questions of household management, maintaining a sage reserve on the subject of the other world, so as not to frighten anyone. For example:

"Are you dead?"

"I might as well be only asleep."

"Why don't you talk about God?"

"I'm not yet worthy of seeing him."

"Will you see him one day?"

"At my fifty-seventh reincarnation."

"Do you know if the weather will be fine tomorrow?"

"Even if it's fine, don't forget your umbrella."

"What should we have for dinner this evening?"

"Veal!"

There were amazements and misunderstandings in consulting him too assiduously; but he turned in a vicious circle where no one could escape him. Once, he had discovered under the castor of an armchair a louis lost weeks before and he had ordered a cap to disappear completely. Jacques, overexcited, consulted Ludovic before deciding to change his underwear, and when his sister could not see him he came to sit down, sadly at the ensorcelled table, feeling its three wooden feet, the repeated kicks of which hammered the floor of the whole dwelling, leaving little round tracks reminiscent of those of a cat with nutshell boots. He lifted it up, ausculated it, sniffed it and finally placed his large hands on it with a conviction so profound that it became touching. Alas, all that was in vain; nothing emerged from the accursed table, no movement or trepidation, not even the internal cracking that they pressed with solicitude and which responded to questions, in the letter rather than the spirit, with an accuracy that was often disconcerting.

Then, Deslandes was afflicted by that new discovery of impotence. No, the poor fellow could no longer think of taming the facetious Ludovic; that was good for women, that supreme domination over matter. Nothing remained to him but curiosity—which is to say, the act of faith; the old curiosity come from the depths of old shoes once placed by the fireside at

Christmas, the dead and disorientating fay that accompanied the old man in spite of all his disillusionments. And he rejected the malicious table to go in search of his sister, who abandoned her saucepans and ran without even wiping her hands to take hold of Ludovic with the air of defying someone, while her brother watched her slyly, vanquished but ecstatic.

The first time that Madeleine, still a little girl, had watched, in their séance of macabre prestidigitation, which she had been able to study from her corner, the different grimaces produced by those faces solemnly leaning toward the lampshade, she had been seized by an inextinguishable mad laughter, and had rolled on the carpet in a crisis of terrible gaiety. Oh, it was too ridiculous, it was too much! She ought to have believed, like them, becoming a fervent follower, lending them the charming naivety of her young awakening imagination, but, unfortunately, she was disposed to find it grotesque that evening and roared with laughter, an effect of the schoolgirl skepticism that, among the pupils of grand modern colleges, goes from bed to bed during the night, brushing many foreheads with its wing of a vicious black bird. She even dared to think, so sure was she already that nothing was done other than naturally in supernatural operations, that Madame Bordes aided the chalk or the table. She did not know the reason for that lie. She knew a pretty fifteen-year-old brunette who swallowed lumps of coal, initially to astonish her audience and later, all alone, for pleasure . . . !

Jacques Deslandes begged his sister to no longer manifest before that disrespectful child. Well, there were games for little girls and games for grown-ups.

And Julia was still scandalized. No! To laugh like that was idiotic. In the scatterbrain's place she would have been afraid, horribly afraid, whereas children, at present, only writhed with laughter. She made a scene of dignity, declared that she would not tolerate henceforth anyone, schoolgirls or maids, laughing at that subject—after all, they did not know what Ludovic was. He might attract misfortunes, make marriages fail, prevent you from inheriting—in short, spoil an entire future. Science or black magic, she believed that Ludovic had authority, becoming a sort of occult uncle, a power comparable to that of a spiritual bogyman father. She spoke for two hours standing before the table, until Madeleine had a desire to weep, like the girl who ate coal, without knowing why.

Deslandes, fearful of family scenes, watched over Ludovic. He locked him up in the drawing room with the forbidden books, and the experiments took place behind closed doors. Only, when Madeleine attained her twentieth year, she had not entirely renounced the unhealthy recreations of the keyhole!

The drawing room of their new residence, a magisterial provincial drawing room, seemed truly destined for those meetings of ridiculous old sorcerers. Everything was hung with green damask silk, passing through all the cadaverous shades permitted to a fabric dating back at least a century. Seen from the threshold it was anguishing; the gaze entered into it as into a forest. Emerald-green at the windows, dead-leaf in the depths of the panels and verdigris around the doors, the room was dismal as a church closed for a long time, was furnished with a dresser in the form of a confessional, a stiff sofa with skeletal arms and two armchairs vomiting their horsehair in the two corners of the fireplace. A heavy bronze ring hung down from the ceiling, centered with a floral rose of damp plaster. There had presumably once been a chandelier there, but no one was sure any longer. Sometimes a stray ray of sunlight made that ring gleam discreetly, and one wondered whether it had ever sustained anything: a bizarre ex-voto, a large primitive bracelet forgotten up there by an eccentric. There was no carpet and no garniture on the mantelpiece; a mirror, also green, the green of dormant water, was buried in the hangings, as distant as the perspective of a path seen in the rain. That made the drawing room flee before you frightfully, giving the vertigo of another, much larger room elongating in a corridor, falling into a gulf all the more obsessive because one knew it to be fictitious.

The only ornaments the Parisians had added were the famous table and a bust of Monsieur Thiers, the favorite household god of Jacques Deslandes. The parquet creaked underfoot, white dust flew up on all sides—a special dust filtered from who knows where, which was sticky, like a greasy substance. Voices made echoes at certain times, according to the position that one adopted in the two large punctured armchairs.

Every morning the windows overlooking the garden were opened, but neither the healthy scents of the countryside not the equivocal perfumes of Aunt Julia's stews arrived to expel the sickening odor of damp that saturated the green cloth, and they took up residence in the dining room, so inhibited were they by the funereal reek of that drawing room. A perpetual damp combined there with some secret putrescence of the soil to spread an acrid taste that caught you in the throat and deposited an exasperating bitterness on the lips. It was necessary not to think of coming into it after a meal if one had an impressionable stomach.

Deslandes and his sister sat down nevertheless facing one another in the armchairs, pushing the mahogany table between them, which gave the impression, in the middle of the somber room, of a huge brown mushroom, a poisonous plant sprung from the earth of a cemetery. Madame Bordes attacked Ludovic with a peremptory gesture, while Deslandes extended his hands faithfully, joining the thumbs and concentrating his will with all the power of his little, slightly squinting eyes. Ludovic made them wait; he had these futile coquetries.

"Dear spirit," commenced Deslandes, always very polite, "are you ready to respond to us on the subject of our child? You know that it's a matter of her health? It isn't going well at all . . ."

Julia Bordes brushed the hair from her forehead, shrugging her shoulders. "He thinks it wrong to interrogate him for a trifle."

"Why did you advise me to interrogate him, then?" murmured Deslandes, vexed.

"Because you wouldn't be tranquil until he'd told you not to fetch the doctor."

Deslandes sniffed the odor of damp very softly. "But how do you know in advance that he'd share your opinion?"

"Oh, that's easy to divine. Look, do you see this wood?" She rapped the table with her fist. "It's hard, like a piece of iron. Usually, when Ludovic is content, it yields under a fingernail like butter. I'll wager that he's going to play some trick on us."

"Anyway, let's see what happens. All the same, he could get us out of difficulty, indicate a remedy to us. I don't want to keep such a pale girl—no, no, I'm aggravated by that pallor!"

In a curious state of mind, difficult to explain, Deslandes had just slyly tried with his fingertips to push the castors in accordance with his means, and started swimming to try to aid the being, secretly, by means of the pressures that he imagined—with the best will in the world, but involuntarily. The table oscillated, but Madame Bordes straightened it with an abrupt movement. Ludovic could only obey her fluid, and she would not permit any error of that sort. Anyway, the table, which never marched of its own accord, sometimes had crackles of ill humor that were incomprehensible. He also played his particular comedy. Julia tamed him by wondering every time whether the roles might be inverted one day. She sat down before the table, to which she alone had the veritable key, with an idea in her head that certainly could not have been dislodged for all the gold in Europe. It prowled within her like a wild beast in a cavern; she had a superstitious fear of the black idea: What if it ends up becoming possible? What then?

She closed her eyes momentarily, trembled in spite of her nature of a cook manipulating satanic cauldrons, and then escaped very rapidly from the tenebrous spiral. Oh, the odious fearful idea, ever ready to insinuate itself, like a screw, behind her nape of an incredulous woman!

"Let's see, let's see, dear spirit," Deslandes repeated, cutting short the argument. "Don't be obstinate, or I'll be forced to call the doctor, and a provincial doctor, which you. mistrustful on principle, surely wouldn't want?"

The table, flattered, started to zigzag slightly, like a table that had been drinking. *Crack, crack!* Yes, yes! *No, no!* Ludovic was doubtless having trouble in his mahogany prison, for nothing reasonable could be extracted from him, either because the young woman's health left him cold or because Madame Bordes had not had time to put a brake on her brother's obliging pushes; they could no longer understand one another, everything was going sideways. Motionless, like the sibyl on her tripod, Julia frowned, straightened her square frame, her violent stature a fairground woman, an ex-acrobat in a broken-down caravan, and wisps of hair crowned her like a primitive diadem.

Ludovic remained coy. A majestic silence reigned; the two augurs looked at one another, disappointed. With a last respectful gesture, Deslandes rapped the center of the table in order to take his leave. A vibrant shock responded to him, formidable in the silence of the large room, an impact so rude that they jumped and the parquet exhaled a cloud of dust. All the woodwork groaned an echo; the bronze ring shook in the ceiling; Madame Bordes was seriously alarmed, while the unfortunate Jacques, although accustomed to the invasion of the supernatural, clung to the back of his chair, his mouth dry, believing that he saw Ludovic arrive in person, or in phantom. For half a second, Aunt Julia imagined that all their pocket phantasmagorias were about to mutate into a colossal specter, a palpable and irrefutable avenger of sincerity. Poignant doubt, frightful doubt, more frightful than fear itself, a glacial frisson, shook them both; they dared not look at one another.

Finally, the drawing room door yielded, its bolt fell off, making a strident metallic noise, and Madeleine surged forth—a frightful Madeleine, upright in her rigid black cashmere dress. Like a sword suddenly standing up under a mourning drape, fists clenched and eyes fulgurant, her hair putting ardent russet reflections around her pale physiognomy, like the flames of a conflagration, and she cried to them in a lugubrious voice that was surely no longer her own:

"I forbid you to evoke the dead here!"

It was Life, beautiful tearful Life, precipitating toward them, arms extended; all of miserable, beautiful Life, howling like a bitch, already wounded, which was afraid of death and divined it in a moonbeam before scenting it in the wound in her own loins, all of Life revolting against the stupid trap of dread, crying for mercy to the paltry speculators on infinity, who, poring over their stupidly rascally work, had not sensed the true Mystery welling up beside them!

IV

SITTING in the large dining room between an open window and a laundry-basket full of linen, Madeleine was mending passionately, no longer even raising her head, continuing to tangle her chimeras with her thread. A mute peace reigned in the street, devoid of carriages and passers-by, a warm tranquility that permitted the bees in the garden to make a tour of the house in order to come and buzz above the streams of household water. The horizon was limited by the gendarmerie, a narrow low barracks painted dark gray, a hostile, rocky gray, solely decorated by loopholes bristling with spikes and a portal with a door in imitation bronze. From time to time a gendarme dressed as a stable-hand, in a blue blouse and dirty twill trousers, stuck his head out of semi-circular vent whistling a tune: "Coco's boot! Coco's boot!" And that persisted, monotonously, circling the vent with the bees and Madeleine's chimeras.

The furniture of the dining room consisted of a table, six chairs and a faience vase standing on the mantelpiece, seemingly stark naked. In spite of its modern furniture, however, the room retained an attitude of old nobility; from its plinths to its cornices it was paneled with polished oak: Louis XV panels, tenderly oval, florid with wreaths and garlands, scattered with doves fluttering beak-to-beak and miniature swooning amours. All that pompadour, in wood flowing like fabric, was velveted by a venerable dust reminiscent of rice *à la Maréchale*; and the severe brown walls presented you with the slight shadows of things forever defunct under a veil, a transparent shroud, with which no feather duster could ever have reckoned, giving the appearance of forbidding you to touch it. The two sash windows veiled their dirty panes with curtains that were too short. Aunt Julia said, looking at them with a curious expression: "Here one doesn't feel at home; everything is higher than nature!" The six wicker chairs seemed too yellow. The table formed a shiny disk of waved cloth that confused the eyes; the faience vase, with its big pink flowers on a bed of moss, was positively blinding.

While the gendarme opposite droned "Coco's boot!" for the tenth time, the dining room door—a magnificent door with two battens whose sculpted moldings conserved traces of gilt—opened gently and Monsieur Deslandes stuck his head through.

"Do you know that he's coming? Are you ready to receive him, eh?" he said, in an ill-assured tone.

"Yes, yes, I know," Madeleine replied. "It's quite unnecessary. I'm not ill today."

The door closed again, Deslandes desiring, above all, to avoid another argument. And the young woman put her needlework down with a gesture of chagrin. For an instant she examined the room from right to left, as if troubled to have been woken from her dream by a disagreeable shock; then she got up and went out in the other direction to go in search of flowers that she wanted to put in the stout vase on the mantelpiece in order to make the lack of comfort less obvious: a worldly coquetry that she imagined she owed to the intruder in the same way she owed the traditional *bonjour*. It was difficult to receive visitors in the drawing room because of the odor of damp, and Madeleine could not tolerate anyone in her own room, making her bed herself and occupying herself with her petty housework in reclusion, which cut off all commerce with the outside.

She came back, bringing a lily in a sheaf of wild oats; she arranged her bouquet very skillfully, masking the garish colors of the faience with a few dangling twigs, and stepped back. The whole room took on a graceful physiognomy. Now she felt more at ease to subject herself to the chore; while looking at the wild oats she glanced at her reflection in the mirror behind them. There was no lack of mirrors above the mantelpieces of the house, but it still required a certain skill to see oneself therein among the patches of damp that spread along their dull crystal. Madeleine twisted her chignon, undid the little lace headscarf that she had knotted around her neck, trying to hide a slight scratch near the ear, and sat down before the linen-basket. A strange ennui curbed her figure, making her fold up in her sad dress of black cashmere, worn in the sleeves; she would have liked to bury herself in the sheets and napkins piled up in front of her, all the laundry that never ended, overflowing over her for a month and drowning her with its white flood. Oh, not to talk any more, not to hear, above all not to be obliged to give precise answers to precise questions!

Doctor Edmond Sellier came in, a trifle ceremoniously, because he had been warned that he was risking a poor welcome. He coughed, seeing that Mademoiselle Deslandes was continuing to ply her needle without budging.

"Here's Monsieur Sellier," muttered Deslandes, rubbing his nose with his habitual gesture. "I hope you'll furnish him with a few explanations regarding this singular condition." He paused, and added, raising his voice in order to render it more authoritative: "Yes, Monsieur, a young person who no longer eats, no longer sleeps, no longer goes out; who has livid cheeks and terrible rings around her eyes! Oh, it's not a matter of a simple sprain this time! I want you to prescribe her a serious treatment. Unearth a good tonic for her, ferruginous water, and above all walks—they don't cost anything, walks. For myself, I wash my hands of it; I've said all I can . . ."

He slipped away, blushing at that *coup-d'état*. Money? He had enough, damn it, since one never went out anywhere, no longer got dressed up, ate so poorly—and country doctors, it was said, only sent their bills after five years, He, Jacques Deslandes, was the head of the family; he had responsibilities, and when well-brought-up young women started breaking down doors, a father had to do something! However, he avoided passing through the kitchen, where he knew that his sister was peeling vegetables.

Edmond Sellier, still clutching his hat with a slightly confused gesture, waited for Madeleine to say something, striving to find this sort of reception natural, a sharp curiosity in his eyes half-hidden by a particular crease of his eyelid. She saluted him with a cold nod of the head.

"Mademoiselle," he said, smiling involuntarily, "Believe me, I am not here to force you to swallow some bitter drug. I encountered monsieur your father yesterday evening; we chatted; he claims that you no longer want to speak or eat. It's a caprice, I presume?"

She indicated a seat to him, but made no reply. Doctor Sellier sat down, making his decision, and continued in a cheerful tone: "Your sprain has had no consequences then? You haven't had any further accidents? I've often noticed your perron, those three shaky steps are so high that I have trouble getting up them myself, a man? When there's ice they're a veritable death trap! The notary who rented it to you ought to make repairs. It isn't cheerful, is it? Tell me, on rainy days don't you feel any pain in your ankle?"

He drew nearer, and she shook her head negatively.

"I think it might well be nothing," he went on, talking in order to break the ice and stringing together the first phrases that occurred to him; it was very difficult at first, but that disappeared quite naturally. "It's necessary to wear good shoes, wide, without high heels. Here it isn't like Paris; our streets are poorly paved; I'm sure that you don't go out because of the accursed cobblestones? But there's the countryside, Mademoiselle, the beautiful countryside, so close to you; one is outside the town on the other side of the garden and you can reach the meadows and the mountain. In your place I'd get up at five o'clock every morning and I'd go at a run all the way to the rocks. A charming walk, which will make sure of your foot permanently."

He stopped, disconcerted, for he was speaking in a jovial tone that was not his own. He had a horror of capricious invalids, detested nervous women and did not pose in the least as a hearty doctor.

I must seem stupid, he thought. Even so, he risked one last opportunistic phrase, hoping to extract a stunned exclamation, in order to conclude the visit in an appropriate fashion.

"Come on, let me take your pulse; you certainly have a fever, Mademoiselle, since you've lost your appetite."

She held out her hand, without a word, her lips disdainful. He took her pulse, briefly, and started looking at her with a kind of stupor. She was not ill, but she must be dissimulating some extraordinary chagrin. What an appearance she had of a faded, miserable creature! Her waist, curved and excessively supple, testified to an excessive lassitude, and her face, although of a rare regularity of features, sank into a leaden hue, changing and tinted green in the rings around her eyes—gray eyes whose violet pupils radiated vacillating gleams, like falling stars in a mist. Might one not have thought that beneath the dark and slender arcs of the eyebrows a storm of tears or lightning-flashes was rising? Her coppery red mouth was shining like a thin pepper, at the corners of which there was a last desire for life, but so distant!

From his winter visit Doctor Sellier remembered a beautiful young woman, slightly pale, with blonde hair. This one had russet hair, a dark red with lighter tints, like streaks poorly applied by a painter. No, the bright sunlight scarcely reached her, the poor child; she was destined more for the crepuscular troubles of Parisian evenings. He thought momentarily of asking her to put out her tongue, as one asks stupid little girls. Did she imagine that he might be wasting his time? In any case, she was not ill, her pulse was strong . . .

Nervously, he got to his feet, desirous of putting an end to it.

"Mademoiselle, I believe you're making fun of your parents; that isn't reasonable. Your father is desolate; your aunt too—she loves you very much, doesn't she?"

Then the desire to smile loosened the corners of her disdainful mouth; he saw her cheerful, with a cold, malevolent gaiety. She stared at him; the obscure stars of her pupils emerged from their fog; her teeth emerged from their red pepper sheath, and he stepped back anxiously, not knowing why she scared him. She was not mute, so it was necessary at any price to obtain a phrase from her, a yes or a no, a stupidity or an extravagance. Neurosis or chagrin; it was necessary to clarify that right away. He remembered clinic sessions in which headstrong girls were often brutalized, and he made an angry gesture.

"You want to say something!" he said, seizing her arm.

But suddenly, the violet eyes capsized in a cloud of tears, the mouth quivered, her complexion became diaphanously white; she stood up in her turn, put down her scissors, her needle and her thread on the linen in the basket, bowed and then drew away; and Edmond Sellier remained alone, annoyed by his false situation, and even more upset by the tears that were doubtless flowing out there, on the other side of the door.

"In truth, I don't understand any of this. It's a challenge!"

He strode back and forth in the room, pretending to be taking inventory of the sculptures of the woodwork. Was she coming back? It was scarcely probable. Would he see the father or the aunt again? What funny people! The stable-hand intoned his stupid refrain again: "Coco's boots! Coco's boots!"

Edmond Sellier shrugged his shoulders. All these petty crises of spoiled demoiselles left him indifferent. He would leave in ten minutes; and he consulted his watch with a habitual movement. A regulation visit lasted a quarter of an hour, which he did not count, for he perceived that these Parisians had no fortune. One never saw them, either in the Cours or the homes of the neighbors. They hid, living without a domestic, in a crudely furnished house. Oh, how life turns around and around in the same frame; the gendarmes whistle a little tune, the flies buzz, the dust thickens slowly and one fine morning one dies, the soul full of secrets one never dared confess to anyone!

Doctor Sellier's face darkened; his head leaned toward a nest of minuscule Amours, to which an enormous dove was extending its beak. Wasn't everything ridiculous and lamentable in this bleak little town? Not yet thirty-five, he felt as old as the world; his hair was already going gray, so much did the dust of the roads traveled by night and day weigh upon his pensive head. He was not happy, and not unhappy either, but it was necessary to live without any motive, and that became irritating at length; it made one dream of chimerical crimes, *killing time*, for instance, and to do what, good God?

Monsieur Deslandes came in on tiptoe.

"Well?" he said, rubbing his left nostril furiously.

"Well, my dear Monsieur," murmured the frustrated doctor, "our invalid didn't say a word. I'm no further forward than you; but don't be too alarmed, young women have whims, a few vapors. It will pass; it's necessary to distract her."

Jacques Deslandes shook his head sadly. "Distract her? How do you expect me to do that. She has a hard heart; she isn't amused by anything. In Paris, excursions exasperated her—because of the men who always follow lone women, you know. Now, she argues with her aunt all day long, about the cooking, sewing and washing. Can I prevent her from detesting her aunt? She doesn't like anything, Monsieur, that's the truth!"

Jacques Deslandes stopped abruptly, regretting that he had said so much to a stranger. He became dignified.

"You understand, if I changed position, I could take her to the sea-baths in summer and invite people to the house, but at the moment, my work as a librarian forbids me voyages and receptions. I require silence . . . yes, a great silence."

Sellier thought about poor consumptives to whom a physician advises a prompt departure for Italy. While searching for his cane in the corridor, he sighed. It was the eternal disappointment of an educated, coquettish, proud girl who finds herself sinking in the muddy pond of mediocrity. Wallowing, my princess, with the geese, the ducks, the frogs on the fetid mire stirred for centuries by the same dimwits. One finds hours of acute desolation there, where one would like to end it all and drown oneself, but no opportunity for a beautiful catastrophe presents itself; the pond is not deep enough to permit the drama.

Having finally found his cane, the doctor had to deal with Madame Bordes. She launched herself out of the kitchen brandishing an onion, her hair spiky and her cheeks lit up; she looked him up and down with the chagrined gaze that all women have for men that are still young.

"You've been disturbed needlessly, haven't you, Monsieur? I knew it! She's a perverse creature, and you don't have any idea of the trouble she's given me in bringing her up since she emerged from her mother. I'm sure that there's nothing wrong with her, but my brother is a weakling . . . he listens to his daughter! Tell me, Monsieur le docteur, will you take something in my kitchen, informally?"

She drew nearer, her manner soothing, holding her onion under Sellier's nose, as he headed for the door.

"No thank you, Madame."

"It's so hot. A glass of cherry cordial?"

Jacques Deslandes became expansive. "Yes, it's an opportunity to taste our new syrup, Monsieur Sellier, so do us the honor . . ."

The physician was in torment. Now he understood the bizarre smile of the young woman when he had talked about the affection her aunt must have for her. An affection of a cook, all slaps and drops of grease. Delicate children detest dirty people; like cats they are enemies of bad odor. She had a fine reek, the aunt!

"I'm in a hurry," Sellier murmured. "Another day, I'd certainly have pleasure . . . *Au revoir*, Monsieur Deslandes."

He went down the high steps, one of which was broken, in two bounds, jolting all his joints, and reached the hospice situated to the north of the house.

"You see, he's very discreet," declared Deslandes.

Madame Bordes pulled a face. "Pooh! What I said was to reduce the price of his visits. You send for the doctor without even informing yourself of the bill. I hope he won't come back again. With the sprain, it will come to twenty francs at least."

"In the provinces it's another matter; he'll ask us for his money in five years. I know the customs, my dear. The concierge at the library explained to me yesterday that Formel, our landlord, hasn't settled a doctor's bill for typhoid fever for twelve years—not that one, another, an old man, who doesn't even remember any more. Oh, the provinces . . . !"

And Deslandes, convinced of the immemorial stupidity of the province, went back inside to get his briefcase of a serious librarian. He needed silence; his important work demanded it. "Yes, yes, Monsieur, I require a great silence!" As soon as he was alone he stuffed his pipe, sat down at his desk and, with the aid of a buzzing fly, went to sleep.

His back slightly stooped, Edmond Sellier shaved the walls of the street, anxious to avoid the searching gaze of old Madame Bordes, and especially the reek of her onions. That was twice he had gone into the home of those Parisians, and twice their kitchen had reeked of fried onions. It was very strange. In the end, one has one's little faults, in Paris as elsewhere. No, the young person could not be completely happy, even though she still seemed whippable, in spite of her twenty-two years. She was near to crowning Saint Catherine, poor thing, and had all sorts of vapors.

Sellier lived on the Cours with his mother, a pious, distinguished woman with a grave manner and extinct eyes. They had comfortable lodgings, a ground floor whose shutters touched the trees of the promenade when they were opened. The promenade was always deserted, and nothing was darker. Save for the bronze plaque on their door—*Doctor Sellier, consultations every morning*—no ray of light filtered through.

From the consulting room the stout black columns of fabulous elms could be seen, lustrous with oily water, planted six meters apart and jostling one another, foliage to foliage, overhead. On Sunday slow shadows went by, of messieurs in frock-coats and ladies in skirts dotted here and there with flecks of jet, which gave the impression of black fish swimming in an aquarium. In autumn, leaves strewed the ground with a marbling of blood and gold; then the black fish filed past in an even more melancholy fashion, two by two or three by three, followed by young ones, fluttering, already with a certain dignity. The widowed Madame Sellier liked that corner of the Cours; for her it was one of the best frequented, and she had forbidden the children of the school to play there because they damaged the bark of the elms. The white marble perron was washed by the maid every morning; the door, painted blue, always shone with fresh varnish; the copper rim of the letter box was reminiscent of a ferocious mouth barking mute and sententious things.

One divined from the threshold the meticulous neatness of the apartment, which had narrow rooms like glove-boxes, where all the objects had their definitive places but were wiped tenderly several times a day. There were little suspensions of old flowery Sèvres and natural florets, which were surrounded, along with their living plants, by a mosquito-net of silvery gauze. The branches and corollas were neatly arranged in their cage; whenever a branch, emancipating itself, threatened to make a hole, it was cut and everything returned to order. Dressers and shelf-units were encumbered by little colored religious trivia, as appetizing as baptismal candy-boxes. But for the fact that one could not see there, it was an agreeable place for a siesta in summer. Sellier's desk scintillated with a furtive gleam and the parquet was resplendent; light muslin curtains bathed the barred windows with their fresh foam, and the beautiful medical bookcase reflected the other items of furniture scrupulously. A religious peace reigned from the kitchen to the drawing room; one could not hear the footsteps of the maid, who was shod specially in fur slippers. Madame Sellier gave her orders in a low voice. Edmond Sellier, knowing that his mother could not abide muddy footprints, was careful to take off his boots when it rained. They were not rich, but comfortable in a cold security, a routine wellbeing that seemed to have been perpetuated for centuries; and every Sunday Madame Sellier dispensed bowls of thick soup to the needy of the town through a door opening on to a smelly back street on the other side of the house.

The old lady's only regret was not having their horse and their tilbury at home, the pretty carriage being garaged at the Post Office at the end of the Cours, there being nowhere to put it in the apartment under a mosquito-net. That carriage, a source of pride, was part of the family, and Madame Sellier languished in knowing that it was exiled out there among the Vandals.

On entering, Edmond Sellier found on the corner of his work-table a pitcher of beer and a tall sculpted crystal glass dating back to the first Doctor Sellier, his father. He drank, satisfied in being in his study, where everything was so neat and orderly, where mysterious hands cared for him at a distance, flattering his little vice: drinking a few mouthfuls of blond beer at about three o'clock in the afternoon. Afterwards, he smoked a cigar. Her mother surprised him as he was finishing the tankard, clicking his tongue.

"Be careful, Edmond," she said, in her soft voice of a resigned person, "you like beer too much; you'll get fat."

He started to laugh. "Come on, Mother; it's stifling outside."

She said "Ah!" with an astonished expression. The warmth outside was good for those who did not have a chill inside; she never warmed up, in winter or in summer. Thin-waisted, she always wore silk, fabric with shiny surfaces as glacial as her skin, which was very smooth and white, without a wrinkle or a bump. She chose austere shades for preference, Carmelite plum or episcopal violet, and sewed jet tassels thereon, which she had a mania for heaping up in profusion, which took up a great deal of her time. With her handkerchief she wiped the spot where the pitcher had been set down, putting a ring on the desk and asked: "How is the demoiselle Deslandes?"

"Mademoiselle Deslandes," replied Sellier, sardonically, "is suffering, I believe, from a family scene."

"Nothing more?"

"My God, no."

Informed of all her son's comings and goings, Madame Sellier asked about everyone's health, out of blessed curiosity, on condition that it never involved repulsive maladies. Deep down, an anxiety gnawed her, the secret malady of her soul, a need to know from one hour to the next what her son was doing, who he was visiting and what they wanted of him. Sometimes, although the doctor had his free pass, she watched for him until he returned. His nocturnal voyages were quite rare, fortunately. Then Edmond grumbled, shook chairs, gripped by impatience. People had no idea of that—worse than a babe at the breast! Was he capable of going astray in the streets of the town, did anyone suspect that he was out of bed now? Then the old lady calmed down and withdrew on tiptoe, closing the doors quietly, and Edmond, calmed by the great silence of the benign house, regretted his outburst of anger. She was a very gentle woman, a careful mother, and yet he could have dreamed of a less gentle, less careful one. He did not reproach her for inhibiting his liberty, thank God; he always reclaimed his masculine liberty at the decisive moment, but she spoiled him with a delicate sentiment, showing that confidence in manifestations of affection. Perhaps she loved him too much for her own good. He earned a living for both of them comfortably; was she afraid of seeing her share diminish one day?

The next day, Edmond, confused by having ruminated egotistical things, became a small boy again and forgot himself to the extent of tapping her cheeks, in order to rid her mind of suspicions that she had perhaps not had. In any case, Madame Sellier was hermetic, and what he held against her most of all was that she did not tell him the true cause of her fears.

"They're funny people!" sighed Madame Sellier.

"The Parisians? Yes, very funny people," Edmond replied, unsealing a letter and opening a ledger.

Without persisting, she left him.

V

SELLIER was going through a little wood in the carriage, allowing his horse to go at its own pace, because he was making a rather pleasant journey to a village on the hill that overlooked the town, and from time to time he addressed felicitations to him:

"There! Very good! He's a good Marquis, that horsey! Yes, a very good Marquis! But he doesn't like flies. Poor coco! And he'd like to browse a little tender grass, eh? Come on, come on! No gluttony! Tender grass gives horseys a tummy-ache!"

Marquis, a young horse with a very white coat, with a large tuft of hair on the forehead that one might have thought powdered, so snowy was it, beat his flanks furiously with his tail, sometimes turning, nostrils open, in the direction of a plant, the damp odor or which gave him an appetite.

The man and the beast never fell out. Each knew that the other was not malevolent, and they understood one another marvelously as soon as they were alone in the open air. Fundamentally, was not the conciliatory physician a creature of soft appearance, like his horse, with the same resigned philosophy of life? *It's necessary to eat every day*, they both thought, and, that task accomplished, they took a quarter of an hour's grace to respire and contemplate green things. They were wise!

The little wood masked the top of the hill and the rocks looming over the town; it was a peaceful spot before the tormented landscape of the summit. One was sheltered there from the wind, the sun and the indigenes. Above all, one experienced a delightful sentiment of security after having traveled through the bleak fields of wheat, flamboyant under the ferocious August sun.

When the little wood ended, one began a steeper climb, jolting, going uphill between disagreeable brushwood, and then the rocks were uncovered: the *Shepherd's Table*, that flat stone, yellow when it was dry and as black as ink when it rained; the *Chairs* of scintillating granite; the *Stools* as round as loaves of ammunition; and finally the *Stairway*, tumbling solemnly down a volcanic wall. To descend that spiraling pebbly route Marquis needed the feet of a goat. At the bottom of the hill the town was grouped, its pointed steeples bristling like a pin-cushion; the town, which seemed from above so isolated from the rest of the Earth, so quiet, so unworldly that one might have thought it a great convent in which each monk had his own little house.

It was a poor abandoned burg far from industrial centers; railway trains sped through its station as often as not and only small objects were manufactured there in sculpted bone, frail patient endeavors that no one bought, at least in the shops of its own streets, futile objects, the considerable efforts of sad artisans who preferred to the robust handles of pick-axes the slender paltriness of some skeletal debris. Before the town came the terrace of the old house of the Parisians, a crumbling wall hardly sustaining the soil of their garden bordered by hazel trees. The perpetual menace of the rocks above their roof seemed to have so horrified the habitation that it was collapsing very gently.

Edmond Sellier stopped Marquis as they engaged on the rocky slope in order to light a cigarette. His mother detested the odor of tobacco; he took advantage of his last minute to savior another one. While lighting it he made a reflection, almost aloud: "Yes, they're funny people, the Deslandes."

He thought about the Deslandes because, as he passed before their terrace on that morning in August, he had perceived their daughter under a blue umbrella. He had felt obliged to salute her with a slight tip of his hat, and she had not even bothered to respond. Doubtless she was still annoyed by his visit. And yet, in spite of papa's invitations, he had not returned, understanding that he would only aggravate her petty familial miseries. Papa persisted, having received discreet assurances that he would never be sent a bill. Oh, that singular marionette, with his squinting eyes and his gestures of a court usher! That vile old lady stinking of frying and decked in extravagant camisoles! "Yes, they're funny people." Always anxious, always making scenes with the postman, and incessantly peering into space, protecting their troubled eyes with their hands, a veil that ought to bring deliverance.

All the same, their blessed lair needs repair, thought Sellier, *but that Formel is an old miser. I'll wager that he'll end up selling it as it is. I would have bought it myself if*

Maman had wanted; it pleases me, that place, and Coco would have his stable!

Sellier adored the vast rooms, where one had air, and room to turn round. He had sacrificed himself for a long time to his mother's graciously paltry tastes, but he suffered for himself and for Marquis. Impossible to have a dog, of course, because it would be so dirty!

She was difficult, that child, for not being happy on her terrace! How life went askew! He saw the blue umbrella again, lying in a clearing in the hazel trees, like a fabulous flower blossoming in hemlock. From up here, the demoiselle seemed even paler, aureoled by her nimbus of blue. She had a pretty, supple figure, though, which did not prevent her bosom from developing easily, her hips from being firm, and she was definitely terribly blonde. No woman of the town sported blonde hair like that! There were the bizarre eyes, of course; of what could she be dreaming, sitting on the gray stones of the old wall, her gaze lost, drowned in a mist of tears?

The doctor was about to lift the reins to make his horse set off when a heart-rending cry resounded, followed by feverish appeals, strangled in the depths of a contracted throat. It made him shiver, and simultaneously gave him an instinctive desire to turn back.

"Good God! Someone here is being murdered!" said the young man, straightening up as if under a whip-lash.

Her cries drew nearer, maddened; it was surely a woman. The physician got down from the carriage, while his horse pricked its ears, curiously. Sellier soon recovered his professional sang-froid and got ready to help the person who was being murdered, or raped— for one never knows what might happen in deserted corners of the countryside. He heard someone coming from the left, a rustle of skirts flying through the brambles.

A path descended from the rocks, and a woman bounded from that direction, hectically, holding a blue umbrella in her hand. It was Mademoiselle Deslandes. Madeleine had the appearance of a madwoman; she often looked behind her, fearfully, her eyes staring, and the umbrella fluttered, wide open, expanded like a huge flower swayed by a storm wind, curbed and crushed. The umbrella fell; Madeleine paid no heed to it; she crossed a ditch with a more violent bound, and stopped in front of the physician, repeating in a hoarse voice:

"The dog! It's the dog! There's the dog!"

"What dog?" exclaimed Sellier, who could not see it.

It was probably a matter of an angry dog chasing the young woman, or even a rabid dog that had already bitten her. With a rapid gesture, Edmond passed his hand inside his jacket to his belt, into which he had the habit of sliding a loaded revolver, the precaution of a man who sometimes travels by night.

"Don't be afraid. Mademoiselle. I'll take care of it! Has it bitten you?"

"No, it didn't touch me."

"It ran after you, then? But where is it?"

Madeleine, out of breath, looked behind her. "It's . . . up there, on the rocks. I'm quite sure I saw it there."

She put her hands on her breast; her staring eyes closed. Edmond thought she was about to faint, and put his arm around her.

"Let's see! *Sacrebleu*, since it hasn't bitten you, you're safe!"

Madeleine pressed against him momentarily, and then pushed him away nervously.

"My apologies, Monsieur. It's passed; it's nothing; I was very frightened, that's all." She tried to smile; her poor face was tinted by an unexpected rosiness. "I must seem to you like a madwoman, don't I? No, no, Monsieur, I'm not mad . . . I'm certain that I saw that dog."

"Of course, it's easy to encounter furious animals in this heat! Wait—I'll go take a look myself."

Resolutely, Edmond set forth along the path, clinging to his rabid dog—an idea that was quite natural, and which explained the atrocious terror of the woman, unused to rural surprises. Having arrived with a few rapid leaps in the middle of the Shepherd's Table, from which one could see the countryside and the town at the same time, he found no trace of a dog, either in the brambles or around the rock. The young woman's screams had made it flee, or it had hidden nearby as soon as the young man appeared. Edmond replaced his revolver in his belt, not liking to prolong bellicose attitudes too long. He kicked a few pebbles, threw some toward suspect points, and then went down the hill again wearily.

"In truth, Mademoiselle, I don't know where your dog has gone, but it can't be found. Are you quite certain of having seen one?" he said, smiling in order to reassure her entirely.

She was leaning against the carriage, bleakly, her arms dangling and her eyes uncertain. She had picked up her umbrella and closed it; the hand that held it was trembling frightfully. At the hint of mockery in Sellier's voice, she drew herself up to her full height, her eyes glittering.

"You're asking me if I'm certain that I saw it?" she said, dully. "Why ask me that?"

Edmond examined her attentively. The woman did not speak like everyone else; she emphasized seemingly insignificant phrases with a strange insistence.

"I'm asking you . . . well, one forges illusions, doesn't one? One believes that a tree root is a snake, that a rock forms the silhouette of a man. At dusk I've often mistaken an unfortunate sheep-dog for a wolf . . ."

Madeleine seized his wrists abruptly and cried: "I saw it! I saw it! I was sitting on the side of the town; I was tracing signs in the gravel with the tip of my umbrella. I said to myself: *It would be extraordinary if* . . . No, I won't repeat it to you, because that only concerns me, and I was quite calm, quite lucid. Above me, a large bird was soaring whose abdomen reflected the sun. A mildness seemed to emanate from the bird all the way to my forehead; I was admiring it, and my eyes blinked, dazzled by so much light. When it flapped its wings, my eyelids beat in unison; I felt my eyes flying away, ever further; I was floating as if in transparent, delicious water. I can't express the charm of that total mental repose! Have you ever had a day trickle through your fingers in little droplets, caressed like pink satin, with an odor of honeysuckle, suddenly, in a gust of breeze, while you don't wonder what has become of it? Oh, you can't grasp what I'm saying! That's a pity. Well, it was all those mild things combined into one! As soon as I lowered my head, stunned by pleasure, I saw the dog, standing on the flat stone, the Shepherd's Table . . . the dog . . ."

She interrupted her sentence to look behind her, and continued, in a less ardent voice: "In sum, I saw an enormous dog, with a square skull, a kind of Great Dane with shiny short hair—you know, one of those dogs that eat children! Yes, I saw it . . . and I ran away, screaming I don't know what!"

She shut up, but her lips did not cease quivering. Edmond Sellier disengaged his wrists carefully. He was stupefied. Like Molière's mute, once she began to speak, she didn't stop!

"You're very excited, Mademoiselle Deslandes," he murmured sliding his arm under hers. We're going to walk along the path for a few minutes, and then we'll drink a cordial. I have my pharmacy here. Hush! Be quiet." And he added, slightly in jest: "That doubtless won't succeed, any more than it did when I ordered you to talk two months ago!"

He kept hold of her hand and was able to convince himself that she did not have a fever. The pulse was steady. Was she mad? No. She really was afraid. Her manner of explaining herself did not lack logic, after all, although it gave evidence of a literary mind. She was, like many isolated creatures, intoxicated by herself, excessively sensitive, vibrant for a glimpsed bird, or brushed by a ray of sunlight, or a respired perfume. He even searched for the name of that kind of neurosis but could no longer recall it. One rarely encountered such unusual cases in his poor little town.

They walked together for a little while. Sellier, his head tilted over his shoulder, did not take his medical eye off her, marching at measured paces, sustaining her vigorously in spite of herself. Madeleine kept her mouth closed, obedient by virtue of education, but he divined that she was restive, ready to escape, having a nervous horror of his contact, perhaps simply because he was the unknown—which is to say, a man.

"Are you feeling better?" he asked, stopping.

She forced herself to smile. "Yes; thank you, you're very kind. I'm confused, having deflected you from your route. A physician never has the time . . ."

"I assure you that I'm in the full exercise of my functions; you're a patient," he replied, in order not to alarm her.

She raised her eyes, and said coldly: "A madwoman you mean? Admit it."

Sellier made a curt gesture. "I believe you're more unhappy than ill."

She looked at him. The man was very good, very just, very sympathetic. He had the handsome and grave physiognomy of a devoted and reasonable companion. His brown gaze was sensually youthful, in a face of meditative resignation. He was, above all, normal; he represented a providence, a refuge, and his broad chest and energetic arms testified to his strength, pleading the superb cause of his health. She almost had the desire to make him a full confession. Alas, he let fall a banal phrase that curled her up again.

"Let's see, can a charming young woman like you lack admirers?"

She found that vulgar, and stiffened. What right did he have to touch a wound in her heart?

"I won't abuse your complaisance any longer, Monsieur. Permit me to go."

"What about my cordial?"

"No, thank you. I'm in haste to return to the house. *Au revoir.*"

"And your dog?"

"You can render me a service," she ventured, anxiously, "by enquiring about its master. Oh, I beg you. I saw it, therefore it exists. You're a local man; try to discover who has a Great Dane in the town or the surrounding area . . ."

"Gladly."

He had a strong desire to propose to her to go back up the slope on the carriage with her, but he thought that it might be inappropriate. He bowed to her very respectfully, took Marquis from his sly debauches in the tender grass, and drew away at a little trot.

Before entering the town, the doctor turned round; he saw her in the distance, descending from the rocks with a weary stride. Her blue umbrella was still swinging behind her shoulder, and its periwinkle blue was diluted in the hue of the sky, so that he no longer saw anything but the slightly tragic dark silhouette of the woman. Why did she wear such a sad dress, so worn in the sleeves, too long, hiding her feet, which made her surge from the ground itself in an unnatural protrusion? Oh, nothing was natural in the conduct of that disoriented creature! Her voice sounded false, as poignant as a plaint; her eyes had obsessive gleams; her hair . . . yes, her hair reeked of sulfur, the tint of which it conserved in places. That young woman was ill, with an amorous chagrin, he would swear to it! An immense pity invaded him, and he wondered what he could do.

"My God! In the meantime I can ask about that dog . . ."

He did not say anything about his adventure to his mother. All that was romantic and shady, which would not please the old lady, who was alarmed by the slightest incidents. He contented himself, at dinner, with questioning their maid.

"Do you know anything about a big Danish dog, Marie? A kind of colossus that has been seen roaming in the surrounding area. Peasants have told me that it was rabid."

"My word, Monsieur, no. There are no big dogs in the town. They're all thin hereabouts."

"The tax-collector has had one for three weeks," said his mother, "but it's not a Great Dane, it's a basset hound."

"Then the one I saw must belong to someone is a nearby village, on the other side of the hill; it looked frightening."

"What—you've seen it?" cried Madame Sellier, terrified.

"Yes, I saw it," murmured the doctor, without much conviction.

In the evening, Sellier went out for a walk outside the house. There he encountered, as usual, notable people of the town: the tax-collector smoking his cigar; a captain of the gendarmerie; a few priests who went past, saying "*Bonsoir*" in low voices, ladies leading big thin girls, pushed too rapidly, dazing into empty space like solitary goats, and a few other slow individuals to whom no one thought of explaining themselves. Sellier made the captain party to his discovery.

"A rabid dog? Outside the town? Excuse me . . . excuse me," he murmured, slightly disconcerted. "My men would have already reported it to me."

"A very big dog, a Great Dane," Edmond insisted.

"Has it bitten anyone?"

"No, I hope not."

"Then, permit me, how can you expect me to have its description?"

Followed by the tax-collector, they went into a little café shaded by wisteria, as green as the inside of a bottle, with a billiard table that gave the impression of a fake lawn in the middle of a room strewn with yellow sand. The tax-collector asked for a green menthe, and for the sake of politeness the captain took one too. Reluctantly, Sellier accepted a similar consummation. They chatted, very mildly, about possible catastrophes, not hurrying either to drink or make a remark, adopting the expressions of men certain in advance that nothing would happen, who had lost, so much were they lost in the shadow, even the hope of seeing anything happen, good or bad. Then suddenly, while the tax-collector finished swallowing his peaceful green reflection, Sellier stood up impatiently; a sudden malaise had invaded him on finding himself with those flaccid individuals, leading the existence of a naïve population of an aquarium. He paid the bill with an abrupt gesture.

"Excuse me! Excuse me!" muttered the captain of the gendarmerie

"We won't excuse . . ." objected the tax-collector.

But Sellier fled, already far away. Leafing through an old medical book in his solitary corner seemed to him to be a preferable distraction. The doctor had never sensed the banality of their conversation and the emptiness of their heads, and perhaps his own, more clearly than that evening, Oh, to commit a crime! To kill . . . time!

VI

MADELEINE pushed the gate with a decisive gesture. She went straight ahead, no longer looking
back. running the risk of dying on the way. To be free!
My God, how many times had she dreamed of being a
beggar, without relatives, without direction, wandering
along the highways, having no other care but that of
stealing forbidden fruit! And yet, she had never dared
to realize that dream, because there were *the principles
of education*—principles in which she had scarcely believed for a long time. No, alas, one could not simply
accomplish certain actions; mysterious powers held
you back at the last moment.

One evening, out there, she had run away from
their Parisian dwelling and walked on the boulevard
until midnight, excited, firmly resolved not to return,
to let herself be picked up by the police; but she had
gone back, head bowed and breast swollen, forgetting
why she had left. She had found her father waiting on
the stairs, a candle in his hand, that little light flickering
so tremulously in the darkness, illuminating the poor
solemn face of Jacques Deslandes so dolorously that
she had started to climb at a run in order to throw her

arms around the old man's neck, begging his pardon. Now, perhaps she would return again, but she would no longer make apologies, for something irremediably cold froze her heart. She no longer loved those people. They no longer counted, and she was not astonished that they were finished in her memory.

She told herself that the family was bound to perish morally by virtue of an excess of intimacy. They knew one another too well, and how could children not be disdainful of grotesque parents, whose cerebral activity always had need of enthusiasm, only alimented by the splendor of beauty in all its forms. Moral bonds did not have the strength to enchain young souls with the mild fictions of tales of enchantment. Did a mother or an aunt incessantly wear a crown of stars? Did a father kill a famous dragon vomiting flames every day?

The young woman would have liked to be born of heroes or marvelous criminals, but she did not even have the consolation of complaining about them in the role of victim, since they had never beaten her seriously.

Was it also the deadly education that aided her to tear the sacred veils? What certain science did she possess, anyway? At present, she did not understand anything at all; a thick smoke, issued from her muted anger, blurred her best memories, and she felt incapable even of analyzing her childhood. At least she had not remained, in spite of numerous serious studies, the anguished child in the depths of the dark cupboard into which Aunt Julia had often thrown her, more to get rid of her than to punish her. Oh, the distant rancors that had taken root in the shadow of her first fears, her first audacities of revolt, and were now producing venomous flowers!

Having gone through the gate, Madeleine set forth into the mown meadow that separated her from the hill. During her daily walks she had traced a path a foot wide through the thick grass, and that route unwound its narrow elegance, as subtle as a pretty snake, through the liberty of the deserted fields. She went for a walk every day, not in order to follow the ingenuous advice of Doctor Sellier but to flee family crises.

This evening, a strange sunset reddened the horizon. The summit of the rocky hill was adorned by a diadem of pink cirrus clouds, and at the center of that diadem, directly above the flat stone, a well of pale blue sky opened, in a watery light ready to inundate the town. Over the road, the woods and the fields, somber clouds whose sinister leaden gray tint was colored here and there with sulfur yellow extended with an evil and devouring allure. A heat like that of a forge rose from unknown vents that must pierce the skin of the earth at intervals, already so lamentably cracked by dryness. The hazel trees of the garden, the poplars of the road, the elders bordering the meadows, and even the sprigs of wild mint took on a phantasmal immobility.

Madeleine looked behind her, according to her habit of an anxious creature, and could hardly perceive the house, which had become the color of ash, like the clouds covering it with their bat-like wings, enveloping it and swallowing its roof. No sound was audible, neither the rolling of rare carts penetrating the town, nor the chirping of birds preparing for their night.

There would not be a storm, because all that had been turning around the hill for three days and there was no reason to expect an imminent denouement. A vague perfume of honey and odors of drains mingled in the boiling vat of the atmosphere. One did not feel, however, prey to a ferocious breath retaining either life or death.

Madeleine traversed the hedge of elders without awakening the swarm of bees that normally plundered its pearly white umbels, no buzzing sprang forth, the pure virtuous insects had gone home, retreating with horror from the slow poisoning of the baleful hour. As if harassed by malevolent powers, the young woman leapt over a ditch, her eyes full of challenge, and climbed the hill angrily. Beneath her, impatient hot stones crumbled, a sort of thin calcareous foliage, and broke, with the harsh rustle of creased papers. The rock that formed the framework of the hill protruded though the soil over its entire surface: a yellow clay, rarely damp, in which nothing could grow, neither grass nor bushes. Only a species of gray moss, an imperceptible lichen, a living dust at the most, carpeted that malevolent and miserly terrain. On palpating that treacherous velvet, one felt a painful heat, like a slight urticary fever.

From time to time, Madeleine slipped; a pebble rolled down the slope, sometimes falling on to the main road. sometimes on to the mown grass, and she resumed her ascent, always experiencing a singular new fury at making the assault of that natural Calvary, where she came to live her passion of isolation. Up there she was tranquil, no one having to go to the rocks in order to labor there. Flocks found no pasture there and peasants and town-dwellers preferred the detour of the road to the rocky path cutting across the summit.

Half way up, Madeleine looked back again, desirous of embracing the panorama of the town with one last glance. She had a frisson of grim joy, seeing it almost buried under a troubled vapor, timidly starred by the poor light of lamps lit behind windows and veiled by pale muslin, like gazes covered with blinkers or filled with tears. The window of the drawing room of their old house shone with an indistinct redness, like the sly furnace of an alchemist.

"They're consulting Ludovic!" she murmured.

Dinner having finished, Aunt Bordes and Deslandes, knowing that no one would any longer come to disturb them, had probably started making their table turn. Mocking laughter shook Madeleine, who was penetrating at that moment into the crimson region of the sunset. She was illuminated as if by a firework. And she had the pride of seeing herself radiant, while at her feet creatures deprived of true light were vegetating. This evening, she believed herself capable of not going home again, for she was not at home among them, and in order further to affirm that resolution, she recalled the scenes of the day.

In the morning her aunt had given her an order to clean the drawing room from top to bottom, and the young woman had promptly lost her taste for that occupation of a maidservant, already fatigued by having washed the floor-tiles of her bedroom on her knees. Incessantly harassed by the shrill voice of Madame Bordes, which seemed even more vulgarly noisy in that tomblike house than in Paris, Madeline became exasperated, for her part, by trifles, and refused the household chores, unable to amuse herself like simple folk.

Soon, a cloud of dust, an inexplicable white powder that made the fingers sticky, had risen around her, dissimulating the furniture, settling on things that had just been wiped and stinging her eyes. Of that banal physical irritation her cerebral irritation was born. She remembered, in fact, that from that moment on she had lost her head slightly. In order to tidy the drawing room, had she not taken it into her head to unhook the wall-hangings? But when she tried, the green damask resisted with more vigor than she could have anticipated on the part of old cloth, causing such an abundance of dust to fuse from all its fissures that Madeleine recoiled. The big mirror over the mantelpiece sent back her image, tarnished, her brow covered in sweat, disheveled, with cobwebs soiling the gold of her chignon.

She called her aunt. "Would you care to help me?" she said, curtly. "We need to unfasten all this and beat it in the open air, in the garden; otherwise I'll give up."

"Unfasten the curtains!" roared Madame Deslandes, raising her eyes to the ceiling. "Are you mad? It's sufficient to brush them, I think, climbing on a table."

"It's futile work," Madeleine had declared, harshly. "I'll spend my life on it without result!"

"Climb on a table, I tell you," repeated the aunt, "and brush! You're young, you need exercise, and it's even more necessary to you than contemplating the beauties of nature."

"So be it!" the niece had replied.

And, perhaps with a very insubordinate intention, she had dragged Ludovic against the wall and then, armed with a stick, she had hoisted herself up. Naturally, the storm had burst, for Aunt Julia did not permit that kind of profanation.

"Let's see," sniggered the young woman, beating the damask, which rendered bizarre sounds under the blows, "you wouldn't want me to climb on Papa's desk and stave it in?"

She was obliged to get down, pulled violently by the skirt, and she confessed that she had had enough.

"You have only to get in a daily woman," she said, shrugging her shoulders, "and for a measly twenty sous you could have your drawing room cleaned. As for me, I give up!"

The scene continued. Aunt Bordes was beside herself. All the reflections on the ingratitude of pretentious girls who preferred caring for their hands and their figure rather than their parents' house passed through it, and then the invectives on the subject of the false savante whose education served for nothing.

"If I were your father I'd send you in apprenticeship to a dressmaker or a mender. You could be a school-teacher and earn your diabolical living rather than encumbering ours, but you prefer dreaming, and you'll end up going to the bad one day. Idleness is the mother of all vices!"

Madeleine took refuge in her room. She was idle, and yet she often made efforts of which no one took any account! Madame Bordes sent her to her room, for the medium, full of down-to-earth ideas that she considered as a plan for future happiness, catechized her niece with the best will in the world. A serious woman ought to interest herself in stews, peeling onions tenderly, getting excited about the quality of butter and putting pieces of flannel in her silk dresses. Unfortunately, Madeleine was distracted, feverish, and she did not perceive her own faults, so much did she suppose herself superior to others! And then, when one had reached the age of twenty-two, one tried to create a reputation as a good cook. In the country, it was claimed that that attracted husbands . . . etc., etc.

"Furthermore, don't hope that your figure will get you married without a dowry," she concluded. "They don't like redheads in the country, you know!"

Standing in a corner of her room, her arms folded over her breathless bosom, Madeleine shut up. But her teeth bit her tight lips and her eyes darkened to violet black, emitting fulgurant sparks. Her father no longer defended her now because if she had had recourse to him against her aunt she knew full well that he would respond: "We'll both be eating in the kitchen when she's finished with us! Is it you that can attend to the spit?"

She had often thought of a position as a petty schoolmistress, but where would she find it? In the town where they lived that would have produced a scandal, and one would have gone voluntarily in quarantine, either out of modesty or by disdain, rather than beg people for favors. No, it was necessary to continue to tread water and avoid poisoning the arguments— but Aunt Julia, tormented by inadmissible thoughts, needed arguments to purge her blood; she made use of insults and scenes as natural outlets, and once the expectoration was concluded, she went to market, the sole goal of her excursion, her firm pace and sacerdotal attitude being to unearth some dubious piece of fish that she could bring back triumphantly, crying: "I've had a stroke of luck! He let me have it for five sous less because of the heat!"

At dinner on that stormy day, the father had augmented the bad mood of the women by announcing that it was necessary to invite Doctor Sellier to dinner the following week.

"I can't, in my official situation, owe visits to a physician whom I don't know. Fortunately, he's a bachelor . . . you'll arrange a very simple repast. You, Madeleine, will make up a bouquet in the middle of the table, by way of compensation."

Them Madame Bordes yelped, furiously: "Has he cured someone, this Monsieur Sellier? Has he prescribed the slightest purgative? To demand payment would have been theft. This is all it needed!" And the vocal outbursts were renewed.

Madeleine said frankly that she thought it ridiculous not to send his bill. Julia declared that she wouldn't lay the table, her, the sister of a librarian; and abruptly, it was discovered that all the crockery was at fault; they only had one fruit-dish, the soup tureen was chipped, the large oval plate was furrowed with brown cracks and the fake silver plate was showing its copper.

"You're annoying me!" growled Deslandes, at the paroxysm of terror. "These are quibbles! I have said what I have said; I don't want to be treated like a leper!"—for he could see clearly that his sister still had the upper hand, and his customary timidity excited him to shout loudly in order to express an opinion.

Afterwards, he went into the drawing room, where he found the furniture all over the place.

"Well, it's your noble daughter," explained Madame Bordes. "You're both puffed up with vanity. One wants to regale the whole town and the other doesn't like getting her hands dirty sweeping!"

Hoping to rally his sister, Deslandes got terribly carried away against Madeleine, and but for the spontaneous disappearance of the latter behind a curtain he would have ended up administering a slap, so unhinged was he. Oh, this silent province, looking out, certainly, to tease them and their poverty, curdling all their blood!

And Deslandes, his face crimson and his little squinting eyes bloodshot, repeated: "Go to the devil! Idle, brazen, evil creature! Yes, go to the devil!"

With a light bound, Madeleine was in the garden. She headed for the gate at a run, knowing full well that a simple explosion of tears would have calmed everyone down, she as well as the others, but she was subject, for the moment, to the recklessness of the atmosphere, which, saturated with a dangerous electricity, would rather poison itself than resolve itself with a salutary downpour . . .

The young woman, therefore, climbing the hill with an anxious allure, went to the devil, determined not to return. The sun had completely disappeared. The crimson clouds gradually paled, taking on an orange tint and then a sulfurous yellow, and the entire landscape was clad in a livid hue similar to a reflection of muddy water. The vapors veiling the town became denser. Directly above the flat rock, the hole of blue sky reformed.

Contemplating the panorama, Madeleine thought about the cruel remark: "They don't like redheads in the country!" Why did she bear on her head that derisory golden color—she, a girl without a dowry and devoid of hope? A muted revolt germinated within her against humanity, brought her closer to the solitary nature that she saw all yellow and accursed, in her image. She did not like anything, and nothing liked her, according to her heart, and what was the point of being held to her own family by frail threads of prejudice? She knew that by now her parents were no longer occupied with her, even in order to insult her, that they were, in any case, too confident in her education, too cowardly with regard to society, to doubt her return.

The worst of it was that her unhappiness must be that into which all young souls were plunged, intoxicated by desires and enthusiasms by the nullity of mediocre life. And with the tip of her angry foot, Madeleine sent pebbles down over the sad little town, over the melancholy house, over the bleak roofs of the hospice.

When she drew near to the rocks known as the Chairs she sat down between their hard granite backs, leaning on the fissures and gazing at the sky. No more azure and no more star, nothing but a hermetic vault of russet clouds. She let down her hair, made it float in the fiery air, and imagined that the torsades, in scattering, were spreading out madly from one horizon to the other. A bitter smile creased her lips. In Paris too, people did not hold redheads in high esteem, although very fashionable women tinted their hair with henna in order to obtain the accursed hue artificially.

How absurd everything in this world was! Lowering her head she fixed her gaze on the flat stone situated opposite her, a broad uniform surface marbled with inky veins, a kind of colossal oval flint, which the rains of numerous winters had polished like marble. Madeleine found herself there in her own realm, where she reigned with the birds of prey, and where, intoxicated by her beloved solitude, she was always waiting for something, if not someone. It was there that she had seen, or believed that she had seen, the Great Dane one August afternoon. My God, was she going to end up doubting herself? She tilted her head backwards; her eyes ablaze with radiance closed, for she was inexplicably weary. Her breast heaved effortfully, her limbs became weak, no longer able to support her in order to go back down the hill. Well, she would spend the night outdoors; no one would come to look for her, and she had no fear of being disturbed by travelers.

While abandoning herself as if for sleep, she murmured: "Yes! He's there! I shouldn't be astonished! From behind the rock a dog might surge forth unexpectedly, without one having heard him coming . . . neither him nor . . . his master."

In certain periods of exaltation, one fears surprises less, and one sometimes welcomes one that ought to make you shudder, shaking your nervous system sufficiently for you to forget the dolorous monotony of existence.

A distant church bell spelled out the hour slowly, the chimes falling into the religious silence of the evening like the syllables of a psalm, and that knell sounded in the depth of her heart the remembrance of mysterious sadnesses. Was not the lugubrious sky, full of evil omens menacing her by displaying the color of lionesses? If it made her the queen of these summits, perhaps it also announced supreme battles. Was her electrified brain not about to give birth to the monster, the myth of amour, and wrestle cruelly against her virginal pride? There are moments when nature, separating itself from humanity, becomes formidably supernatural, crying out to you that the laws of reason are finally going to be violated, that all social bonds must finally be broken, for, floating through the vivacity of the mountain breeze is the incomprehensible vertigo of pride. Oh, the bitter desire to encounter the handsome cavalier, astride the palfrey of legend! Would one not have the skill of the devil? Yes. if. perchance the devil were to show himself in the features of a seducer, would she not follow him, in spite of her instinctive repugnance of men?

Madeleine dreamed that, costumed as Cendrillon, she was sweeping an immense dusty room, and while she removed the cobwebs soiling her red hair, a crimson strip of cloth slid from the clouds all the way to her forehead . . .

When she opened her eyes again, she perceived *the dog*.

VII

IT was really there, the dog, standing on its four paws, taller than ever. Black and shiny, against the sulfurous sky, like an animal sweating some mysterious poison, it darted an enigmatic gaze at Madeleine, either malevolent or desperate, and then it advanced silently, undulating in the fashion of images deformed by water, and its frightful maw opened, without letting any bark escape. Did it want to howl? Did it simply have a desire to yawn? The young woman did not understand, but she stood up straight, frightened, her hands joined and her eyes fixed. Then she heard a word pronounced, behind her shoulder, very close to her, against the rock, imperiously, but very softly:

"Silence!"

The dog stopped, lay down along the stone, and started to crawl, seemingly vanquished. Madeleine dared not turn in the direction of the man, whom she sensed in her shadow, making, so to speak, a single body with her, doubling her. A convulsive frisson seized her. She murmured in a prayerful tone, ready to crawl like the beast: "Who are you?"

"The dog's master," he replied

"Why did you just say *Silence?*"

"Because it's his name. He's soundless."

The sensation of horror that Madeleine experienced was augmented in spite of the charity of the stranger's language. She dared not turn round, although she habitually looked over her shoulder frequently. Was she still dreaming? Was it necessary to flee without asking for a more ample explanation, or to remain under this infernal sky, the livid reverberation of which prevented the night from closing in and spreading definitive repose? She had thought she had seen this dog; she had seen it. She had thought about its master, and its master had come! All that might be an ironic machination of chance, a passer-by having the right to pass over the hill every evening, but the hour did not permit logical deductions.

Weakly, she added: "Why are you prowling around my house so late?"

He repeated the same sentence, like an echo, in a jesting tone, mocking her or interrogating her with the same question: "Why are you prowling around my house so late?"

She took a step, perceived that he was holding her by her hair, and shook her head violently, trying to tear herself away from him.

"You're hurting me!" she moaned, trying to turn round.

The man let go of her hair, a sheaf of which he was holding as he might have held a bouquet of flowers

"I find it beautiful," he said, coldly, observing the quality of an object that had ceased to preoccupy him for the moment, which he was no longer keeping in his possession.

Madeleine leaned in the granite back of the Chair. An almost divine joy inundated her now, and her mad terror changed into a sharp voluptuousness. He had mentioned her hair! This strange passer-by liked red hair! Blessed be those who are able to lack respect for you appropriately, my God! She collected the scattered strands, rolled them up with a rapid gesture, and knotted them in a chignon as best she could.

"I beg you, Monsieur," she stammered, "to tell me who you are?"

"Oh, I exist," he replied. "Here's my hand; touch it."

He divined, therefore, what she did not say—her doubt in believing that he was real—and that was more disquieting than the proof . . . of the contrary. She saw him emerge from the shadow of the rocks, offering his hand, his long, bony hand, very white, and she pushed it away with a feverish gesture, finding his proposition too masculine. He folded his arms, still cold and disdainful, no longer looking at her, perhaps in order not to frighten her again.

With his back to the rock, he seemed unnaturally tall, so slender and swaying so rhythmically on his two stems that one might have thought him a species of prodigious plant bearing a human head. He was dressed in a somber costume, neither gray nor black, as shiny as the coat of his dog, a costume that molded his youthful forms, following all his supple lines without a rupture or a crease. His felt hat, designed for travel, with a slightly inclined rim, left his face in darkness, and one could only distinguish his gaze, darting the gleams of a lamp veiled with mourning. A sleeveless mantle, a kind of exceedingly soft drape, of silk or wool, hung down all the way from his shoulders to his feet, continuing him in the earth, causing him to melt into the rocks, confused with the other shadows. And his dog, still flattened on the ground, watched him with its yellow eyes, shining with a grim, monstrous passion, a passion that the master only tolerated from afar.

Madeleine examined the two tenebrous individuals in turn. She told herself that the sky, still coppery, was the cause of their fantastic appearance. Nothing, that night, could proceed naturally. Dead things, like living things, were colored by a mysterious hue in the expectation of solemn events.

"Do you often traverse the mountain?" she said, finally, in order to hear herself speak, for the soundless dog and the man who was no longer opening his mouth, encrusted on the rock like a tortuous serpentine root, were making her fall ill.

"I'll be here, Madeleine, every time it pleases you to encounter me," declared the stranger, in a dull voice.

The young woman's blood froze.

"How do you know that my name is Madeleine?"

"What does it matter, since I know it?"

"Have I arranged to meet you, Monsieur?"

"Perhaps."

He took his hat off slowly, and his arm fell along his body, as if suddenly broken. She saw that he was blond, that golden blond that tends toward red, and which is known, for the sake of politeness, as Titian blond. But his hair had more metallic reflections. Some was a purer gold, which appeared tarnished by copper alloy.

"You insult me, Monsieur," she said, courageously. "In order to arrange a meeting with you it would at least be necessary for me to know your name, and you have refused to tell me!"

"So be it; my name is Hunter, if that is agreeable to you."

"Where do you come from? You're surely not from this town or the surrounding area."

"My homeland . . . ?" He paused, looking at her attentively, seemingly seeking a response in the depths of her eyes. "How many futile phrases you demand of me, Madeleine!" he added, smiling.

She straightened up, trembling with impatience, her fear mutating gradually into anger.

"I forbid you to call me Madeleine, do you hear?"

"My homeland is the earth," he confessed, very softly.

She made a gesture of rage. How prompt he was to avenge himself! "Oh, not that! Shut up. Leave that ridiculous game. Are you not a man like others?"

"If I were a man like others you would be scornful of me, Madeleine. I don't want you to be scornful of me. And then, doesn't a passing traveler have the right to say that he inhabits the whole earth?"

The young woman, confused, had a desire to turn away, but a vertiginous curiosity retained her, motionless and quivering, before him. He advanced his arm again.

"You're wrong not to touch my hand. I tell you that . . . I exist."

She seized that white, dry and cold hand between her own, so feverish that they were moist. She exclaimed: "Yes, yes—I doubted you . . . I'm mad."

Hunter knelt on the rock, collapsing all of a piece, detaching himself from the surface of the Chair like a shred of curtain. He seemed to fold up on himself and no longer to be anything but a head level with the woman's feet.

"Are you afraid, Madeleine?" he murmured, smiling from below, making the irresistible flash of his surprisingly beautiful teeth gleam.

To tame her, no doubt, and perhaps also to play with her at closer range, he raised himself up again, with infinite precaution, crawling like his dog Silence, metamorphosing entirely in a perfidiously graceful caress.

"Madeleine, Madeleine! I've come and you flee me! I speak and you don't understand me! Yesterday, I was some passer-by, today, I think I'm your friend, and I know you better than your parents, whom you've expelled, better than Doctor Edmond Sellier, who is a boor, and better than yourself, who is . . . a child! I know everything! Yes, that astonishes you! Think! Your hair, your splendid red hair, has brushed my face! Its heady perfume has told me everything, I found myself close to it, as if caught in a trap, and I saw immediately that you hadn't let it down in vain! You were asleep there, in your bed of rocks, confident, having set your snare for the storm wind and, in spite of its fragility, your snare captured the bird of prey. You're a sister that I'm seeing again after a long exile. Do I not have a duty to attempt to console you? Oh, once we lived together, Madeleine!"

The young woman listened to him, paralyzed and fascinated. The man's voice had tender, suddenly feminine intonations, like the voice of her own imagination, whispering dreams of ideal happiness to her. If she had been able to project her brain, in the form of a flatterer, it would certainly have been that seductive prince of darkness. No, she was no longer frightened. Dream or reality, she accepted the marvelous adventure And although prevented from prowling around their house, for a motive she did not know as yet, he had heard the family scenes, and when she had not supposed him to be there on the August day when Doctor Sellier had protected her against the dog, he had been able to divine various things while hiding in the thicket of the little wood. A little psychology did the rest . . .

In that supreme moment, could she not explain the inexplicable? However, she had one last timid objection.

"Where did we live together once, Monsieur?"

He burst into harmonious laughter, a musical laughter that, singularly, did not disturb the nearby echoes.

"In the stars, Madeleine!"

She lowered her head, tears streaming from her hot eyes, calming and deflating her heart, her poor woman's heart, amorous of the impossible, swollen with the desire for all forbidden fruits.

"I'm dreaming . . . don't make fun of me, whoever you are, because I might wake up and I'd have a terrible awakening. I've been suffering for some time, my nerves have a desire to kill someone! But where are we, here? At times I seem to hear a distant sound of a hurricane in the valley. I'm weeping . . . and if I had touched my cheeks, I would have thought my tears were raindrops. Where are we?"

"We're *on the mountain*, Madeleine, and at the height we've just attained in a single bound, I won't waste my time occupying myself with what's happening in the valley, or making you an impious list of my powers! Satan once showed his kingdom to Christ, but a twenty-year-old virgin has no need to affirm amour! Madeleine, I love you! It's me who asks to prostrate myself and adore you."

She leaned over and looked at him for a long time, simultaneously charmed and horrified. Huddled in her black skirt, he was entirely black. The night closed around them, changing her russet veils into crepes. Nothing stirred or made any sound. The enormous rocks shielded them from the wind, which had freshened, and funereal birds, circling them discreetly, beat the air with their warm fans. An extraordinary odor was disengaged by the fissures in the Chairs, the odor of immortelles, of that frail yellow flower born of a little sand and a great deal of sunlight in the most arid corners, a flower fond of wild liberty: the immortelle, that drop of light that one goes to pour, once picked, over the obscurity of tombs in order to recall the pride of having lived.

"Hunter!" sighed Madeleine, as if spelling out that name in the hermetic face of the kneeling man.

That face appeared resplendent to her, in spite of the black atmosphere, and she studied its features in their divine radiance of joy. He had profound blue eyes, slightly sunken, blurred below by a bistre line that went to join, above, the fine arc of the eyebrows, circling them with a rim of shadow, which magnified them frightfully. The narrow nose, very noble, was slightly tilted upwards at the extremity, but that sufficed to form a harsh, macabre angle. The beardless mouth cut across the bottom of the face with an excessively red wound, the ardor of which was ill-matched to the unhealthy pallor of the cheeks, and he had the forehead of a woman, as smooth as a mirror of snow. He must have been very handsome, since he scared her. Studying Madeleine with his steely blue eyes, he followed her slightest gestures, held her hands tightly, watching through the obscurity for the moment to speak without causing her a disagreeable tremor. He knew that he was redoubtable and feared that he might make her flee. Oh, he knew her well, in fact, for he did not risk embracing her and only proffered the most chaste words: *My sister . . . in the stars . . .*

"No, Hunter, I can't love you!" said Madeleine, in a whisper, so quietly that it only had the modulation of the cooing of a turtle-dove.

"Liar, like the night!" he murmured, squeezing her fingers, like those of a plump child, between his skeletal phalanges.

"Why . . . like the night?"

"Are you not treacherous and as deceptive as can be desired, Madeleine, when you claim not to be able to love me? Do you not already love another? And the woman with the leonine mane that I saw a little while ago twisting her arms, evoking amour, like a beautiful warm day, is transformed at present into a brunette woman, firm and cold, like a desolate twilight, a brunette woman I'm obliged to approach on tiptoe, fearful of the precipice of a crisis of nerves. Yes, liar, liar . . . like the night!"

He put his head on her knees, abandoning her hands.

"I'll wait!" he added.

And while he made that threat, Madeleine felt an abominable damp caress run long her open left hand from the palm to the wrist. It was the tongue of the soundless dog, which was licking her, imploring her on behalf of its master, his idol, the mute monster no longer having, alas, any other means of proving its faithful tenderness. Madeleine uttered an exclamation of disgust, in spite of her flesh being moved by that bestial homage of servility.

"Oh! Your dog, Hunter, send your dog away!" Then, anxiously, she said: "I already love someone?"

"Edmond Sellier," he replied.

She was astounded. "I swear to you, Hunter, that I've never thought that."

"You will think of it, Madeleine."

"The idea of marriage revolts me, and you can't think me capable of . . . behaving badly?"

The young woman's peremptory reply contained an entire program: neither a wife nor a mistress. Hunter started to laugh softly.

"Ah," he said, as if talking to himself, "if the stars were eyes, and if eyes were stars, if swallows scented roses and if roses could fly!" Sliding his thin arm around Madeleine's waist, he said: "Will the pact not be ratified tonight, then? Listen to me, my sister! I'm accursed, and you're accursed. We ought to be glad. Let's hasten to understand one another completely. I'm very old, by virtue of having once come from the stars. Time is pressing. I only want your soul, but I want the whole of it. You can give your amour afterwards to whomever you please."

"I can't grasp what you're saying very well, Hunter, and be careful. Don't try to frighten me; I'm not a naïve little girl. I'm scornful of vulgar acts."

"You're an angel, Madeleine!"

"I shall only love you on one condition, which is that you forget that you're a man and that I'm a woman."

"The pact!" he cried, suddenly, in a voice so loud that she got up, bewildered.

Bounding to his feet, he drew her to his bosom, and she did not have the strength to resist him. At their feet, the dog agitated in the depths of the shadow, darting eyes like bloody coals, eyes that seemed to be laughing.

"We shall love one another thus, and I shall live!" said Hunter, triumphantly.

He continued, lowering his voice, proffering his syllables, so to speak, directly into the woman's brain, so close was his mouth to her ear.

"You have wanted it, Madeleine; I have finally emerged victorious from your entrails, rotten with death. Summoned by you from so far away, your adorable charity has extracted me again from nothingness. You love me; *I am*. Oh, my pale sister of folly, I will have drawn, in the golden harvest of your hair, the sacred aliment. I will drink all my eternity at the bright fountains of your eyes! Henceforth, you see, my desires will grip your white neck like furious birds striking their cage with their beaks! Understand well! The line of your white neck will be the limit . . . the limit, Madeleine. The hour has sounded for realizations of the impossible! You and me! The rest of the world no longer exists, and one day . . . one day, I will carry your head down there in my two hands, like a chalice! Your predestined brain will have flowed into me, and in order that none of that intoxicating liquor can escape me, I shall put on your mute lips the seal of purity that is called the bitterness of tears! You will weep and you will cause weeping! For infinite despair gushes forth, Madeleine, the great, the only voluptuousness!"

He had taken her head in both hands, really like a chalice, and plunged his somber gaze into her dilated pupils, only sustaining her any longer by her delicate neck, carrying her away, already trying to decapitate her in order to separate her forever from her miserable body of a poor suffering young woman. His long powerful arms, from which the flaps of his supple cloak fell all the way to the ground, enveloped her without brushing her. There was no longer a horizon, no more sky and no more rocks. A profound night surrounded Madeleine, and that appeared to her to last for centuries. An immeasurable pride now enabled her to penetrate the mysterious meaning of his musical phrases; she stripped them, in order that her understanding could become much more subtle, of their superficial absurdity, doubling herself, presenting, like faceted mirrors, a multitude of rational senses. Sometimes she recognized the man and sometimes she admitted the god. A delicious intoxication made everything that she said turn around her in living images, and she believed that she had returned to the age of simple credulities, in which the astonishing fictions of fabulous stories became concrete.

As a little girl she had wandered in legend, carrying in her innocent heart the flower that opens in sepulchers, which is also the key to treasures that make you love the king. She did not think, could not even suspect, that this adventure of darkness could reach a banal denouement. Was he not, in himself, the exact expression of her maddest dreams? Why would she have suspected him of playing such an atrocious comedy, since she had dictated this role to him in the secrecy of her soul? In any case, was not that young being, whose Aeolian voice took on the accents of the most sincere passion, *the man*—which is to say, a monster that had the mission of taming the woman? No, she would neither be the mistress nor the wife of that man; she divined that he would not ask the figure of her dowry after having offered so respectfully an amour outside nature! This would only end in an eternal embrace . . . but what did it matter? According to the admirable expression of the saint, everything that finishes is too short for cold creatures, the coldness signifying that nothing can suffice for them. Had she not dreamed once of loving a second self in order that their purely cerebral passion, having arrived at its paroxysm, would never have the right or the duty to descend to the brutal prostitutions of the flesh, which determined while luring the senses? And if she had slipped at the last minute, it was because she had insurmountable repulsions in the presence of vice. But her heart, a devouring furnace, conserved demonic appetites. She would not recoil before a demon.

"Hunter," she murmured gravely, "I'm yours, take my soul!"

Meanwhile, an intense emotion gripped her throat, her limbs flexed, and she was obliged to sit down on the rock.

"Thank you, Madeleine," Hunter replied, dully, whose extended arms fell back with a strange lassitude.

Then she saw an expression of hesitant anguish pass over his arrogant physiognomy of an eloquent jester, an expression wholly imprinted with humanity, although so fleeting that she was unable, later, to remember it in a precise fashion. Did he hesitate before the silhouette of his own youth, looming up in the form of a virgin woman, who would doubtless bless him for having vanquished her? Was he afraid of what he had said, for any slightly resounding speech must project an irrevocably physical conception through space? Did he experience a remorse or a new desire? Did he recall oaths exchanged in identical circumstances? Was he on the point of admitting odious things, lies?

The self absorbed everything: shames or anguishes! He drew away from Madeleine, made her a bizarre sign, the index finger extended and then brought back toward his mouth in a gesture of imperious command.

"Silence!" he added, in a faint voice, as if stifled, already departed.

The dog leapt on to the flat stone, immeasurably magnified, and suddenly disappeared; its master did likewise. Madeleine remained alone in the shadow.

"My God! My God!" she cried, putting her clenched fists to her temples. "Is everything finished between us then, Hunter? We're at the dawn of our happiness, and you're abandoning me? Hunter! Hunter!"

She ran to the Shepherd's Table, and fell to her knees desperately.

"Hunter!" she implored, beating the air with her arms, "I order you to come back! One more word! Say one more word to me! Why flee me, who loves you?"

One word, only one word, reached her, like a regret, an echo, perhaps from underground and perhaps from above the rocks,

"Dawn!"

"Dawn?" she stammered. "What do you mean?"

Was it to him that it was necessary to attribute that distant syllable, like the sound of church bells reverberating several leagues away? Turning instinctively toward the east, she did indeed perceive a pale light bleaching the thickness of the clouds, opening in lips the first light of the dawn, where she imagined that she saw the horrible white smile, the beautiful teeth of the stranger's death's-head—and Madeleine fainted.

VIII

"YES, I'm coughing a little," she said, coldly.

She was sitting on the wall of the terrace, still holding her umbrella by the handle and a corner of the cloth with a gracious movement, thus forming an azure nimbus that rendered her more blonde and roseate. She had put on a little calico peignoir whose poverty was carefully dissimulated by lace linings; more lace swelling around her arms made the most of the elegant curve of her shoulders; her waist was tightened in a wide blue silk belt, the same shade as her umbrella, and her hair was put up in the Chinese style, which suited her well, giving her a child-like appearance.

Doctor Sellier had just stopped his carriage outside her garden, he was playing his whip negligently over Marquis' ears, who was not setting off and was shaking his head in a bad temper.

"It's necessary to pay attention to these little coughs, Mademoiselle Deslandes," he said, addressing a benevolent smile to her. "By the way," he added, hastily, fearing to abuse the right he had to ask for news of her on passing, "I've carried out your commission; I've searched for the owner of the dog—you know, the famous Great Dane?"

As he looked at her attentively, finding her pretty, perched on that wall, like a bird of paradise displaying its plumage, he thought he saw her go pale. It was a pity that she had a complexion that spoiled so easily. A reflection of sunlight in the hazel trees was sufficient to decompose her features—yes, ferociously capricious, did she hold it against him that he wanted to meddle in her affairs after having asked him to do her that favor?

"And do you have information?" she queried, her voice even more detached from the things of this world.

"In fact, no. I haven't discovered anything about the dog or the master. I think that it must be some beast escaped from a traveling performers' caravan.

She smiled ironically.

"Acrobats never have dogs like that, Monsieur; they cost too much to feed."

The remark seemed to him to be just. Confused, he let the conversation lapse and lifted the reins in order to get Marquis moving. The horse was obstinate. Mademoiselle Deslandes was able to add: "Thank you all the same, Monsieur, for taking the trouble."

"Oh," he replied, "I didn't dare come expressly; I thought that . . ."

"Indeed," she interrupted, swiftly, "you would have been wrong to come expressly, for I haven't mentioned it to my family."

He suspected as much. They must live perpetually on a war footing in the old house at the end of the town. He was thinking about whipping his horse when an appeal reached him from one of the windows of the drawing room, where a gesticulating Jacques Deslandes was framed.

"Monsieur Sellier! Doctor!"

Madeleine turned round, annoyed, knowing in advance that her father watched for the opportunity every morning, having not so far attempted anything to favor it.

"Why, it's your father! What can he want with me?" said Sellier, astonished.

"I don't know," the young woman replied, indifferently.

Deslandes stepped through the ground floor window and started running toward the terrace.

"That damned doctor," he exclaimed, out of breath. "One can never get hold of him. Let's see, Monsieur Sellier, it's not a matter of running away without drums or trumpets; I've got you and I'm not letting go until you've promised me to stay to dinner this evening, taking pot luck. It's agreed, yes? As you have to go past us on the way back, I'll wait for you at the corner. There!"

"But I assure you," murmured Sellier, alarmed by the prospect, "that it isn't possible, Monsieur Deslandes. I have a high fever in the village of Hotteaux and I won't be back until late, very late. You're very kind, but . . ."

"Let it go! A high fever doesn't prevent one from dining, especially when it's with a client. My sister will make a little feast to welcome you, and she charged me very frankly with inviting you, without any ceremony."

Poor Deslandes, while insisting, looked at his daughter furiously. She had an engaging expression, that one! A fool for having put them—him and Julia—in that piteous situation.

"Well," he said, nudging her elbow, "what if you were to try to persuade him, Madeleine? Perhaps you'll succeed! Come on, come on! I warn you that we're having veal with peas, nothing more! I'm counting on you."

He pulled down his straw hat with a resolute gesture and turned round solemnly, slightly offended, in sum, that this modest country physician should think him a derisory client—him, a Parisian of distinction.

Madeleine swung her umbrella.

"Why don't you want to come to dinner with us?" she said, in a mocking tone. "Does veal frighten you, Monsieur le docteur?"

Sellier was touched by her effort. It would be ridiculous to have to be begged to spend the evening, when they thought themselves obliged to invite him to a feast prepared a long time ago. She finished ingenuously: "Myself, I propose to you hard-boiled eggs, the only thing I know how to make!"

"I surrender, Mademoiselle. Hard-boiled eggs made by you . . . is too much joy." He started to laugh, bowing. "It's agreed. This evening, about six o'clock. But don't worry Madame your aunt with regard to the high fever. I'll be punctual."

Marquis broke into a trot, a twig between his teeth, and his master sighed, perplexed.

"My God, what a chore! What will my mother say?"

Then, in spite of everything, he thought that blue definitely suited the red-haired girl.

There was quite a fuss in the old house to prepare that impromptu meal. Julia Bordes, while skinning a sole, roared that it wouldn't do, that it would be necessary to make futile expenses, that Deslandes was mad! With

118

a salary of a hundred francs a month he wanted her to feed, dress and lodge three people—one of whom was a girl who would not consent to sweep the rooms, and see how she treated people into the bargain! She tipped up the saucepan in which the veal was cooking, which reduced the juice proportionately and forced her, by harsh necessity, to add water as a last resort. Deslandes had declared that he would not present himself before the doctor again—a matter of avoiding recriminations. The unfortunate fellow, trapped in an existence of despairing monotony, rejoiced secretly in his escapade, especially in seeing flowers on the tablecloth, brighter crystal, whiter napkins and polite guests.

Finally, toward six o'clock, Madeleine, not having warned anyone, set the table and made a large bouquet. She went down the shaky kitchen steps, her waist girdled by a dazzling apron, in order to prepare her hard-boiled eggs, and the bewildered aunt contributed the clove of vanilla that was asked of her, yielding to the calm gaze of her niece. When she had finished, fearing accidents, Madeleine stacked the eggs in a pyramid on a soup-plate, and as she went through the antechamber she met her father, followed by the doctor. There was amazement on the part of the two men.

"What!" cried Deslandes joyfully. "We have a new cook now! Would you like to go and hide with your wretched apron? Have we arrived too soon?"

"On the contrary! Mademoiselle is charming like this," murmured Sellier, very surprised to find the sympathetic silhouette of a modest housewife. Her hips stood out beneath the waxed apron; her complexion had color, and a few droplets of sweat were shining like diamonds on her temples at the roots of her russet hair.

She smiled at them without any embarrassment. "I promised you," she said to the doctor, "to enable you to taste them. They've come out quite well, haven't they?"

He was flattered, without quite knowing why, and regretted less having been obliged to run home to warn his mother.

Madame Bordes received him worthily, from the height of a pink tulle headscarf that gave her crimson face an even deeper hue than usual. The beginning of the dinner went well. The doctor, between Julia and Madeleine, multiplied his attentions, waxed ecstatic over the sculpture of the wood-paneling, praised the excellence of the atmosphere of large rooms, discovered that autumn, this year, would end without rain, and that, after all, the position of librarian was an enviable employment, a true sinecure.

"A little more soup?" said the aunt, in a shrill tone that she had once adopted in society and which had made her best friends detest her.

"Yes, yes, take a little more soup, my dear doctor!" exclaimed Deslandes, speaking loudly, as he did whenever he was anxious. "No? Without ceremony, what! So much the worse for you; I've warned you."

Deslandes' preoccupation was focused on his neighbor's empty plate. Who would take it away? The medium had declared that she would not serve a man younger than her. He was amazed again on seeing Madeleine remove it promptly, with a touch-me-not air.

"Be careful with the fish sauce when you bring it!" said Madame Bordes, beaming under her pink tulle headscarf.

They had crossed the Rubicon now. The father filled his glass. The aunt set about giving orders and eating like a grand dame who knows her personnel and knows that it is necessary to put on airs from time to time. Madeleine came and went, her hands agile, her mind elsewhere and her eyes calm, slightly atonal, looking inwards. Edmond felt sorry for the young woman, in spite of the mission appearing to him to be quite natural, in that servile role, which lowered her in his presence and embarrassed him; but he would gladly have reattached around her waist the strings of the white apron that she had just thrown into a corner, on her father's order. He had been enthused by that apron since crossing the threshold.

"Oh!" murmured the father while she carved the famous veal with peas in the kitchen. "If she wanted, we could make her an accomplished little countrywoman—but she has singular whims and doesn't possess the good health of your provincial women."

"I've heard Mademoiselle Madeleine coughing, in fact. Is it chronic?" Sellier hastened to ask, trying not to emerge from his role of physician and to be useful to them, if necessary, in order to pay his due with regard to the severe Madame Bordes.

"Pooh!" said the aunt. "That child has been cracked since the cradle. Didn't she run around outside all night during the big storm? You know, the one at the end of September?"

"What?" cried Edmond. "She was outside in that storm, which uprooted the finest trees in the valley?"

"Exactly, Monsieur!" emphasized the aunt, without seeing the signs of ill humor that her brother was addressing to her. "She ran away for a word, for one of papa's pleasantries. Almost nothing, for God knows that he doesn't scold her often enough. She does what she wants here! And she came back at five o'clock in the morning, soaked and dirty, her hair down her back, a veritable barbet! I gave her a good welcome! I made her go to bed with an eiderdown over her. If she didn't catch anything worse than a cold, it's not her fault."

"You understand," said the librarian, "I thought she had come back. About midnight I heard a window close. My sister shouted to me from her room: 'Don't worry! There she is! I forbid you to go to her. Dignity is necessary before childish caprices.' So I didn't go. Anyway, there was such a squall, Monsieur, that I couldn't believe that she was walking up there on the mountain."

"Hmm!" said Sellier, disconcerted. "That was hardly prudent."

Again the scene darkened. The funny people resumed their appearance of shaggy creatures, malevolent or mad, perhaps hypocritical, trying to misrepresent their intimate dramas.

"Hush!" said the aunt. "Here she is!"

Madeleine, with a gesture full of ease, placed the oval plate on the table, and Madame Bordes exclaimed: "There's too much juice. Lord God, you must have added water."

"You know that I didn't, Aunt," replied the young woman, placidly. And she turned slightly, sat down and tried to eat.

"It's necessary to ausculate her, eh, if she wishes," muttered the father, anxiously.

122

"Certainly—with your permission, Mademoiselle?" asked Sellier, who was becoming impatient with these marks of pity toward a young woman who had been left outside on a stormy night.

"I don't have any objection, Monsieur, but I'm not ill, I assure you. A cold in the head; it isn't serious."

The father rubbed his hands. Good! Everything was all right. The child was making amends; the doctor was complaisant, and the dinner seemed passable.

"You see," he sighed, leaning back on the back of his chair, "I like family meals; good simple cooking eaten by simple folk. No fuss! And a little wine, which rejuvenates you, my word! We must do it again, doctor. You make good wine in your satanic province! My digestion has improved since I've been drinking it!"

A discussion ensued on pure and adulterated wines, the doctor furnishing all the technical terms he knew and the librarian citing recipes for *sulfuring* and *cutting* that he had read that morning in the départemental revue. The aunt risked: "A good label! Old wine drowns young chagrin!" but she regretted the Mère Moreau's cherry brandy. While her husband, a *bon viveur*, was alive, it had been her birthday present. A hundred-sou bottle of cherries. Monsieur, neither more nor less, but what cherries!

Edmond smiled and straightened up, his head sinking a little less than usual between his slightly vaulted shoulders; his brown eyes blinked slowly, as if trying to pierce the mystery around him. He examined those simple folk and was astonished to see them becoming more and more complicated. Having conserved from his patient and useful studies a mania for rational analysis he induced a heap of singular things from the banality of their remarks and ran into irritating contradictions. The father had a big jovial nose with little naïve brown eyes and a mimicry of importance, probably obtained from an itch of noble desires. The aunt's bestial face bore all the stigmata of vulgar rapacity, the acquisition of property, persons and the direction of souls, with, in the depths of her ink-black pupils, a sort of evil afterthought of malign destruction, or a fear of what she did every day. As for Madeleine, she was an absolute enigma. One could only extract blank gazes from her.

At dessert, everyone softened over the boiled eggs. The doctor complimented their author courteously.

"Come and kiss me, child," exclaimed the father, wiping his mouth. "This makes up for many things!"

Madeleine had an imperceptible movement of recoil, which only Edmond noticed, but she went ahead. Liqueurs were poured, a bitter cassis manufactured by Madame Bordes, and then coffee.

"What if we were to go into the drawing room to drink it?" said Deslandes.

Feeling in a confidential mood, he took Sellier's arm familiarly, explained to him in a tearful tone that they had sold the piano before taking refuge in the province, and that it was a pity for the child, who could already play Chopin.

"Yes, Monsieur, she's had lessons! She followed complete courses, but those chic boarding schools spoil you; they're brought up with rich demoiselles and acquire the tastes of princesses. Madeleine knew the daughter of an ambassador, but when she got married she didn't associate with her any more because of the mediocrity of our situation, Madeleine was very chagrined."

"I understand, I understand," Sellier repeated, annoyed by the fuss that was being made of him, and finding that the atmosphere of the drawing room, in spite of its vastness, was unbreathable because of a musty odor.

The two women brought a lamp and little cups, already full, that were placed on Ludovic. Madeleine sat down in the embrasure of the open window, staring contemplatively at the somber rocks dominating the hill. My God, how high they were, by comparison with the roof that sheltered them! Were they not going to collapse, precipitating upon them to annihilate them, shutting their insignificant stupid mouths? Now they were talking about old houses, vanished nobility, the immortal principles of 89, the heap of people that they owed to the guillotine . . . The doctor replied in a cold tone, feeling more directly the icy contact of Madeleine, behind whom he was placed, standing. He saw her breathing with difficulty, and her blue-green eyes, descending from the hill suddenly darkened, passing to violet-black, launching gazes almost similar to those of Aunt Bordes, in the depths of which a horrible idea lurked. Her lips contracted in a malevolent rictus. A sentiment of hatred zigzagged across that young face all the way to the blonde hair, radiant with wild reflections.

She coughed.

"You're suffering, Mademoiselle!" said Edmond, anxiously. "It's quite visible; don't deny it!"

"It's necessary to allow yourself to be ausculated, darling," declared the father. "The air is fresh this evening; close that window, or come away from there. During the consultation I'll go in search of cigars. You smoke, don't you?"

The doctor declined, but Deslandes protested. It was necessary to struggle against the odor of damp, and he had a desire to celebrate; decidedly, they shouldn't stop. He went out, accompanied by his sister, muttering surly phrases. Outside the drawing room they disappeared momentarily, and doors were heard slamming.

IX

EDMOND SELLIER was still looking at the young woman.

"I beg you, tell me why you're coughing?" he said, affectionately, dreading in advance her capricious hostility.

Madeleine shrugged her shoulders. "This house is damp, I believe. And then, as you see, I'm always at the window."

He sketched a half-smile. "Or on the mountain during storms!"

She straightened up, white with anger.

"Who told you that?"

"Your aunt, just now. Don't get annoyed if I'm indiscreet. It's my duty."

She folded her arms. "No," she said, dully, "there was no storm. That's a ridiculous invention. Rain, perhaps . . . I don't want you to occupy yourself with that adventure any more, Monsieur."

"You don't want . . . me to question you about that nocturnal excursion? That's all right. I have nothing to say about it—but on the subject of the cough . . .

may I not ausculate you, Mademoiselle? Is it still a bold enterprise?"

He was joking, becoming nervous, and, imagining that the shadow of the great sad drawing room was weighing upon them with all the weight of its ambient melancholy, he tried to react, as much for his sake as hers.

"I don't want anyone to touch me," she riposted violently. "Not you, or anyone."

"Good, good! That's sufficient," he stammered, intimidated by her burst of savage energy.

He took a few steps, his hands clasped behind his back. He, a physician, treated like a boor because he wanted to ausculate his patient! The young woman's neurosis really was going too far—for she was neurotic, that pretty pale Parisienne; she had a secret hunger for society; she missed the daughters of ambassadors, the gossip, the pianos, the dresses, and, no longer having anything to satisfy those unhealthy appetites, she had fallen from the height of her exasperated disdain upon the poor provincial, who only wanted to do her a little good. Oh, it was too much!

He drew away, frowning, haunted by a sudden desire to hit her. Anyway, did they not hit one another, in her family? Were not those vulgar people, scarcely touched by education, dissimulating evil things beneath the hypocrisies of naïve apes, capable of martyrizing her behind closed doors? A softening brought him back to her.

"Come on, Mademoiselle, I'm not an ogre! You must be suffering, and even outside all the usages of my métier, I've never been able to divine suffering, physical or mental, without trying to remedy it. Believe that

I'm not animated by any inappropriate curiosity. We physicians are blasé. We have seen so much that the worst situations leave us cold. However, there are cases of cerebral delicacy in which we need to demand confidence before offering our care. Do you take me for a man? I've already noticed your horror of pleasantries . . . let's say gallantries, if you wish. Do you suppose that, in wanting to ausculate you I lack respect for you?"

He was speaking to her in his an amiable tone, trying to recover his medical aplomb on the presence of a badly brought-up child who did not know what she wanted, or what he wanted of her. In reality, a bizarre disturbance emanated from the thick obscurity of that drawing room, confusing them, which he would have had difficulty analyzing. He had, however, dined better than usual. The wine and the liqueurs in the Deslandes house were not especially heady. Whence came this particular overexcitement, this imperious desire to push her into her last entrenchments, to palpate her physical or mental wound? He felt aggressive, borne to care for her by force, perhaps to humiliate her. Just now, in the middle of the rococo dining room, disguised as a maid-servant, she had seemed so welcoming, so full of good will . . . and abruptly, she had changed her appearance, haloed by her red hair like the diadem of an offended queen, adopting a hermetic physiognomy, forbidding things to him, a poor devil trying to ameliorate her fate. Oh, he had no luck. He had always mistaken his route in life, and his rare affectionate manifestations, crises of a worthy fellow weaned from amity at his age, always failed piteously.

Madeleine stood there with her arms folded, seemingly imprisoning her bosom defending herself against all those who might permit themselves to observe the beating of her heart.

"No, I assure you," he repeated, striding back and forth. "A physician is not a man, Mademoiselle."

"It's pointless to say that, Monsieur. It's already too much to have to affirm it."

She uttered that remark in a dry voice, whistling like the crack of a whip through the somber atmosphere.

Edmond stopped. In fact, her judgment was sound. He was dazzled by her perspicacity. Why raise that dangerous subject? He desired her confidence and he was creating chimerical suspicions. What stupid ineptitude! He hastened to veer away.

"Listen to me seriously; it's necessary not to play with pneumonia. It's romantic to run after I know not what poetic fantasy on stormy nights, but it would be less amusing, I assure you, to die of consumption. In the beginning, it's interesting to cough; later, one spits blood, and that's nasty!"

"What gives you the right, Monsieur, to believe that I run after a poetic fantasy?" she said, haughtily, her violet eyes launching fiery darts at him.

He shivered involuntarily. This was no longer a capricious girl standing up before him threateningly; it was an angry woman, who had decided to make him lose footing in order to get rid of him more rapidly. She was afraid of Danish dogs but she would not yield in the presence of a man when the latter had the stupidity to testify a slightly keen interest in her. Yes, she belonged to the cruel race disdainful of males, scenting all their weakness instinctively. How to get out of that vicious circle?

Edmond had sweat on his temples. God, how dark this drawing room was! It seemed to him that he was entering into night, the profound and mysterious night of the feminine brain, a gulf bristling with poisonous thorns, the obscure trap extended since the beginning of the world for unfortunate beings who were simply kind. One wandered, groping in order to seize a white hand, with was taken away without any apparent reason, solely for the pleasure of refusing a pleasure, that of aiding the blossoming of a healthy, normal joy. And in spite of that refusal, all the phantoms of dolor and all the seeds of madness were engendered. Without any possible explanation, one suffered, perhaps, on either side, separated by darkness, simultaneously stifled by tears and pity.

"Mademoiselle Madeleine," he murmured softly, "you have a grim character. So be it; let's not talk any more about your state of health, since you're quite well. As for your state of mind, I don't have the right, I confess, to occupy myself with it, and I offer you my apologies."

He expected to see her smile at him spontaneously, out of flattered pride or vain coquetry, but she remained impenetrable, her malicious eyes riveted to his, gradually forcing him to lower them. Mechanically, he drew away from her, heading for the back of the drawing room, still obsessed by that fixed stare.

Well, he thought, *I've just made an enemy. Doubtless I should have had more intelligence, but I got bogged down in my explanations. Young women from out there*

*don't like imbeciles . . . understood! In addition, I'm no
longer master of my nerves because of that damned reek
of mildew!*

He pretended to examine the wall, taking inventory
of the folds of the old damask, sounding them and
touching the dusty, slightly moist fabric with his fingertips. Strangely enough, he could still see her, looking at
him with he knew not what tragic determination. That
heavy gaze rose up along his spine, tenacious, full of
magic; it bit the nape of his neck, plunging into his
most sensitive fibers and devouring his brain. That
imaginary pain became, for a moment, so atrocious
that he was on the point of turning round and shouting
insults. Fortunately, Jacques Deslandes came back in,
bringing cigars. That broke the charm.

"Child, I need a pen-knife," said the father.

She rummaged in the drawer of a desk and cut the
golden yellow favor that bound the packer of cigars
herself, then went out, crossing paths with her aunt.
Edmond sighed. They started to smoke. Madame
Bordes tapped Ludovic, her fingers grating on the varnish of the wood. She took her part in the new expense,
hoping that the coffee might be forgotten, which she
could serve again to her brother the next day, Sincerely,
the doctor had no further desire to drink. His nervous-
ness increased, gripping his throat and squeezing his
stomach, and he searched for a polite pretext to withdraw, to go outside and breathe pure air. Deslandes, for
his part, was meditating another species of debauchery,
scratching his big nose as if he were itching to make
new confidences.

"Doctor," he finally rushed in, seeing that his daughter did not return, "are you interested in magnetism?"

"In the province," replied Sellier, lightly, "we scarcely have any opportunity."

"And spiritism?" said Deslandes, his eyes shining.

"I don't see what connection . . ."

"What! What connection . . . ! You physicians don't know about spiritism, but you tolerate the phenomena of magnetism, which are its feeblest manifestations?"

With that, Deslandes bestrode his favorite hobby-horse, while Madame Bordes, nodding her head, punctuated his discourse with signs of intelligence. The librarian related the prodigious exploits that he had witnessed (possibly): tables floating up to the ceiling, photographic visions, pieces of chalk moving on their own over a slate; the whole series filed past, and Aunt Julia, suddenly illuminated by a diabolical joy, concluded: "Ah, Monsieur le docteur, you're an unbeliever. Well, I, such as you see me, can convince you!"

"You're going to make a table turn?" said the young man ironically, resolved to make fun of her, for he did not know the extent to which he had dammed the flux of revelations about which those people could no longer shut up. He thought that the pleasantry was inopportune, gave way to a moue, and permitted himself to look toward the door, but Aunt Julia brandished her fist victoriously and brought it down on Ludovic.

"Yes, Monsieur! This one!"

That was the limit! A veritable madhouse! There was a silence. For several minutes the dull irritation that was tormenting Sellier had been giving him a migraine. Furthermore, the cigar proved to be detestable, with a bitter taste and acrid smoke that burned his lips. He dared not throw it away and bit it, stupidly, with the tips of his teeth, not listening to the explanations of the two monomaniacs, so much was he hypnotized by that fiery dot. He shook it, and aspired it, no longer able to distinguish its odor from the ambient odor of the room. Finally, war-weary, he took it between his fingers, posed it on his tongue, and savored it meticulously.

"Where did you buy these cigars?" he asked Deslandes suddenly, in a curt voice from which all mundanity was excluded.

"From the tobacconist on the corner," said the librarian, shivering. "Why do you ask in such a funny tone?"

"Because, my dear Monsieur, they're impregnated with arsenic!"

Madame Bordes emitted a shrill scream. Deslandes opened his arms, hastening to spit out his own.

"What!" he stammered "It's a joke! You're not serious!"

"Cigars at thirty sous a packet!" hissed the aunt.

The doctor approached the table and set about studying the suspect objects one by one, blinking, as was his custom as soon as he entered his medical functions, forgetting the fearful expressions of his hosts, very intrigued by his discovery and not yet having had time to become unduly alarmed by it.

"Strange," he said, "Very strange!"

He passed his hand over his forehead. Did he have all his lucidity?

It resulted from his examination that his cigar alone was poisoned. He did not fear the consequences of that minimal intoxication, but it seemed to him that the certainty he had acquired was more frightful than the poison itself. He had taken all the others in the sugar-tongs, had turned them over and over, and tasted them; they remained wholly indemnified. Only his own reeked of arsenic!

A kind of somnolent torpor took possession of Sellier. In the home of these naïve people, fundamentally welcoming, if not reasonable, who could have had the idea of poisoning him, who knew them so slightly, being almost a stranger in their house?

"Well?" said Deslandes, anxiously.

"These are good, I observe," replied the doctor, indicating the rest of the packet, "but mine has been rubbed with arsenic. One can't mistake the pronounced odor of garlic that it gives off." The physician looked up at Madeleine's father, darkly.

"That's quite a story!" murmured that latter, already reassured.

"Oh, this drawing room sometimes smells of garlic," objected Madame Bordes. "I've noticed it in hot weather."

Sellier was struck by that reflection. A gleam of joy shone in his eyes.

"Oh!" he said. "I've picked up a trail," he exclaimed. "Finally! I'd rather get out of this nightmare right away. Lend me your lamp, I beg you."

He ran to the hangings on the wall, at the same place where he had been a little while ago, and stood there sadly, his fingers wandering over the creases of the dusty damask while Madeleine had looked on with her cruel gaze of a proud woman. He had clenched his fists angrily, and perhaps torn the fabric without taking account of it. He had received the poison there in his moist hands!

"The walls of your drawing-room are distilling the arsenic," he declared, tranquilly.

"We're in a fine mess," moaned Madame Bordes.

Monsieur Deslandes raised his arms toward the ceiling.

"Repairs are necessary," the doctor continued, "or seal the room and nail up the door. As long as you don't eat in here, there's no danger."

He formed a mute laugh, relieved of an enormous weight, for he was truly suspected someone in this crazy house. There are neurotics capable of anything when their obsessions are disturbed.

"You'll permit me, won't you, to go and wash my hands. I've been punished for my curiosity. That green damask seemed so silky, and I must have handled it too much."

"Go, go, doctor! Oh, my poor Monsieur Sellier! What a story! I'm mortified," replied Jacques Deslandes.

"I might have swallowed that too! Arsenic on the walls! It's necessary to come to the provinces to see such things! Madeleine will give you what you need," added Madame Bordes.

Sellier slipped away gladly.

The brother and sister looked at one another for a moment, idiotically.

"Do you think it's true?" breathed the medium.

"Bah!" said Jacques Deslandes. "Since he affirms that it isn't dangerous, we needn't occupy ourselves with it any longer. I've never smoked my pipe in here." He looked around with less terror.

"Oh, these doctors!" muttered Madame Bordes, "they see poison everywhere. Besides," she mused, philosophically, after a pause, "it will be a good means of keeping Madeleine away from Ludovic."

"What if we were to consult him?" risked Deslandes, whose little squinting eyes began scintillating again in the shadow.

"Yes, it's an opportunity. I'll take the coffee, the glasses and the cigars away in the meantime."

Madame Bordes hastened to clear the table, realizing a dream of economy. The coffee could be utilized the following day.

Sellier did not want to call Madeleine. He found a carafe of fresh water, washed his hands and rinsed his mouth, then went down into the garden, glad to breathe at his ease. The night was very pure, a beautiful melancholy autumn night, almost glacial, and the moon inundated the stony hill with white reflections— the hill that one might have thought enveloped in a long shroud with stiff lines, harshly ridged by bony angles.

"Everything is natural," sighed the young man. "Isn't life also a poison?"

As he proffered those words he encountered Madeleine standing in the winding path through the box, a spectral Madeleine the color of amber and gold—transparent, so to speak. She had let down her red hair, which dressed her like a radiant mantle. She was contemplating the rocky summit, and her pale face, a mirror of polished snow, reflected all the white reverberations of the mountain. Why had she let down her hair? Was it coquetry? No, for the thought she was far away from the man who might admire her. Perhaps her proud head was weary of its role as crown-bearer! Perhaps she was deploying the magic net in which great night-birds might be caught!

"Mademoiselle," said Edmond, in a respectful voice, "you're committing another imprudence by delivering yourself bare-headed to this fresh wind."

She turned round, shivering. Her eyes were abruptly drowned by tears. She coughed.

"I'd like to be dead already!" she replied, in a heart-broken tone.

"Oh well," he sniggered, "go and respire the green drapes for a week; I assure you that you'll be satisfied."

She looked alternately at the young physician and the drawing-room window, which framed a couple leaning toward a lampshade: her father and Aunt Julia interrogating Ludovic.

"What do you mean, Monsieur?"

He explained the adventure of the cigar, sometimes sardonic, sometimes desolate to sense that she was indifferent to everything that was not her own chagrin.

"Oh, yes," she stammered, "death surrounds us under all in its multiple perfidious forms and prowls around the house, in the streets and on the mountain. It's all the same to me. I don't struggle; I consent to allow myself to be devoured."

"But *sacrebleu!*" he said, his teeth clenched, seizing her arm. "You must react, Mademoiselle! If not for yourself, for others; beautiful and young as you are, you're capable of spreading your neurosis among all those who surround you. I know very well that life is bleak; I know that the people one loves often forget to love you. Is that any reason to push sadness as far as despair, selfishness as far as cowardice? Let's go back inside, right away. I don't really know what I'm saying to you; I must have poison in my brain this evening!"

With her index finger, slowly raised, she showed him her family. "And what do you think of that neurosis?" she asked, acerbically.

He was momentarily absorbed before the scene in the window. By the slightly ruddy light of the lamp, that glittering bloody eye, against the green background of the walls oozing poison, old Deslandes was breaking his meager spine in two and his solemn nose was outlined at the level of the tabletop. He was listening to the wood. Facing him, Julia Bordes, coppery wisps of hair under her pink tulle headscarf, which had slipped sideways, her large cook's hands extended thumb to thumb, was darting gazes like a she-cat, and Ludovic was oscillating to the left and right, forcing them to totter like drunken people. Those poor maniacs, seized by their fury, were no longer concerned with anything else. It could have been raising arsenic and maladies of the lungs. The essential thing, for the present quarter of an hour, was to warn Ludovic, in order to make him bound like a mad goat, to the great scandal of the laws of nature, represented in their home by a physician.

"Oh, the poor child!" exclaimed Sellier, whose profoundly tender heart was exploding.

"Who are you talking about?" asked Madeleine, sarcastically.

"Do they do this often?" he whispered, heading toward the terrace, no longer daring to propose that they go back inside.

"Every evening, every day; it's their only distraction since they've arrived here."

"And when you were younger . . . a little girl?"

"Of course," she confessed, with an indefinable smile. "I watched them through the keyhole myself."

"My God!" he exclaimed, thinking that there were lunatics who were not locked up.

They sat down on the edge of the wall of the terrace, behind the curtain of hazel trees. A universal peace reined in the countryside. The road, bordered by its tall undulating poplars extended uniformly to their feet, evoking an idea of departure, of distant flight, in the land of religious silence and mild repose.

"You aren't cold?" he queried, anxiously.

"Thank you, no."

She put up her hair again slowly, weary of having to bear that weight on the nape of her neck.

"Give me your hands, since you've finished putting up your hair."

She gave them to him. She had a fever this time, and a very characteristic fever.

"Oh, Mademoiselle Madeleine, if you could only put your confidence in me . . . will you?"

She leaned over the terrace, her eyes searching the shadow of the wall.

"I have no need of you, Monsieur Sellier. I don't want . . . no, I don't want to have confidence in you."

"Invalids are weak; there's no shame for a sick woman in ceasing to be proud."

"I'm neither proud nor weak, Monsieur.

She withdrew her hands abruptly. Her face was illuminated by a sudden joyful light. "Do you hear someone breathing?" she asked.

"I only hear the breeze blowing in the poplars," he replied, shivering at the exaltation in the sound of her voice.

"Me, I know, I know, because I'm a predestined creature, stronger than death . . . Monsieur."

A sharp sensation of suffering traversed Sellier's skull. He looked at her, consternated, his arms dangling. She was as rigid as a statue, seeing only to live through her eyes, her admirable violet-black eyes, and her vermilion lips, the color of a beautiful poisonous fruit.

"Shut up, I beg you."

She uttered a sinister laugh.

"Oh, I pity you too, Doctor. All your science can do nothing here. I have built my temple outside this world. You can't hear what the breeze is murmuring between the poplars? *Eternal amour! Chaste voluptuousness! Eternal amour! Chaste voluptuousness!* I am the Princess of Darkness! You cannot see me as I am, and when you can see me it will be too late, poor seeker of humanity that you are."

"Silence! Mademoiselle . . . !"

"That's the name of the dog; it isn't for you to evoke him, for I alone have that power."

"Let's go back inside, let's go in quickly," begged Edmond.

The young man foresaw that all his wisdom of a sane and robust being would not be able to resist the ambient vertigo. Folly for folly, better that of the family, which was at least ridiculous! He snatched her away from the wall on which she was flexing her supple figure again and dragged her at a run—it was like an abduction—toward the house, where the door to the corridor was gaping. They were engulfed within it.

"What did you see out there?" she said, bewildered by his brutality.

His eyes wide, he replied: "I didn't see anything, but I believe, Mademoiselle, that I was afraid for the first time in my life! Excuse me."

Nodding her head meditatively, she said: "Be careful! It's dangerous to be afraid . . . because fear is the commencement of the supernatural."

He had had enough. He went to salute Madame Bordes ceremoniously and take his leave of Deslandes.

"What a pity," piped the medium, "that you're quitting us so soon. Ludovic is marching . . ."

She indicated the occasional table, now immobile.

That blessed Ludovic! He's becoming farcical, thought the librarian.

He retained himself, thinking that perhaps it was him who was losing a sense of reality.

Once he was in the street he hastened his steps, as if pursued . . . and, in fact, a remark made by Madeleine pursued him, attaching itself to his flesh like a sucker

"Fear is the commencement of the supernatural . . ."

X

SLENDER and black, the delicate skeletons of branches in the clumps of trees made the bright golden color of the foliage stand out. The entire little wood was yellow, like a treasure heaped up at the foot of the rocky slope, a treasure forgotten by some giant who had climbed back up to his throne on the hill. Here and there, leaves drier than the others were rattling, giving the illusion of a metallic sound, and in the thickets a light breeze was shaking the bushes, seemingly counting coins mysteriously, letting them fall from above, rustling the twigs in a cascade of new louis. No birds were singing. All the nests were dead. Only the insects wandering on the bark or buzzing in the air were perceptible, padding it with an amber mist. Over that corner of artificial nature, one might have thought that the malediction of some pretty perverse fay floated, whose wand was mutating the poor plants into gold in order to deprive them of life subsequently without their suspecting it.

A large tree, a beech, had fallen across the path, the one chosen by the last storm of summer to bear the sins of all its brethren; and lying like a long cadaver, its arms still hanging on desperately to two powerful offshoots of the stump, it displayed a colossal brown, charred wound with lips crevassed with sulfur, having been disemboweled along the trunk all the way to the crown. The entrails could be palpated and the open veins touched where the lightning had drunk, at a stroke, all the honest vegetal sap. Thus laid down, it formed a comfortable bench surrounded by a tangle of branches on one side and inciting travelers on the other to repose under a tent of creepers shading its bare trunk. In front of it, the narrow path wound, leading who knew where, dotted with leaves fallen from a plane tree, which the recent rain had already stripped and furred with a saffron ermine of lustrous moss in the oblique rays of sunlight like the pelt of an animal.

Madeleine was sitting there, her gaze lost in the distant perspective, her hands joined on her knees. That magical landscape of gold, amber and sulfur, blurred by the transparent vapors of the imminent dusk, which opalized it, rendered it fluid and filled it with an artificial jewelry of dream, flattered her melancholy, separating her further from the rest of the world. She isolated herself with things suddenly struck by insensibility, funereal straw only waiting for a stronger gust of the light wind to sink into the oblivion of the mud. Tomorrow, perhaps, she would rediscover the skeletons of black branches, but the enchantment of the golden foliage would have disappeared forever, and she would be able to contemplate, behind the bodies of twisted trees, the sad tableau of the poverty of the fields. All the soul of November had taken refuge, the desolate soul of the agony of the roses, the last sighs of the nightingale, the bitter odor of chrysanthemums that are spread over graves; it huddled, shivering, in the line of bright gilt, haloed by a false splendor, trying to soften the sunlight, and one felt that even the searching wind had not dared to chase it away, so intense had the bleak despair of adieux become.

Gold, amber and sulfur, Madeleine's hair matched the yellowed tones of the little wood. It was as if the young woman were wearing a crown of dead leaves on her dolorously tilted head.

"It's finished," she murmured. "I shan't see it again."

Tears filled her eyes. She raised them toward the sky, scintillating like two aquamarines, superb jewels embedded in the immense gilded mass of the landscape. Her pale hands were trembling and her feet, in their pointed black shoes, were extending toward an imaginary departure. Her entire woman's body, in a black dress, like those of the slender young trees surrounding her, writhed with the bitter terror of abandonment, while in the distance, beyond the deserted wood, beyond the valley, the bell of Toussaint was sobbing.

"It's cold. I shouldn't be allowed out any longer."

She started to weep like the distant bell. A kind of exasperated heartbreak took possession of her. So be it: to die as quickly as possible in order to rediscover herself. She invoked the final uprooting and wanted to fall, like the beech, under an impact coming from even higher up than the lightning. And she saw herself lying alongside the cadaver of the tree, in its wound, making her a crude coffin where golden leaves were weeping, enveloped by the shadowy mist, and where saffroned mosses climbed, velveting her limbs to aid them to bury her. Her fatigued eyes darkened gradually and closed, letting fall their bruised, bistred eyelids fringed with brown lashes, like the petals of white roses that were fading, and she remained prostrate, in the attitude of the broken stem of a beautiful golden plant from which the flower is about to fall, its heart disaggregated.

The bell of that Toussaint Sunday fell silent, in the depths of the horrorstruck atmosphere. Silence reigned over the vast cemetery of Autumn. Madeleine opened her eyes again, and saw a black dot moving in the distant perspective of the deserted path. She leapt to her feet with a hoarse cry, the cry of a wild beast calling her young, a cry of joy and anguish; then she tried to run, but her legs, as in those terrible nightmares in which one is forced to obey laws contrary to nature, refused her their service; she was condemned to wait, nailed to that dead tree, dead herself. The black dot grew and split; now there were two: a man and an animal. Seized by doubt, which can kill if it does not change into the hope of certain happiness, she fell to her knees. At that distance, he ought to be able to perceive her, or rather to divine her.

That thin silhouette becomes more distinct: the man has a trailing cloak. One might think it a dangling wing sweeping the yellow leaves, forming a wake of sulfur, amber and gold foam. Around his head the famous mist forms an aureole like a white halo. He knows where he is going. And his fantastic dog follows him, continuing the train of the cloak. It's really him.

"Hunter!"

She calls to him in a heart-rending voice, and yet he does not hear her cry out. What if he is about to take another path, forking away, disdainfully, without seeing her?

"Hunter!"

"Hunter!" says a second voice, dully, a voice emerging from her own, an echo.

The man still does not press his pace. He has merely removed his hat, saluting her with that brief gesture; his arm falls back along his body with an automatic motion, as if scythed, the gesture that she knows too well to attribute it to another.

And the dog, taking the lead, launched forward, and was beside her in a few rapid bounds, licking her hands, panting with a ferocious and mute joy.

Madeleine had stood up amid the branches of the beech, where she took refuge, trying to dissimulate the convulsive trembling of her limbs. She did not have the strength to repel the animal, limiting herself to hiding her hands under the large black lace scarf that she had knotted feverishly around her neck.

Finally, Hunter joined her and stopped, his gaze fixed on hers, giving the impression of someone waiting for an order in order to speak. He appeared paler still, and yet more human, because he had marched toward her for a long time, rather than being abruptly projected from a curtain of trees or from behind a rock. A smile made his red lips shine, and the incredible whiteness of his teeth completed his transformation of ancient God into new man.

"Why come to me so slowly?" she stammered.

Without ceasing to smile, he answered: "Why have you replaced me so quickly?"

"Hunter! I've been suffering extraordinary torments for nearly two months because of your absence, and your first words are a reproach? Who has replaced you? Who could replace you?"

She held out her hands to him. He did not take them.

"I came back one evening to the terrace of the garden. I found a lover there, Madeleine's garden is poorly defended!"

"You're jealous? You? Hunter, accessible to an earthly sentiment?"

He laughed, frankly, showing his teeth, his eye tranquil, still very handsome, very arrogant, but hiding a dolor under his appearance of an enigmatic wicked creature.

"And I'm very ill," she added.

"I know. Me too. With the same thunderbolt, nature once slew that tree and made us love one another. All that is already far away, isn't it? The seed of amour! The seed of death!"

"Why didn't you come back sooner, Hunter?"

"Since you're saying that to me, I've come back too late. I still obey other laws than yours, Madeleine."

She twisted her arms.

"Your name! Your true name! I want it. Where do you live? Could you not write to me? I would have replied. I need to know what I have to dread, or I'll die."

"I am the traveler who passes by . . . and who goes away, for cold expels me!"

"You're going to abandon me again?"

"I'm leaving you a physician."

"Oh, stop this ridiculous game! You're odious, Hunter. One doesn't make fun of a woman like that. What have I done wrong?"

"You speak when it's necessary to be quiet, and you choose my own rival for a confidant?"

"But you're mad! That evening, perhaps I spoke maladroitly; I had a fever. Edmond Sellier is a doctor, not a lover."

"You'll marry that man, Madeleine . . ."

"Get away!"

". . . Because I wish it. That interests me."

She collapsed on the dead tree.

"Hunter," she begged, "don't talk to me any more. You're torturing me needlessly. I've given you my soul . . . have you come to return it to me?"

"Return the soul!" he sighed, like an echo of what she said.

He had a singular love of repeating the ends of her phrases, and that frightened Madeleine more than any other proof of his special character. She took his arm. Either because his cloak had deceived her, draped as it was over his elbow, or because the arm was exceptionally thin, she only seized a void. Then Hunter coughed—a hollow cough—and a little blood colored the projections standing out from his pale cheeks. Madeleine burst into tears. It seemed that she was weeping for herself as much as for him. When she looked up she found him very close to her, his gaze soft.

"I've come in order to permit you to choose, Madeleine. It's just because I've already lived for a long time . . . in spite of my age! I believe that you're occupied with me, but I know that you love that man. Can

I tolerate that? Yes, if I possess your soul entirely . . . then you and he will become utterly indifferent to me. However, I intend to leave you free." And he added, smiling his smile of a fallen angel: "Absence might plead my cause better . . ."

"Where will you go, and for how long?" the young woman asked, feverishly.

"I swear that I'll be here, in the same spot, when the first violets open their eyes."

"My God! There are no wild violets hereabouts; I've never encountered any."

"If you come, there will be some, Madeleine. Your blue eyes sometimes have the color of violets."

She smiled.

"You don't want to tell me your family name and give me your address?"

He laughed. "Doctor Sellier has rendered you vulgar in . . . caring for you, my darling! Don't you think that we ought to have a tacit agreement never to ask one another certain questions?"

"You're a coward, Hunter."

She straightened up, resolved to attack him in what remained to him of proud humanity, to force him to betray himself. Hunter, that hero of her imagination, was no longer entirely a god, since he walked like a man and showed himself to be jealous, like a lover. In her turn, she would dare to become the demon.

"Yes," he confessed, coldly.

"And what if I put my family on your track, if I revealed my fashion of acting to the doctor who cares for me, if, finally, I threw my arms around your neck to make you my prisoner?"

"Your family," replied Hunter, disdainfully, "are grotesque egotists and idiots who wouldn't budge. I despise them almost as much as you do, their daughter. As for the doctor, I can send my dog to strangle him one day; but he won't know who I am, I guarantee that, and that will be my worst vengeance. I don't measure myself against blind men . . . who have blinded my mistress, for decidedly, there are blind men who win."

"Your mistress? I decline that quality, Hunter."

"Indeed!" he said, ironically. "I thought that a woman talking about throwing her arms around the neck of a man *in order to make him her prisoner* . . ."

She interrupted him violently: "Around the neck of a man who has stolen her amour and abused her good faith . . . around the neck of a man . . . *of a man!*"

She was excited, mad with passion, and she launched the words *a man* like the crudest of insults.

He extended his arm; his long cloak opened in somber wings, and he burst into strident laughter.

"There we are! I'm whatever it pleases you to become, and you aren't content, infernal daughter of Eve, my worthy sister in treachery! Successively Amour or Lover, Demon or God, man or beast. I appear to you as your brain has molded me, not without making me suffer cruelly, and perhaps you'll cause further suffering, and you'll desire me under a new form? Which, eh? You've forbidden me, up there, on the mountain, at the summit of our enthusiasm, to possess you carnally. Is it here, descended into this wood, where the leaves, ready to rot, exhaling poison, that you'd like to deliver me something other than your foolish heart? Must I now prostitute myself to you to be sure in advance that you'd be unfaithful to me with your future husband? Must I fall at your feet with the vain grimace of the ridiculous monsieur to whom you will make the supreme insult of doubling yourself, you in his bed and the child in the cradle? Do I look like a muleteer or a simple country doctor, dreaming of caring for himself in your excessively complaisant person? Have I the ugly appearance of the man who intends to propagate his ugly species?" He raised his hands in a wild gesture. "Look at me! I'm the man you don't know, the greatest of all, the only one you can love sincerely, poor woman, for I affirm that you will never know me—*never*. My strength is eternal doubt! I've suffered, and I no longer want to agonize for you or because of you. My goal is to steal, finally, immortal pleasure from a mortal and to vanish thereafter, in the egotistical pleasure of having been, for one second, more powerful than life! Let some dream of fortune and others of glory, myself I dream of realizing fully a voluptuousness simultaneously intellectual and physical. That's very little, you suppose? Well, I believe that will be necessary to sacrifice our two existences to it! Anyway, what do our two existences of intelligent and refined creatures signify without love, as the priests of all religions conceive it—which is to say, divine? Oh, you have the audacity to renew the scene of the terrestrial paradise! You want to cast down the idol to make the man spring forth from it! But the man, debased and exhausted by you, is united with Satan, they are no longer anything but the same monster! Oh, you want to penetrate my mystery . . . come, then, to suspend yourself around my neck and try to make me pick the beautiful fruit that I judge to be full of ashes!

Come on, child, little woman, and offer me the cup of your lips, varnished with lies, before I've decided to drink from it. Come on! My God, one might think you're afraid, Madeleine?"

She shook her head, horrified but still valiant.

"No, I'm no longer afraid!"

He folded his arms, the somber wings of his cloak folding up again.

"I'm waiting?"

She took a step. Certainly, she would go! Loving that man passionately, it was necessary for her to know, finally, whether she was addressing a dangerous madman or a skillful actor, a patient cunning man, having sworn to overcome her disgust for the male. What could happen to her worse than death? If she were raped, or killed, she would rather die than see him play with her like a sick child who believed herself to be hallucinated . . .

Who believed herself to be hallucinated! She hesitated momentarily, her eyes lowered, thinking that, by means of an inexplicable conjuring trick, he might vanish in her arms, that in spite of the adventurer she desired to absolve, she might only be embracing mist! The unfortunate woman forgot her definition of fear: *the commencement of the supernatural.* She was afraid of the precise, decisive act, sensing herself searched to the quick by the sharp gaze of the human monster; she recoiled, *she doubted,* and as that doubt was, for him, the triumph of his diabolical cause, she declared herself vanquished, no longer even having the desire to act.

"I submit. Whoever you are, I love you, and in fact, the rest is superfluous. Rather endure all humiliations than risk losing you!"

He smiled.

In the dry grass and the dead leaves the dog rolled over on his back, his four paws shaking with a hectic but silent gaiety, its ebony underbelly shining and exhibiting an enormous erection: an animal delighted, it seemed, to witness things it did not understand. Madeleine put her hands together and knelt down on the dead tree, very close to Hunter.

"Good," he said, in an affectionate tone, stroking the flamboyant crown of her hair with his index finger. "Would you like to repeat with me a *Credo* that I shall teach you? Listen to it, and engrave it on your memory:

"God does not exist. The only God is the man I love. The universe is a dream, of which he is the creator. The laws of humanity are abolished because he wishes it. I curse my birth and aspire to death, because it will unite him with me beyond this world. Virgin or woman, I swear to serve him for my happiness or for my despair. If, by chance, my family tread on a corner of his cloak one day, I will kill my family, and if he is thirsty, I will express pure water from the eyes of my new-born in order to give it to him to drink.

"Repeat that, Madeleine, and try not to make a mistake."

She repeated that singular act of faith in a low voice, like a prayer, and then she added, in a clearer tone: "And will he promise me in his turn to return in the spring?"

"So be it," he replied. "You have an astonishing memory!"

He draped his cloak over his shoulders. "Adieu, Madeleine," he murmured, more tenderly. "Night in this valley is cold; save yourself. Here is the delicate crescent of the moon, shining between the branches of the thicket. Truly, one might think that God, offended, were showing us, on his menacing fist, the inaccessible ring of betrothal! Are you afraid of God, Madeleine?"

"I'm afraid of you."

"Then save yourself, my foolish friend, although I sense that I'm more redoubtable than this cold air . . . of which I'm jealous, since it is caressing you."

"Hunter?"

"Yes, I know; I've played my role as a man badly, and you wanted me to be a man this evening. Forgive me. All that I can add to it is to withdraw normally, like a classic stroller, smoking a cigar. You like men who smoke, I believe?"

She shivered, thinking about the accident that had befallen Doctor Sellier.

"Have you heard about that?" she said, already habituated to seeing him divine what, logically, he could not know.

"Of course," he growled, bearing a light green flame to his mouth.

Feverishly, Madeleine shook his arm.

"Yes. Answer me, how is it that a cigar can suddenly be poisoned by arsenic welling from a wall? Is that possible?"

"Everything is possible in my house, Madeleine," he replied in a reserved, almost philosophical, tone. Then he burst into his youthful laughter of a fallen angel. "Adieu, Madeleine, I adore you!"

He kissed her hands nervously, and with a prodigious leap, hurdling the dead tree, he tore himself away from her, and was soon no more than a shadow among the shadows of the path. The dog galloped behind him in the train of his cloak, continuing the man and the fabric like the tortuous rump of a black hydra. All around them fluttered a little luminous blood-red dot, like a fire follet amusing itself in the wind of their course.

Madeleine stiffened, clawed by a nameless dolor. Was she the plaything of a handsome idler or had she really sold her soul to Satan? A sage idea immediately germinated in what remained of her reason. She followed him. No matter what it cost, she would know what path he took on quitting her. Oh, she would not draw away, carrying on her lips the bitter tears of which he had often spoken to her. She launched herself straight ahead with a bound. The route was straight until a wooded curve that she imagined seeing turn in the direction of a distant village. There, he doubtless had horses and a carriage in the depths of some inn, for he must evidently come from some great city. An eccentric traveler habituated to nocturnal excursions he could only be a trickster familiar with a certain extent of terrain. He was unknown in her locale, in a little provincial town, because no one had any interest in paying attention to him and he did not care to go through its streets, but there, the villagers must talk about him . . .

Madeleine came to a ditch, wanted to pass over it, groping her way, and fell, tripped up by a large branch that felled her like a sledgehammer. She uttered a desperate cry: "Hunter!" and lost consciousness.

It seemed that the tenebrous beau was laughing in her ears when she opened her eyes again, but, on due reflection, that could not be exact, since she found herself in front of her bedroom window!

IX

THE vast library, a former convent refectory, was always better heated than their house, if no less sad, and Madeleine came there in the afternoons to devour the books that her father put at her disposal since he had renounced the hope of engaging her in conversation. She sat down next to one of the columns that sustained the vault of the ceiling, enveloped herself warmly in her long black lace shawl and stayed there, her eyes almost closed, over an old romance of chivalry. A religious silence reigned, scarcely interrupted by the gasps of Deslandes' throat, spitting and sniffing for hours in the office next door, or the trailing steps of the concierge descending a stairway.

Sometimes a priest arrived in order to search for a book; he saluted her dryly—she did not frequent his church—and promptly withdrew, as if he had glimpsed the devil. From time to time a subscriber renewed his subscription and the subscriber, always boorish, hastened to go out through the office without saluting at all. She remained alone, quite alone, irrevocably alone. Life, for her, was scarcely supportable any more. She skimped her morning chores, housework and sewing, listened to her aunt's sermons without making any reply, and then ran away on the specious pretext of aiding her father in vague classifications. For what could she be reproached? Did she not have a right to take advantage of the beautiful coal fire that the concierge carefully maintained in honor of his unique reader? The meticulous neatness of that sanctuary of study, where no one studied, comforted her heart a little, and she dreamed that she was a young queen, imprisoned in a sad palace from which the courtiers were exiled in order not to see her weep . . .

One day in January the snow covered the roofs of the old monastery, and through an arched window one perceived a carpet of blinding white that not even the feet of a skylark had brushed. The red stove was purring; a bleak somnolence took possession of Madeleine, sitting in her high Louis XIII chair. She let go of her book, let her arms fall, and her head tilted backwards against the sculpted back.

"My God!" she moaned. "This torture is horrible. I'll end up no longer being able to read."

What she was searching for, in her reading chosen at random, was forgetfulness, a forgetfulness that was not completed, the forgetfulness of everything that constituted her inner life, in her own brain. Often, she sat up angrily in the midst of her momentary distraction, thinking, because of a striking analogy, that she had been tricked. Yes, tricked! That and nothing else! She had been abandoned in a cowardly fashion by a being who mocked her complaisant credulity. Oh, he would not fail in his duty as a man . . . he would deceive her, like all the other men one loves!

And from the depths of her entrails a desire rose to kill or torture someone . . .

"What if he did not exist?" breathed her imagination. "Oh, then he would return, for amour believes easily in the absurd."

She walked for a moment from the window to the large oval table covered in green cloth. What silence! Always the same purr of the coal in the stove, and the pulsation of the milestone-clock planted on the high mantelpiece of black marble, like the truncated stump of a funerary column. She counted: "January . . . February . . . March!" Yes, perhaps in March there would be violets. She finished her reflection in an abrupt laugh that sowed sonorous echoes throughout the hall.

"What's the matter with you, being cheerful?" asked her father, bewildered, passing his head through the gap in his office doorway.

"Me? Nothing. I'm reading a funny story."

And she resumed reading a chapter, further on from the place she had been scanning before. Her father closed the door, disappointed.

Footsteps, younger and firmer than those of the concierge, came up the stairs; finally, someone came in. The individual's large overcoat, with the collar turned up, hid his face. He came all the way to the stove, lowered his collar and saluted her in the indistinct tone of an embarrassed visitor. It was Doctor Edmond Sellier, whom she had not encountered for more than three months. Madeleine held out her hand to him spontaneously.

"I'm glad to see you," she said. "I was absent on New Year's Day when you left your card at our house. I regretted it . . ."

"You're very kind," he replied, softly, his grave face illuminated by a half-smile. "Are you feeling better? You're no longer coughing?"

"No, I come here as much as I can to warm up—our house is so cold! You desire a book?"

"Yes, in a while; there's no hurry. Why do you regret not having seen me on New Year's Day?"

"Firstly, to thank you for your chocolate pralines. They were exquisite. Then, I wanted to beg your pardon . . . I behaved rather stupidly in your regard, one evening. Perhaps you've already forgotten it?"

"I haven't forgotten. On the contrary . . . and I also needed to see you . . . You're happy, then, in this immense deserted hall?"

"Yes. I'm looking at the snow and waiting for spring . . ."

"You're not difficult."

He went to her father's office to look for his book. He did not say any more that day—but he acquired the habit of returning to idle in the library, especially when the weather was bad, with snow or heavy rain. He chatted a little before going into Deslandes' study, in a curt, dull tone, as if strangled, and, suddenly remembering a pressing visit, he disappeared at a rapid pace like a man being pursued. Sometimes he only went to see the father, seeming to neglect the daughter, addressing her with a cold little nod, always marching quickly. And yet he came for her alone, no longer being able to bear the martyrdom he was enduring. The crystallization was complete; the image of that strange woman he carried under his skull, in his marrows and in his flesh, and he struggled like a madman in order not to cry out: "But you must be able to see that I'm suffering! Prevent me, then, from thinking about you, since I detest you . . . since I can't love you, that I mustn't love you!"

When the father had closed the door again, believing him to be already on the staircase, he lingered near the great oval table, leafing through journals, and she, her coquetry sharpened by contact with an amateur more delicate and more distinguished than the others, indicated articles to him, making critiques of books she had read and for which he asked. Caught in the trap of his own capricious spirit, he sat there, his elbow on the green baize, his forehead in his hand, his eyes following the graceful evolutions of the pale and excessively blonde young woman in the mist of the mysterious mourning she was obstinate in wearing. From time to time one of them went to steal the key to the little museum, which was only open to the public on Sundays, and among the Egyptian homunculi, before the carcasses of animals in the natural history cabinet, they had a few discussions in louder voices, teasing one another about what they called their false erudition. Madeleine held forth on the solemn and monstrous divinities of Egypt; he brought her back to the meek science of nature that induces you to believe that bees are pretty creatures full of forbearance, even after they have murdered or chased away the male that they have enjoyed. Singularly enough, Madeleine, although atrociously coquettish, did not think that the physician might be in love; she said to herself in her roguish language of a Parisienne: "One who likes my face! I must be an object of study!"

She was hard on him, as she was on humankind in general, not suspecting that her blows might break a heart.

Sellier's existence was divided between two tortures: seeing her and not seeing her. His passion, born of the curiosity of a worthy fellow who honestly desired to verify a diagnosis, had made such progress in a few months that he renounced the struggle without even thinking of struggling. Yes, the young woman was not a *suitable* party, as his mother, Madame Sellier, would have put it. Yes, the young woman could, rigorously speaking, pass for a candidate for madness, and perhaps she loved someone else, whom she had left out there is the great dissolute city, one of those burning shames the memory of which was etiolating her here, in the isolation of reclusion. Yes, she would have no dowry and one would be marrying, along with her, in-laws who were ridiculous, if not dangerous. The aunt, Madame Bordes, was a species of cartomancer whose principal occupation could be filed under the title: *The art of accommodating the remains of the dead.* The father profited from all flirtations to extort digestive pastilles from him while forgetting to pay for them. But the daughter was extraordinarily, above other women, beautiful with an eccentric, unhealthy beauty, perhaps composed of ugliness, which gripped all the senses at once . . .

Oh, that tawny hair, impregnated with a savage and delectable odor, the odor of a lioness that had the custom of mingling violets in her mane! That nape of a milky whiteness, where gleaming wisps curled like jets of liquid gold! That hand of a little girl with omnipotent fingers, which dug into your pallor with retracted feline claws; that voice, above all, mordant and musical, by turns desolate and seductive; and those eyes, those eyes containing one knew not what obsession, an obsession with steely blue reflections. He admired her mourning dress, always the same, having ended up taking her form to such an extent that he saw her naked with a black skin, like someone emerging from a conflagration.

One day, she allowed herself to be ausculated. That happened quite simply, The father claimed that she had been coughing during the night, and she complained of a pain between her shoulders. They went into the little office. She unbuttoned her blouse and he saw, under the habitual blinking of his eyelids, her two rigid breasts, pointed and seeming to want to pierce her chemise—for she had no corset. He was ecstatic.

"You do well not to wear a corset, Mademoiselle; the corset is the executioner of young women."

She formed a malicious and confused moue. "There's also another reason, which is that a good corset is very dear, and I prefer not to have one than to wear an ill-fitting one."

She said "ill-fitting" so politely! A cloud passed before Sellier' eyes when he had to apply his ear to her breast. He experienced a veritable self-disgust on observing that he did not know what he was doing or why he was doing it, and the traditional: "take a deep breath" would not emerge from his clenched teeth. His hands were burning, as of supporting a bust of lava.

The father did not miss the opportunity to say something stupid.

"Ha ha!" he said, teasingly, "you doctors don't get bored every day, and for you young ones, if you treat many ladies, the métier can't be too burdensome . . ."

"But a doctor isn't a man," put in Madeleine coldly. "Monsieur has already told me that."

The apparent innocence of that remark upset Sellier. She was a coquette, a frightful coquette, and was making fun of him, which was worse. He ordered her to get dressed again in an authoritarian tone.

"No, you have nothing serious, Mademoiselle. Only you don't wrap yourself up warmly enough. Wear thick woolen jumpers for me, then!"

"Oh, you wouldn't want that!" she cried, laughing. "Pullovers like those of peasant women, eh? There's a prescription! Thank you very much."

On the day of the auscultation they did not talk about literature or sciences, and he left without shaking her hand. As soon as he found himself at home again, in his work-room, so neat and so prudish, and his mother came to bring him a lamp, he felt so miserable that he had a brutal desire to smash his head against the wall. His mother! She would die of chagrin on seeing him marry a woman without a dowry. But so what? Can one marry a stranger? For he confessed that he knew her less than ever. He could already see the indignation of Madame Sellier, who dreamed for him of the tax-collector's *demoiselle*, a great horse of a woman who exhibited all of her gums when she talked. He collapsed in his armchair, hiding his face in his hands, to which the perfume of that bewitching creature still adhered. He wept with rage, furious against himself and others. Oh, that virgin truly reeked of a courtesan, for having put him in such a state! The storm having broken, he calmed down.

The following week, in damp and warm weather—it was March—passing in his carriage before her garden, he saw her coming from the corridor of the old house toward the terrace. Instinctively, he stopped Marquis, thinking that she probably had something important to confide to him. It was the day after he had sworn to flee her by all means possible, and no longer to risk himself in the game of literary conversation if he did not have a frank desire to marry her. Madeleine was wearing a mantle with a hood and heading toward the gate to the meadows. She made him a sign to join her at the bend in the rocks on the hill. He whipped his horse, very anxious. A quarter of an hour later, he found her in the Chairs. She was laughing.

"Pardon me, Monsieur Sellier. I have a caprice."

He shivered. A caprice of Madeleine's was doubtless, for him, the annihilation of all his good resolutions.

"What is that, Mademoiselle?" he questioned, maintaining his physiognomy of a doctor in a hurry, but sensing that he was at her mercy.

"Well, here it is. My aunt has charged me to go to the village of Hotteaux to ask her laundress for some bleach, and if you're passing through that village . . . ?"

He was struck by stupor. What! In a carriage! Side by side, in an area where he was very well-known? Madeleine's gaze weighed upon his own, imploring him seductively, like a blue forget-me-not in broad daylight. She had pulled up the hood of her mantle and had put her pale face inside like a white bird in a nest.

"But Mademoiselle . . ."

A litany of politic phrases filed before him; his affairs; a childbirth; an urgent visit to a dying man; then the idea occurred to him that she believed him to be much older than he was because of the graying hair on his temples, and he was annoyed.

"Does your father permit you to go out in such wet weather?"

"Yes, he's the one who is sending me," she said, resolutely.

He could see that she was lying, and experienced a sort of wicked joy in surprising her deceiving someone in order to escape with him, playing truant. My God, what to do? Her pepper-red mouth was preparing a moue for him, her teeth bit her lip and, leaning forward, he discovered that she was wearing little canvas shoes that would not take long to get soaked with damp.

"Climb up, Mademoiselle," he sighed, delighted and desolate at this abduction of sorts.

He got ready to assist her, but she leapt up on her own, like a goat.

"Oh!" she said, clapping her hands. "I've wanted so much to ride in a carriage!"

A whim! However, he reflected, what child of twenty-two would not have a desire to escape, at least for an hour, from a monotonous existence? He tried to conserve his ceremonious tone.

"And she lives in Hotteaux, Mademoiselle, your laundress?"

"No, a house some distance before the village. Her name is Mère Jean."

"Good! I know. She has a scrofulous son."

166

She started to laugh. "Your nasty habit of classifying people by their illnesses again!"

He could not help smiling. Oh, he scarcely saw life in its nicer aspects! As they were no longer separated by the rampart of the big table in the library, they were naturally brought to talk to one another while Marquis made his regular trot sound in the deserted road.

"You'll be scolded when you return!" he said, to tease her.

She shrugged her shoulders. "If you knew how little I care about that! I need to respire up here. Your prescription of excursions on foot is pleasant, but one gets fatigued, especially when one encounters nothing interesting." She took a breath of the cold air and pulled up her hood again. "When one thinks, Monsieur, that I've been searching for one poor violet for a week and can't find one!"

"You like violets very much, then?"

"A Parisian flower, of my own homeland."

"Always Paris! It's very close to your heart."

"I regret it from the point of view of violets, that's all."

"Hmm."

He whipped Marquis, with a little surge of anger that was not addressed to him.

"And then," she said, "in Paris one feels alive, and less afraid when one wakes up on the night."

"What can you have to fear? Tell me that."

"How do I know? Sometimes, in the middle of a dream, I see *the three-legged wolf*; it wakes me up with a start and I can't go back to sleep. It's a wolf that I saw for the first time as a little girl, during a fever. It arrived from afar, as soon as the light in my bedroom was extinct, from very far away, in a nightmare forest. It limped, and held out its paw, which was crushed, streaming with black blood. It was abominable, but it caused me more pity than horror. I wanted to care for it. It appears that I went to sleep every evening cradling my doll and repeating: 'Dodo, the wolf, dodo! Don't eat me; I'll cure your paw!' That's so present in my memory that I can describe every hair of that wolf to you. It had eyes so malevolent and so sad. The night before my examinations I saw it again, and in many other circumstances.

"But there isn't only the *three-legged wolf*, there's also *the game of anguished children*, as we called it at school. Not being able to go back to sleep I lay down full length, with my arms pressed to my body and I held my breath; then I said to myself: 'You're condemned to death! In ten years, or twenty years, or perhaps in one year, you're going to die. Since birth, the being you call the good God has condemned you to death,' and I weep. It's irresistible. It does so much good to weep, my dear doctor. Or I listen to the silence, and I think: 'At this moment, someone somewhere on the surface of the globe is sobbing. Nothing I do can console him, I don't know him, he doesn't know me, and we'll weep, each for our own part, until dawn!'

"During the day, too, one has a right to play the game of anguished children. I often put down the needlework I'm holding and go to place myself between two mirrors that are facing one another in my bedroom, and, I don't know why, I look for a long time at their infinite perspective, murmuring 'Out there, in

168

the last mirror, descending the frames one by one like the steps of a golden stairway, *the little man without a head* is coming . . . There he is . . . there he is . . . He's running . . . he's already crossed half the route; he has pink shoulders full of blood; his legs are molded in a fine leotard of red silk; he's getting bigger, growing.' You can believe me or not, but I've had the illusion until it made me ill!"

Sellier contemplated her, bewildered.

"It's a foolish amusement, your little game. Here, you deserve the whip." And with an impulse that he could not repress, he whipped Marquis conscientiously. The latter took to the gallop, in a very bad humor. They were going through labored fields From the good brown earth rose warm scents of fermentation. A peasant saluted the doctor.

"Put up your hood," he said. "There's no need for him to recognize you."

She obeyed.

"You can explain that I'm a poor sick peasant girl that you picked up on the road!"

"Perhaps I'd only be lying by one word."

"No, I'm not ill; I'm not coughing any more; but I'm bored and I have a desire to run like a poisoned rat, according to my aunt's fortunate expression."

"I can assure you," said Sellier, "that you're not in your normal state, Mademoiselle Deslandes! You're much too occupied with the double mystery of night and death to be as alive as I'd like. Furthermore, your passion for solitude isn't natural."

"The fact is, my dear doctor, that since I've been chatting with you from time to time, I feel less nervous."

He turned round, triumphantly. "You see! When I tell you to have a little confidence in me! Oh, the veritable remedy would be . . ."

He stopped, sensing that he was about to do something stupid. They were trotting now in a dip between two slopes covered in flowering gorse with a fragrance of honey. Marquis quickened of his own accord.

"Yes," she said, "I don't deny that you're reasonable, but that's your métier, not mine. I have no mission to fulfill, myself."

"Get away! To be an obedient child, first of all, and then a good wife and a good mother! Isn't that a mission?" He sensed that he must have wounded her, and added immediately: "Do you occupy yourself with religion, with your mystical character?"

"No," she replied, frankly. "I've even ceased making the sign of the cross every evening."

"Too bad, for it lacks nothing more than that for you to become a stigmatized of the first order. We'd have miracles in the old house at the end of the town and it would be charming."

He forced himself to joke, but he was under torture. For an instant, he closed his eyes and went very pale, for the pithy curve of her hip had brushed him during a jolt of the carriage,

"What can you see?" she said, anxiously. "Is it someone that it would be very disagreeable for you to encounter in my company?"

She looked in all directions.

"My word!" he replied, clenching his teeth. "I see no one but you, at the moment, who could frighten me!"

She burst out laughing.

"That's the *game of anguished children* operating! You'll end up taking an interest in my double mystery of the night and death!"

"That seems certain to me," he grunted, inwardly.

They emerged from the ravine and discovered the village: four or five thatched cottages on the roofs of which guinea-fowl were piping.

"I'm going to get down here," she said, "and we'll meet up again after your visit, won't we?"

"Agreed. I'm going to the Perrons, who have a feverish child."

He breathed out; he had time. His visit to the Perrons would be concluded quickly enough. He prescribed quinine again, which he had judged unnecessary the day before, and when the parents showed him out with many thanks, he congratulated them, in order to say something, for having such fine pigeons on their roof.

"But they're our guinea-fowl!" the scandalized peasants cried.

He ran away, very ashamed. Madeleine was waiting for him at the rendezvous. She was sitting in the flowering gorse and she seemed melancholy.

"Let's go!" he growled. "Has the wind turned? Here you are with your terrible eyes, a contracted mouth and a new black butterfly in your brain?"

"I think," she said, "that I would like to be stupid."

"Ah! That would be a hundred times better, given that it wouldn't prevent you from still being pretty.

The somber violet of her perverse eyes had just blossomed. She had not obtained, in the village, the information that she had come to demand, and apart from her two dark irises, no blue flower was blooming in the poor gardens in the environs.

"You think I'm pretty?" she laughed.

"Is that forbidden?"

"Pooh! If it amuses you. A physician is a man, then?"

My God, he thought. *She talks like a girl.*

"But I'm frightfully red-haired!"

"Say marvelously, Mademoiselle Madeleine. There is gold and fire in your hair, which is the very beauty of your blood."

"Ah! Well, if my dear aunt could hear you!"

He fell silent. Indeed, if anyone heard them, he would be edified on the opportunity of his functions with regard to the librarian's daughter. He laid such a whiplash on Marquis that the poor animal got carried away. They galloped for ten minutes, the wind lashing their faces and making Madeleine's mantle flap. For a moment, a lock of her red hair escaped from the hood to wander over Sellier's face No longer being able to see, he inhaled with full nostrils the maddening odor of that creature kneaded from fire, sulfur and gold, and he was able, thus, his gaze veiled by sensuality, to launch himself into no matter what catastrophe. He tugged the reins, pulling back with all his weight, stopping Marquis so brutally that the latter nearly broke the shafts.

"We're just at the height of the little wood!" exclaimed Madeleine, indifferent to anything that was not her obsession. "I want to get down. Some were perhaps born last night."

He leapt down from the carriage. Marquis snorted, his eyes menacing, very discontented with the turn that things were taking.

"Yes, poor old thing, we'll leave you tranquil," murmured the doctor, stroking his horse's sweaty flank.

Standing on the vehicle, she was smoothing the hair on her temples. "How good it is to gallop," she said, becoming joyful again. It seemed to me that I was traversing the sky like a cloud. I thank you, Monsieur, and I offer you my apologies. You're very reasonable; I must have disturbed you considerably."

She felt the footstep with the pointed tip of her shoe. Edmond put his arm around her waist to help her.

"Oh! No!" she said. "I want to jump down on my own. Don't touch me."

He insisted. She leaned backwards, now wanting to pass over the edge. That resistance exasperated Sellier, already beside himself since the remark that a doctor was also a man. He pulled her from the apron of the tilbury, made her fall entirely into his arms and, without taking account of it, because he was not himself at that moment of vertigo, he kissed her hair, her forehead, her eyes, and finally her lips, her beautiful pepper-red lips, tarnished by the poison of lies. He only stopped when he saw that she was so pale he thought she was dead.

"Madeleine? What's the matter? My God! But she's fainted!"

Frightened, he took her to the bank of the road and tried to sit her down on it. She fell back inertly.

What a boor I am, he thought, desperate at his foolishness.

He made her respire ether. Then she writhed, sinking her fingernails into his neck and howling like a dog.

"I should have expected that!" he sighed, almost calm again now that the physician had regained the upper hand.

The crisis passed quickly. She got up, astonished and smiling.

"You tried to carry me and you dropped me? I'm in a fine state; I can't walk at all."

"Forgive me, Mademoiselle, I beg you," he stammered.

She lifted her arms, the fists clenched. "Ah! You kissed me—I divine it, I sense it."

"Yes."

"An excellent subject of study, isn't it? Me! Me, the Princess of Darkness!" she stammered, furiously.

"A kiss, according to you, is an irreparable crime?"

"I wanted to preserve my lips, you hear, all my life."

He drew her gently toward the carriage.

"Henceforth there'll be two of us to preserve them, Madeleine," he replied.

And, sustaining her with one hand and leading Marquis with the other, he went back down the hill, simultaneously happy and heartbroken at having her so close to him, as if forever. She closed her eyes, seeming no longer to care about anything. When he deposited her outside her garden, he perceived that an old woman was examining them from a bend in the road. He recognized his mother's maid.

"There it is, the irreparable!" he confessed, vanquished.

XII

HE felt sorry for that woman, a frail trinket of the church planted there, upright, in front of him, seemingly waiting for a sentence of destruction. Dusk was falling behind the elms in the Cours—a glaucous dusk—and the windows, always clean, reflected it like a rising tide of troubled water. The rain could be heard splashing softly along the shutters like the wailing of a tearful baby. Sellier turned toward her and sighed. It was necessary to finish, since it was him who had asked for permission to explain himself.

"Well, yes, I want to get married!" he said, looking her in the face.

She had the sensation of the point of a dagger on her breast, and remained motionless. Where to go? What to do? And if she remained with them, what would be her life henceforth with a daughter-in-law? If the daughter-in-law in question were rich, things might be arranged. But if she were . . .

For a moment, she saw her dear porcelains reduced to fragments, her cherished plants dying for lack of care, the kitchen in disorder and the maid forced to leave because she no longer suited the young household.

Why delay, then, in telling her her name? And did that well-brought-up son not have, first of all, a consent to implore, very respectfully? Her fingers clenched on the silk of her dress, producing an atrocious little squeak of anguish, and she dared not breathe a word. For the space of a lightning-flash, she suffered so much that she had a desire to get carried away for the first time in her life, to cry out, to insult and to beat that grown-up son standing before her like a scarecrow.

Edmond divined all that and felt, in his turn, suddenly separated from her by innumerable things that she could not formulate.

"My child," she murmured, having remembered the mercy of God, "you merit being happy, and I hope that the person you have chosen will be as your heart desires."

He laughed, oppressed. "I don't believe, in fact, that I'm a wicked man."

And yet, at that same moment, he was in the process of torturing a defenceless creature. He saw *the enemy* approaching his mother, and he was not hastening to draw her away; on the contrary, he was leading her by the hand, making her enter in order to lie her down under the same roof, to eat at the same table; that was inevitable, and even worse, it was just.

For a moment, the widow, who was silently clawing her dress, had the idea of fleeing, of blocking her ears. He retained her with a confused phrase: "Have I made a bad choice? I don't know, but I love her . . ." Then, letting out his breath like a man who has finally put down his burden: "Too bad! *It's her.*"

He never talked about her, but his mother understood: *her* was Madeleine Deslandes. The detailed reports of her maid—the one who always walked shod in felt slippers—had not induced an error. A flood of tears sprang from her eyes, her lips trembled and suddenly, she found arguments, prepared in advance, which fell densely upon the unfortunate son like rain on the great elms, the water of the downpour with her whimpers of a stifled baby.

"My God, Edmond! No! It's not possible! You're going to marry a girl like that? An invalid! An eccentric! A madwoman! A Parisienne without a sou, whose parents give the impression of fairground performers! Tell me that I'm having a bad dream! You, brought up so wisely, so careful, so reserved! You, the son of an honest man known throughout the neighbourhood! It's madness! It will pass. You're only trying to frighten me . . . Edmond! Look at me! What do you expect to become of me with the derisory income your father left me? But I'll never live with that brazen hussy who runs about the high road in the company of a bachelor. It will be necessary, then, that the two of us separate if you marry her. She has neither a dowry nor expectations, you know? Furthermore, she's almost ugly . . . and as proud as a peacock! Come on, it's a whim of spring that will disappear the first night when you get out of bed! And then, how do I know that you're not asking me to marry your mistress, eh?"

"Mother, you're going too far! Madeleine Deslandes is a young woman living honestly under her parents' roof. How do you imagine that I've made her my mistress?"

"But . . . what about what I want? I want what you want, provided that you don't marry her. Ah! You haven't taken her . . . you were wrong, that brazen hussy is only seeking to go astray! Hasn't she been living all winter in the hall of the library to wait for you and catch hold of you in passing? Do you think, my poor boy, that it wasn't obvious? Didn't Monsieur l'abbé Sevrin see through it immediately? I believed you were stronger!"

Shaken by sobs, she collapsed on an armchair. Edmond tapped his desk with a curt movement. He stared into empty space, glad that the lamps had not yet been lit, for he felt himself blushing and going pale at the flood of incoherent words with which the mother was defending her property as best she could. In sum, she had said certain hurtful things. Yes, Madeleine was unhinged, an invalid, and who knew whether there was still time to erase her malady, a tenebrous flores-cence bloomed in a kiss, the malady of the possessed of Loudun or the lunatics of the Salpêtrière? As for her parents, he abandoned them to her with a clear heart. Fairground performers, perhaps worse!

"You're exaggerating, Mother," he pronounced . . . lightly. "I haven't allowed myself to be chosen, I've made my own choice. And then, who are the ideal spouses that are reserved to me by *your place*, as you put it? The daughter of the tax-collector, the one who contemplates the sun with her teeth? Or the daughter of the merchant of novelties, who isn't healthy, with her wrinkled neck? Or the daughter of my former colleague, Balurier who waddles like a duck when she walks? No, *sacrebleu*, I don't want those pearls! Ugly, Mademoiselle Deslandes? It needs to be a truly hardened provincial to find a woman possessed of such eyes and hair ugly! Let's be frank; you and I reproach her for her lack of fortune. Bah! I'll try to work harder. You'll stay here. I'll go live out there, since you dread her family, and we'll console ourselves for no longer possessing an interior so . . . distinguished, but which has become too small for the two of us."

He emphasized the words *too small* with a gesture of contained anger. It was not uniquely to maintain little plants, prisoners beneath their mosquito-nets of silvery gauze, that he earned his living. At present, he needed space, a hope of better caresses, the divine perspective of building a nest around which flowers, like confessions, would have the right to bloom freely. And he leaned on the corner of his desk with a somber expression. The misunderstanding between himself and his mother had been eternalized thus for many years. Without him realizing it fully, he had been, in that little work-room, prey to a hypocritical passion for the comfortable. At his first attempt at revolt against the yoke, so mild and so patient but so real, of the pious mother who loved him in spite of her monomanias of devotion, he received, like a cold shower the singular declaration that she would pardon libertinage if he renounced legal marriage! Well, pious people sometimes had slightly daring rascalities . . . !

"So," he persisted, intent on making disagreeable things precise in order to be finished with them more rapidly, "Mademoiselle Deslandes could become my mistress without you seeing any inconvenience in it?"

"I didn't say that," moaned Madame Sellier. "I only claim that, if that were the case, I wouldn't think myself in the least obliged to make recriminations. An honest girl has only to preserve herself."

"Hum!" said Sellier. "At twenty, it's difficult to defend oneself against a seriously enterprising man; my dear mother, you're preaching there a conventional honesty, and you know that I don't admit that one forgets good dame nature. Her laws exist for Mademoiselle Deslandes as for all the young women of the town. Remember the unfortunate young Angèle, your last-but-one maidservant. Having no dowry, and not being able to get him to marry her, she ran away with him one morning . . ."

"What are you trying to get at? You've already made me one speech on the subject of that child. I ought, according to you, have increased her wages in competition with a dowry. Oh, you have broad ideas when you put your mind to it! They ran away, so much the better—two wretches fewer in the locale! Does Mademoiselle Balurier, or the tax-collector's daughter, have any desire to run away with a lover? No, no! Sincerely honest girls know how to preserve themselves, I can assure you . . . and they'll coiffe Sainte Catherine, if they must, without having an evil thought on their conscience."

"That I don't doubt . . . opportunities for sin will always be lacking them. Come on, Mother, it's not a matter of those exquisite individuals . . . it's a matter of your son's happiness! I've been reflecting for a long time, I've weighed the pros and cons. I want to marry Madeleine Deslandes or never marry. It's her that I love and her that I need, not another. I confess to you humbly that I can't even think about making her my mistress. If you knew her better, you'd know that she's grim enough, the beautiful child, for one not to have the desire to . . . offend her. That rose has terrible thorns, I assure you."

"That's it," interrupted his mother. "She holds the chocolate-box high, the trick of a coquette who knows how lust can get hold of a man. I'd hold her in higher esteem if she'd yielded to you . . . like the others, in Paris."

Edmond straightened up, his eyes sparkling.

"Yes or no, do you want to go and ask for Madeleine's hand for me, Mother?"

"No! Never! I won't go in search of your unhappiness in her house."

"Very well, I'll go! Anyway, I prefer to take all the responsibility for my future."

He went out, and for the first time a door was heard slamming in Madame Sellier's house. The widow looked at the clock with a stupid expression.

"To think that it's eight o'clock . . . eight o'clock!"

Even more shocked by seeing him depart for a ceremonial visit at eight o'clock in the evening than what he had just shouted to her, she put her slender cold hands together on her silk dress and remained there like a poor cracked thing too abruptly brought down from its shelf by a brutal hand.

A few minutes later, Sellier rang the bell on the rickety perron of the last house in the town. He felt that the slightest delay might engage him to reflect further on the perfidious insinuations of his mother. She did not know anything, but nor did he, and that is what tormented him when he heard the crushing word Paris pronounced.

He found Père Deslandes sweetening the bitter cassis of Madame Bordes in the dining room with the Louis XV paneling. The aunt and niece, fortunately absent, were occupied in lifting the linen from the laundry-basket and laying it out in the grass behind the hedge of the garden.

"Monsieur Sellier!" exclaimed Deslandes. "What a surprise! You call so rarely. Sit down. A little cassis?"

"No, thank you. I've come to talk to you about serious matters."

"Not possible! I'm listening; entirely at your service, my dear doctor."

The librarian, whose closed existence had rendered him insensibly dotty, rubbed his lorgnon, and then his nose solemnly, his eyes squinting at the young man's pocket, from which he almost expected to see the traditional tin of digestive pastilles surge forth. Edmond was still quivering with muted rage. He had just arrived, as if to throw himself into the wolf's mouth, and why not the famous three-legged wolf, which haunted him?

He commenced, in a mordant tone: "Monsieur Deslandes, do you often think about your daughter?"

"What?" said Deslandes, bewildered. "Why should I think about my daughter?"

"You're wrong to forget her. A young woman can never look after herself entirely on her own, especially when she has lived in Paris, where appearances are much freer than in the provinces."

"Oh, my God," stammered the disconcerted fellow. "What stupidity has she committed now?"

"You admit that she might commit one?" insisted Sellier, in the manner of an examining magistrate.

"My word! You know her by heart, don't you? She's capable of anything."

"Even deceiving an honest fellow who adores her?"

"I believe," declared Deslandes with conviction, "that the man who marries her will have a thread to untangle. At least, that's what her aunt says, who is a sensate person, Monsieur."

"Be precise, my dear Deslandes, for the moment has come to tell me the truth. If I have a party to offer you for her, what would you respond to me?"

"Who is your party?"

"A poor devil who is mad about her."

"He's a very poor devil . . . as poor a devil as that?" murmured the anxious librarian. He resumed rubbing his nose, utterly disturbed in his digestion, which had promised to be quite good that evening, wondering what stories these physicians involved themselves with. They bore some resemblance to confessors, thinking it their professional duty to poke their noses into all dark corners.

"I've scarcely thought about Madeleine marrying, Monsieur. We live tranquilly, or almost tranquilly. A son-in-law would inconvenience us greatly."

"Is that all you can tell me? Has Mademoiselle Deslandes not had, back there, one of these amourettes?"

Deslandes shivered. "Be frank, in your turn," he stammered. "Has my daughter confided some secret to you?" She might have committed some enormous stupidity with a good-for-nothing around here . . ." Deslandes got up and came to seize Sellier's hand. "You're a physician; could you get us out of this awkward situation?"

He said that quite naturally, like the excited imbecile he was, without thinking for a moment that the poor devil, although poor, might well repair the error if the case arose.

Sellier, outraged, lost sight of the immediate necessity of his interrogation, jibbing furiously against the band of estimable individuals in league against him in order to show him all the paltry aspects of their affections.

"So that's it!" he growled, folding his arms. "What about great, holy amour? What do you do with it, then, all of the old, who once loved? It's a negligible quantity, then, and it's decidedly futile for you to occupy yourselves with it?" He was ashamed to have allowed his imagination to be soiled by doubts and calculations, he who loved passionately and nobly. "Monsieur Deslandes," he added, in a harsh tone, "that poor devil is me, and I have the honor of asking you for Madeleine's hand. You doubt your daughter, but I have none; I no longer want to doubt her."

The father felt his egotism dissolving, gained, in any case, by contact with individuals more malevolent than he was. His little eyes widened with the healthy dew of joyful emotions. Tottering, he held on to Sellier's torso.

"Madeleine's hand . . . you! Oh, Monsieur Sellier, you would become our savior. Can you imagine that I might refuse? That's a generous action! And you'll take her, just like that, without a dowry?"

"I hope to have enough for two."

Deslandes pirouetted on his heels, ran to the door of the corridor and cried, recklessly: "Julia! Madeleine! Come here . . . Julia! Julia!"

So, thought Sellier, smiling in spite of himself, there was no longer any question of a son-in-law inconveniencing the parents-in-law, nor of the daughter having committed a stupidity with the local good-for-nothing he represented. Everything was effaced, finally, before great, holy amour! Or money? As he went into the garden, he sighed and shook his head, gained by a hesitation.

"And what about *her*, how will she receive me?"

Julia approached, while the young woman, although having recognized the doctor, remained out there, straight and rigid, in the middle of the grass.

"What is it? What's up?" yapped Madame Bordes, her camisole in disorder.

"It's," cried Deslandes, shouting even louder, "that we're marrying off Madeleine! Doctor Sellier has asked us for her. Did you expect that, eh? Had Ludovic told you?"

"Madame," murmured Edmond, "excuse me for acting outside all social regulations, but true lovers have the habit of moving their affairs rapidly. I want your niece; will you grant her to me?"

Nonplussed and suffocated, Madame Bordes clung to her neck, passing from bottle green to fiery red like a boiling punch.

"Lord God!" she groaned, too deprived of speech to modulate a pretentious phrase "One might say that you have a vice!"[1]

---

1 It is not obvious what Aunt Julia means. The French *vice* has a range of meaning very similar to the English word, except with reference to a carpenter's tool; it is sometimes used to means a flaw but refers more frequently to a sexual perversion.

The doctor nearly burst out laughing.

"Oh, my poor Julia! He's saving us! He's saving us. He has a heart of gold! O believe that it's necessary for you to kiss him."

They embraced affectionately, each looking over the other's shoulder, she rolling her wide eyes at her brother, he seeking to distinguish Madeleine's features in the twilight.

"Ah, the sly pair!" continued Deslandes laughing. "They were as thick as thieves in my library! They talked about literature, natural science . . . what do I know? Then, it was necessary to care for the child, to tell her to avoid draughts; he ausculated her, she was pampered. I didn't see that there was fire! No, no, that's what comes of being a birdbrain!"

"I've always told you," said Julia, no longer knowing whether she ought to laugh or bite, "that the girl would make fun of her father one day."

"Come on, it's not like that, we'll discuss it tomorrow; but the young people doubtless desire to talk. Doctor, I give you permission to go and tell her the news yourself. We'll go inside to leave you a clear field."

"I suppose that Madame your mother will design to come as far as the house?" interjected Julia, intending to stand on her dignity.

"Yes, yes," replied Sellier, embarrassed. "My mother will certainly make her visit. I confess that I was wrong to come on ahead of her."

"Ceremonies, with us?" protested Deslandes. "Be quiet, my dear friend. We Parisians have more intelligence than that. Oh, these old women, what blessed crack-brains!"

And he led Madame Bordes away, nudging her repeatedly with his elbow.

Sellier headed toward Madeleine with a resolute tread. Why had she remained behind like that, still strangely nailed to the ground, when she divined very well what was in question?

When he drew close to her she grasped, with her dangling hands, the corners of a white sheet, making the train of a court mantle for her black skirt, and nothing was more bizarre than that young woman standing there, carrying pale reflections in the semi-darkness of the meadow. She seemed to be followed by an immense shroud, which extended, continuing and blending with all the mists of the valley.

"Mademoiselle," stammered Edmond, softly, "Your parents have authorized me . . ."

He stopped, his breath cut off, his eyes closing. How beautiful she was, that child that some called ugly, how proudly she bore her head of a lone princess among malevolent men, and how her eyes, starred with her own darkness, were sufficient to illuminate any situation! Oh, if she was a mystery, it was necessary to bless it instead of repelling it, for mystery emanates from a more delicate pleasure, a finer species of voluptuousness, and happiness is no longer happiness as soon as it commences to resemble all permitted joys!

"Madeleine," begged the young man, contemplating her with an intoxicated gaze.

"What? What do you want?" she said, in a glacial voice.

"Can't you guess? My God!"

"No!"

"You aren't still holding something against me?"

"No!"

"Madeleine, I've come in search of a wife. Is she here?"

"No!"

Those three *noes* resounded like a dolorous knell in the depths of Sellier's vibrant brain. Utterly disorientated, he made a gesture of fright.

"Understand me well, Madeleine. I've come to tell you that I love you"

"So what, Monsieur?"

"And, in accordance with my promise, I want the irreparable to be repaired, since, for you, a kiss is a criminal thing."

"Can you make it that you have not kissed me? I don't believe you. So let me get back to my laundry. I'm only a poor servant."

She went past him, dragging the great sheet, of an implacable and evil appearance. Such pride was illuminated in her humiliated will that Sellier, trembling with stupor, felt precipitated from the height of his dream.

"Truly, that's too much!" he cried, taking her by the shoulders. "I had a right to expect another reception, Madeleine! Why do you amuse yourself torturing all my senses? Yesterday, your coquetry made me your slave. Today, you mock me because I behave like a gallant man. Listen to me, I beg you, and don't play me a ridiculous comedy. People saw us the other day; the curious are already commenting on our excursion in a carriage. If you were proud, this is your punishment. I'm belated, naturally, in putting all that in order. Do you imagine, my dear neurotic, that an amity between a man and a woman can work out in any other manner? You're too intelligent to have wished for any other conclusion. Answer me!"

"I don't wish anything at all."

He strove to find the key to the enigma in her fixed eyes. Suddenly she looked behind her at the long white train scything through the grass, and started laughing.

"You want to marry a dead woman? A strange caprice on the part of a doctor."

"No childishness, Madeleine! I'll take charge of enabling you to live, I swear to you."

He felt that with regard to that romantic he ought to have made declaration either less brutal or less reasonable; but he found kneeling juvenile leads on the stage cooing sentimental idiocies repulsive.

"Reflect, Madeleine, be reasonable," he said in a hoarse voice. "I won't marry you against your will, that's certain, but it's your future and mine that you're risking at this moment for the sole pleasure of saying no to a man who's imploring you. I've had to struggle against the will of my mother, and if I have to combat yours, I'll go mad. Think of your family, very happy about this marriage, and then . . . ask yourself, in a whisper, whether I was entirely in the wrong when I stole a kiss from your lips. You are, my dear child, redoubtably perverse. Oh, unknowingly, I'd like to believe, only . . . Madeleine, one last word: I'm convinced that you need to marry, if only to get out of the unhealthy dreams that haunt you. Yes, a doctor's caprice, a doctor who has thought about your happiness before his own, cruel jester!"

"Oh, delightful! You're giving yourself to me in the quality of a remedy against amour?"

"Madeleine! You don't love me, then?"

"Me!" she burst into sonorous laughter, which resounded throughout the valley. "Why do you want me to love you?"

"Is it not for the great honor I'm doing you, Mademoiselle, by offering you my name, of begging you to become my wife, when I don't know whether you're worthy of it?" he retorted, beside herself.

Madeleine's arms were raised, extending the white shroud like a flag.

"Ah, there we are! He loves me, but he's doing me an honor by loving me. It's a chore to struggle to obtain me. And he hasn't yet mentioned the duty he would be doing by marrying me! He asks himself whether I'm worthy or not. Those are, my dear Monsieur, very petty considerations. I can't interest myself in this any longer. It's cold, I'm going inside. In any case, you're too late . . . much too late."

And letting the folds of her lugubrious virginal standard float audaciously, she fled, abandoning the consternated Sellier in the midst of shadows.

XIII

"MY GOD, my dear Monsieur Deslandes," said the devout woman,[1] draping her stiff silk dress around her, "you've guessed what brings me here? I didn't want to let my son engage himself completely before discussing the question of interest. That concerns us, we old folk!"

Deslandes, very perplexed on the subject of his daughter, whom Aunt Julia was keeping from view in her room, fearing new extravagances on her part, and who believed, in addition, that everything was "botched" now, was caught on the hop. He scratched his big nose, thinking that a son of thirty-four could row his boat on his own, damn it—and that an explanation between old folk would probably finish ruining the edifice . . .

However, she did not give the impression of doubting the marriage. The widow's assurance returned his own.

"Madame," he said, recovering the fine manners of a senator's secretary who opens the door to solicitors of distinction and furnishes them with patience, "I'm glad

---

1 I have translated *dévote* literally as "devout woman," but it is usually employed euphemistically to mean "bigot."

to see that something remains for us to discuss, which will procure us the pleasure of making your acquaintance more amply."

They bowed to one another then, with the little short breaths of beasts at bay, pushing their chairs closer together from either side of the fireplace in the salon. Madame Sellier lifted her veil above her prune velvet bonnet, and Deslandes consolidated his lorgnon as if it were a fencing mask. The odor of damp was not encouraging and they were trembling like criminals awaiting a severe condemnation.

"Here it is," said Edmond's mother. "We are all simple folk who don't put on airs, are we not? My son must have told you that he only has his clientele to enable us to live. An honorable position . . . but a pretty young woman, a trifle coquettish, it goes without saying, and who brings no solid dowry . . . I fear for the future! One gets married in order to have children! There are already three physicians here, a place without importance. What if Edmond were to lose his clientele one day? You see him in a tilbury and you say to yourself that he has means! It's a great sacrifice, you know. It's me who has given it to him, who engaged him to buy it in order to help him obtain patients in the surrounding area. Without that he wouldn't be considered."

"We don't care about the tilbury," murmured that librarian, naively, "and if you want to take it back . . ."

He was breathing more easily now he saw that Sellier had not informed his mother of Madeleine's monstrous refusal.

"It's not a matter of that," sighed Madame Sellier. "A mother never takes back what she has given. I only want us to establish accounts. My son wants to acquire or rent this house. I would gladly live on the first floor and we would organize the ground floor for you and the young couple. We would thus have a maid and a domestic in common; the horse and carriage would be lodged in the outbuildings, which are very large, it appears, and we would do our cooking, separately or together, in the basement. Also, since we could not avoid . . . promiscuity, we would try to make arrangements . . . but . . . but . . . it would be necessary to send away Madame your sister. There is no reason, it seems to me, for you to keep her, now that your daughter has no further need of her care. I'm even astonished, Monsieur Deslandes, that you, a man so well brought-up, support the . . ."

"The what?" interrupted Deslandes, bewildered,

"I know that I'm mingling with intimate things, and I know that I ought not . . . however, the interests of my son and your daughter command me to speak. No, I don't care about the tilbury, personally, and I'm certain that you will quiet your scruples of a good parent to obey a measure of prudence. Your sister, Monsieur Deslandes, is not a woman of . . . your rank, of our rank. If we all want to live together in good intelligence after the marriage, it's necessary to engage her to return to her own home."

"But her home is here! Where would she go? Since she lives my life, my dear Madame. My sister has no fortune; I took her in after her husband's death, and since then she has eaten my bread. She doesn't even have the idea that she could live anywhere else!"

"Hmm! Hmm!" coughed the devout woman. "Is it entirely natural to eat into your small income to house and feed a person who could, I'm sure, earn her living elsewhere? Furthermore, I insist on this point; Madame Bordes has manners that would not suit my son. I believe"—here the old lady lowered her voice—"she practices table-turning."

"Pardon me, Madame, is it your son who has charged you with telling me these stories?" interrogated Deslandes, annoyed and seeing that he was a hundred leagues away from what he had supposed,

"No!" murmured the widow, her white porcelain cheeks blushing. "Edmond is so smitten that he's no longer thinking about anything. I haven't been able to get a word out of him for three days, but I know him well enough to know that he'd be satisfied by that departure. You should know, Monsieur Deslandes that I've had a few arguments with my son. I won't hide it from you that the idea of this marriage upset me, at first; I had other dreams. I am making all of you an immense concession in accepting it with a good grace. My principle, Monsieur, is to submit to the laws of Providence and never complain of it. However, a first concession summons a second; I hope that you will help me bear my cross!" She had a slight tremolo in her throat and wiped her eyes with a fine handkerchief trimmed with Valenciennes lace. "You're separating me from my child . . ."

"I can't throw my sister out, Madame."

"Would you like me to look for an employment for her? A petty employment, well-paid and . . . discreet? A bursar in the hospital of deaf-mutes, for example?"

Certainly, the devout woman had not received the mission of expelling Aunt Julia. Her son, entirely delivered to his chagrin, was incapable for the moment of heading toward the old house at the end of the town with any other intention than pacifying the excessively proud young woman as much as possible, of temporizing, of leaving her the opportunity to reverse an insensate decision. But now that Madame Sellier felt that she could not prevent the marriage, she thought of reserving a corner for herself in the new fortress. In getting rid of useless mouths, she charged herself with taking command of the garrison there! The librarian, almost lame, did not appear to be the most terrible enemy, and if he promised never to set foot in her quarters on the upper floor, she would be consoled. It was for her son above all, she told herself, with the best faith in the world, who could not live happily without his habitudes and the traditional comfort of waxed floors.

Deslandes scratched his nose anxiously. He had just perceived the sound of a mouse trotting behind the drawing-room door and although he knew that, a common circumstance for an old dwelling, there were no rats in their abode—doubtless the arsenic oozing from the walls, or the odor of damp, drive them away—he was beginning to regret inviting her to enter it. The doors fitted poorly and the windows sometimes opened silently of their own accord. So why surround themselves by so much mystery themselves?

"In sum, Madame," he growled, "What do you desire? Formulate your request clearly."

"I desire that you accept the petty employment for your sister. I have powerful connections in the town.

Monsieur l'abbé Sevrin directs the religious exercises of the hospice, and I'll speak to him about it, quietly. Will you authorize me to do that, Monsieur Deslandes?"

"But," said the increasingly anxious father, lowering his voice, "why don't you take the discreet employment in question for yourself if, once your son is married, you'll be ill-at-ease in his house? We're not bad people, and if my sister is . . . a trifle lively in character, she wouldn't swallow without chewing!"

She was about to respond, sharply, that she could not tolerate tables turning in her vicinity, when the door of the drawing room opened brutally and Aunt Julia appeared, her gaze ferocious and her face ablaze, carelessly dressed, with her greasy camisole awry and her hair dangling over her left shoulder.

"Are you completely mad?" she roared, planting herself in front of her brother, her fists extended.

Terrified, Deslandes, leapt forward to protect Madame Sellier, who, deathly pale, imagined that she heard the hour of the last judgment sounding. Yes, this was the lair into which her son, such an orderly man, had just landed!

"First of all," stammered Deslandes, his hands twitching, "you must be listening at doors now! You listen at all the doors here! I'll answer for anything I have to answer for . . . calm down! You'll poison things! We'll never get out of it, this marriage! No, you were doing it expressly! To miss such an opportunity . . . I present my apologies to you, Madame; but you understand, she's my sister! Oh, I'm utterly desolate . . . Madame!"

Edmond's mother was still looking at Madeleine's aunt, who was still exhibiting her frantic fists, and howling:

"Yes, get out, priests' hag! Get out, Saint Touch-me-Not. I'll leave the floor to be cheated by the son and the father-in-law! You're giving away my place! You're leaving me nothing but my skin! Oh, I make tables turn? That's what offends you? Is it rustic enough? And you, are you not taking a step to make your son's money turn in the direction of the holy altars of godliness? You find me too much? I'm not of your rank, I look like a dish-washer, and you want to lock me away with the deaf-mutes? But I'm neither deaf not mute, me, and I'll give you some news that will hammer in your nail, my good woman! You're waving your arms in vain!" She turned to her brother. "It's finished! I've had a bellyful of your chic marriage, and I believe that for once the girl is on the right track! Yes, Madame Sellier, my niece doesn't want your scoundrel, and I've been mounting guard outside her door for three days to prevent her from getting mixed up in your visits, if you chanced to deign to render us one! Anyway, I'll go fetch Mademoiselle; it's not worth the trouble of charging me with her commissions—she can spit in your face herself!"

Deslandes, panic-stricken, threw himself across the threshold of the drawing room.

"It's a furious folly, Julia! You know very well that Madeleine is ill! You mustn't exasperate her, for now! Think, my sister! It's her future, the future of all of us!"

"It's the last time I get involved in your machinations. And since Madame has dreads, with regard to her money, I'll prove to her that we can do without them."

Madame Bordes ran, breathlessly, to her niece's room, threw the bolts open, and returned, dragging her by the skirt.

"There's the object!" she laughed, pushing her into the middle of the drawing room.

Madeleine had had a crisis of nerves during the night because she had been forbidden to go out for three days, and she was veritably incapable of seeming to be in her right mind. Shivering with fever, her eyes haggard, her hair hanging loose down her back, she had a fixed stare, clenching her fingernails like a beaten animal about to pounce.

"Is it true, Mademoiselle, that this marriage is no longer agreeable to you?" asked Madame Sellier, believing that she was witnessing the frolics of two lunatics in the depths of a padded cell.

"I implore you, my child, not to say anything stupid, of which you'll repent," stammered Deslandes, pitifully.

Madeleine smiled. "I'll respond to you, Madame, when the violets have responded to me."

The widow made a gesture of bewilderment. No, it was impossible! Her son wanted to marry a lunatic, and he did not perceive it!

"That suffices, Mademoiselle," murmured the devout woman, who retired, making a last sign of the cross, beneath her veil.

Fortunately, she had come on this mission at sunset. No one would see her leave.

And while Madame Sellier escaped, without saluting anyone, into the corridor, Madeleine, quitting the nightmare of marriage for the dream of amour, launched herself through the window of the drawing room into the garden. She was free! Free to go to the rendezvous in the sacred wood.

She arrived there, breathless, her hair whipping her back, her cheeks poppy-red, her ears ringing, her dress torn and her little feet bruised. Before the fallen tree she dropped to her knees, almost dying of joy. In the hollow of its wound someone had spread violets, a profusion of embalming flowers! Did she see them? Was it only her intense desire to see them that accomplished the miracle? But no, she could smell them and touch them, and from the profoundly sweet scent, from the hue of that somber explosion of violet, that purple of mourning, rose a voice calling to her mystically, darkening her further with its intoxicating caress.

"Hunter! Hunter! My beloved! Come! Save me from life!"

She fell, her face drowned by the flowers, and remained thus for nearly an hour, prostrate, in an exquisite intoxication.

An imperious finger was posed on the nape of her neck.

"Here I am, my lovely bride!" said the man she was still imploring in a whisper.

"You!"

She got up, unsteadily, and buried her forehead in his breast without any longer fearing the discovery that no heart was beating there. He kissed her, irresistibly, with full lips, on the nape of her neck, where he had tapped her with his index finger, willfully, like a bird desirous of finally breaking the bars of its cage. And his kiss, simultaneously furious and soft, made her hang her head for a long time in the rapture of a saint at prayer.

Hunter set her down, as easily as he would have done a little child, in the midst of the scattered violets, and he knelt down in his turn before that coffin of a virgin died of amour.

"Here I am, my beloved, here I am," he repeated in his musical tone, still slightly guttural. "Here I am, with the first violets and the first breaths of renewal. My soul has come to flower again next to yours. Feel how my hands are burning. I've brought you all the flames of the sun of passion. Bonjour to you, my sister and my mistress, my bride or my spouse! I have stolen from the entrails of the earth the secret of blossoming, and in order to see you again I have forced the heavy chains of the misty night. Here I am, and the dusk becomes the dawn! I have heard the nuptial mass sung in the trees. *Salut*, blessed and accursed daughter! *Salut*, perverse and frank madwoman! *Salut*, pretty lust of my meninges! *Salut*, triply pure monster, little witch that casts lots from the tips of her black lashes! You are the naivety of horror, the supreme joy of torture! I adore you among all women and scorn you for all men. Alas, my impeccable sinner, I have drunk from the poisoned cup of absence, and I am wounded by all the needles of voluntary chastity. Your memory sticks to my skin like a silice of clinging silk studded with rosebuds; I have rolled on the rutilant vision of your blonde tresses, have eaten, in dream, the pulp of your warm lips, and have drilled through spaces, your gaze with mine, so that my eyes have become your eyes; we could unite ourselves, I believe, by the intermediary of a single mirror. But I think that, and since, as well, we love one another less the more we say, do you also love me?"

He held her pale hands together in his own, contemplating her with his staring eyes, which had the acuity of an eagle's. Oh, his pride would not change if it were humanized!

"Hunter!" she said, suddenly confused. "Perhaps you know what has happened to me? Must I really be married?"

"No! I don't know anything, except that you are beautiful, my princess in a torn dress, my little empress of the highways!"

"Well," she sighed, dully, "I confess, then. "Doctor Sellier, while you were dreaming about my lips, took them, quite truly. He loves me and he wants me."

"Perfect! You fainted, I hope . . . or made a semblance of it?"

"Don't laugh! I nearly died of regret, not having been able to keep my mouth intact for your return."

"Glory to you, for you could have kept silent and offered me a lying mouth. A woman ought to have admitted the truth, once, in the name of amour!" He was silent for a moment. His eyes darkened, anger replacing ecstasy. "And when one thinks, Madeleine, that you could equally well have given me the charity of silence . . . of silence!"

Almost at the same moment, a black form surged forth from the frail bushes, scarcely veiled by a transparency of nascent foliage. The young woman made a gesture of repulsion. It was the dog, Silence, which was crawling slyly, having caught its master's last word on the wing.

"O jealousy! How faithful you are to me!" mocked Hunter, turning his head away. Then he shrugged his shoulders and started to laugh. "And do you remember clearly," he said, "the pleasure experienced? Tell me, my adored darling, can you enable me to enjoy it in my turn by means of a savant description, complicated by the ignoble underside that it's necessary for me to divine?"

She raised herself on one elbow, her cheeks ardent.

"Coquette, perverse madwoman, so be it! But I have my virginal dignity. In betraying you I would have betrayed myself, Hunter. I have not sinned against you, I remain entirely yours."

He scattered flowers around her, throwing handfuls at her face.

"Yes, yes! Entirely . . . for the space of three or four months. That's prodigious . . ."

"What are your orders?" asked Madeleine, seductively, stopping his hand full of violets.

"Marry him . . . and reserve the wedding night for me!"

"Oh, Hunter! What are you saying? It would be simpler not to marry him, while reserving a similar night for you."

"I don't like simple things."

"You want me to belong to that man?"

"I want it, and if you belong to him, you will be mine much sooner!"

"What if I disobey you? What if I don't marry him?"

"You'll become his mistress, and you ought not to have two lovers!"

"But it's Hell that you're proposing to me, Hunter?"

"I can only propose Hell to you."

"My God!"

"What God are you talking about?"

"I'd like at least to understand. Will you scorn me to the point of not explaining anything to me? Hunter, I have vertigo merely in looking at you! I'm afraid."

"You believe you're seeing your reflection."

She closed his lips by putting the entire mass of her hair on them.

"Let's be quiet," she moaned, "and let it be thus, since that is your wish, my divine lover!"

They played in the flowers, chastely huddled against one another, the great beast, wallowing at their feet in order to remind them from time to time of the lasciviousness of cruel beasts. Hunter appeared bolder than before in regard to caresses, but all his movements remained so unctuous, with such a good grace of a poet enthused by beauty, that Madeleine forgot to defend herself. One stormy evening he had said to her: 'Your neck will be the limit . . . *the limit.*' And he scarcely went any further, scything her head with a long kiss, which fell inertly on to her breast like a ripe ear of corn. Then, weary of weeping and laughing, she went to sleep in his arms, murmuring: "Take me back to my window. I'm tired, you see, and I know that you have wings! Oh, lend me your wings, Hunter!"

When she awoke, she was lying on the grass outside the garden gate. She got up. It was warm. The moon was resplendent. She extended her arms, with a locking smile.

"When one thinks," she said, "that I've descended from the heavens!"

Pushing the garden gate, she perceived by the light of the full moon the silhouette of a man standing next to the terrace. She had a vague idea that Hunter had retraced his steps in order to come in search of her and carry her away definitively in his open arms, on his somber wings, but the silhouette became more precise and thickened; it was only a poor human, quite normal.

"You here, at this hour, at my home?" said Madeleine, haughtily, while Doctor Sellier advanced, very timidly, directing anxious glances from the road to the house.

"Yes, me, Mademoiselle Deslandes. Excuse me; it's absolutely necessary that I talk to you."

"You've chosen your moment poorly, Monsieur."

She joined him on the terrace, where the curtain of hazel trees might, strictly speaking, have hidden them from curious eyes, if it were not for the brightness of the spring night. Edmond took her hand gently—the hand still burning with the other's kisses.

"Listen to me, Madeleine! I couldn't come to your family after today's scene. Then I had the pretext of a visit in the neighborhood and I stopped my carriage under the terrace, knowing that you like walking in the moonlight. Then, on seeing you, I leapt over the wall, for, in truth, I have set about scaling enclosures like a good thief. Oh, wicked girl, what will you soon have made of me? Me, I can no longer wait; I'm suffering too much. I've lived centuries in three days . . . it's necessary that we have a decisive explanation. I've reflected that I've become a veritable subject of torment for you too, and from everything my mother has told me I've only retained the portrait she made of your dear face in distress. Your family exasperate you, and I can understand why. You only have one word to say to me, therefore, and I'll go away. I'll leave this country, where you are, and where I can't live without seeing you. Madeleine, reply to me frankly; you love another man, don't you?"

She remained upright and motionless under the limpid moonlight, seemingly unable to hear, and laughing, the pretty mute laughter of a statue.

"I beg you," he stammered, inclining his forehead over her pale hands, which he held united in his own. "The moment is grave, Madeleine! Don't respond to me lightly, in accordance with your deplorable custom. I can't make beautiful phrases, but all that I can certify to you is that I'm holding here, between my poor trembling fingers, my entire future, my entire life. If you take back your hand, can I at least ask you again for a serious reason, whatever it might be?"

"Why do you suppose that I love someone else?"

"Because I feel atrociously jealous, Madeleine!"

"An excellent proof! No, Monsieur Sellier, I don't love *another man*."

He straightened up, palpitating with joy, and added, in an altered tone: "You doubtless imagine that I would be unhappy if I married you. It's by virtue of a kind of crazy generosity that you're refusing me? Oh, have no such scruple. If I don't have you, I believe that I'd kill myself. I no longer want to play the role of a reasonable man. If you don't love me, so be it; I accept your indifference, and I'll try to make myself loved after the marriage as best I can, but I repeat to you that my only misfortune would be no longer seeing you. Now that I think of it, is it my estate as a physician that you find repugnant? You're so bizarre, although you're an intelligent woman."

"No, it's all the same to me—everything is all the same to me."

"Madeleine, Madeleine, you're a very profound night!"

"Illuminated by this, however!"

And with a rapid movement, she made her floating hair undulate. For an instant, he saw her as resplendent as a star, whose radiance mingled whiteness and fire, her two violet eyes making two dark patches, the blackness of the gulf, in the lunar whiteness of her face. He drew her to his bounding breast.

"Coquette! Odious coquette! Oh, it seems that all the blood of my heart is flowing in your hair!"

Madeleine shivered, astonished; he had the musical, slightly guttural voice of Hunter! Did not the demon, in order to possess her really, need to take the form of that normal man?

She let herself fall back, her head on his shoulder.

"So be it; I surrender. But let us pose our conditions, my dear fiancé; you won't demand the impossible?"

"What impossible?"

"That I become entirely your wife."

"I confess that I can't quite grasp . . ."

"Oh," she interrupted, huddling in his arms, insinuating and seductive, "I want to remain entirely free. I want to run through the fields by night, with you or without you! I want to remain a virgin—in sum, I want to remain the beautiful Princess of Darkness!"

At that solemn hour of irrevocable decision, Edmond Sellier glimpsed the task that was incumbent on him. He would remain much more the guardian of a madwoman than a husband. He had a sad smile, and then rediscovered the unctuous and consolatory speech that he sometimes adopted at the bedside of the dying in order to promise them a cure.

"Well, yes," he declared, with fervor. "You'll remain the beautiful Princess of Darkness, until the day . . . when you renounce your crown of your own accord. By the way," he added, frowning slightly, "you don't like children, Madeleine, naturally?"

She lifted an indefinably troubled gaze toward him.

"If my lover was thirsty and he ordered me to express pure water from the eyes of my new-born to pour it into a cup for him, I would obey."

Sellier uttered a cry of horror. "Oh, shut up, shut up! And go into the house quickly. I'll see you again tomorrow—yes, tomorrow! I prefer to encounter you by day, word of honor!" He took hold of his temples momentarily, his eyelids closed "You upset me to the point of making me lose the desire to be happy, Madeleine!"

"*Au revoir*, then, my dear fiancé. Don't forget that it's you who will have wanted it! Come on, give me the kiss of betrothal—here, on my neck." She parted her hair. "I permit you; that's the limit. You must cure the red traces there, the traces of my fingernails, which I dig in there when I have my crises of nerves, or you're not a good physician."

For all response he leapt over the wall of the terrace and fled. Soon the sound of Marquis' hooves striking the sonorous pavement of the town told Madeleine that, like a prudent fiancé, the doctor was already far away. She turned round, chagrined . . .

A sinister shadow was detached from the hazel trees. It formed a monstrous group of a dog and a man, a colossal dog that its master had trained to stand still, having taken hold of the shiny coat of its back with a firm hand, before launching it irresistibly against someone . . . Hunter released Silence, which fell back heavily, flattening itself out, in the middle of the sand.

"My felicitations, Princess," said the veritable lover, finally. "You have just behaved like the last of prostitutes!" And with an elegant gesture, he bowed all the way to the ground.

"What are you doing here, with that dog?" she questioned, alarmed.

"I was going to strangle your future spouse. He departed just in time, for I would have deplored my fit of ill-humor. He's a worthy fellow."

Hunter laughed—a high-pitched laugh, only irradiating the extremity of his beautiful, dazzling teeth.

"Ah! You're not content?" said Madeleine, folding her arms defiantly. "What do you want? I'm acting like a damned soul, who's amusing herself!"

"Abominable girl!" he growled, smiling incessantly.

"Well, embrace me yourself, then!"

"Damn! I'm no longer sufficient here!"

He leaned over his dog, which was still crawling on its belly.

"Here, Silence," he hissed, "do you see this woman? She belongs to me, but I no longer want her, this evening! Go, my good dog! Go and embrace her, and don't stop until I call you back."

Before Madeleine had taken a step backwards, the dog, with a formidable light bound, knocked her over on the ground, crouched over her, simultaneously respectful and obscene, licking her face humbly and covering her entirely with its black body. Poor Madeleine shut her eyes, finding the desperate courage to keep quiet, until she lost consciousness, while a rhythmic beat of the joyous animal's enormous tail struck the sand.

XIV

THE two men were chatting in a dark office, situated below street level, from which the legs of passers-by walking level with the ceiling could be seen through the thick iron grille of a vent. Boxes overflowing with stacks of yellow paper, cluttered the room, which was already too narrow, spreading their special stale odor, and a smoky lamp, lit at four o'clock in the afternoon, combined it with the reek of bad oil. The notary, sitting before a little work-table, resembled a very honest old miser who did not care about anything, closed to events that did not bear directly on his métier. He had congratulated the doctor in a discreet tone on his forthcoming marriage, without even asking the figure of his future dowry, foreseeing, indifferently, that it would perhaps not bring him any dowry at all.

"Monsieur Formel," said Sellier, smiling, "you might as well confess to me why you don't want to sell it to me."

He was astonished by the refusal of that individual, who had the secret reputation of depriving himself of a fire in winter, pretexting that the lamp, which he was obliged to light then from morning until evening, produced enough heat to the clerk of his study, which did not penetrate the rooms, vaulted like cellars.

The young physician had come to him in order to try to flatter his chimera of an aged chicken sitting on golden eggs, and had run into polished defeats accompanied by singular head-shakes. Sellier, certain henceforth of his marriage, desired to purchase the house at the edge of the town, where he would carry out a few embellishments in order to distract his dear Madeleine. He was dreaming, more and more, about it being entirely his own, and since his mother did not want to hear any mention of . . . promiscuity, he would let her care for the consulting room; she would remain in her obscure lodgings in the Cours, and as soon as the last client had filed through, he would return out there to the conjugal nest, which he would take care, at modest expense of rendering entirely comfortable. Only the old miser, in spite of serious offers, still refused.

"There is, therefore, an extraordinary reason, Monsieur Formel, which is close to your heart?" said Sellier, intrigued.

"In truth, my dear doctor," replied the notary, placing his glabrous chin on his two hands, joined inversely—which was his favorite position—"I'll confide the thing to you. As you are, by profession, not every talkative, you won't spread it around. Besides which, it's not of a nature to reflect badly on me . . . at my age. The blessed hovel doesn't belong to me—or, if you prefer, I deem that it doesn't belong to me, pending more ample information."

Sellier started in surprise.

"Have you the leisure to listen, to me, doctor?" added the notary.

"My God, yes. I've come to settle a business matter, but if you want to tell me a story and it's interesting . . . I'm listening, my dear Monsieur Formel."

Slightly suspicious and slightly vexed, he veiled his medical gaze with his habitual blink of the eyelids, pricked up his ears, and leaned against a pile of dusty files.

"This is the story," Formel commenced. "The house at the end of town once belonged, when I was a clerk in this study—and I'm talking about a long time ago—to a noble lady with a funny name, Comtesse Roberte de la Messiale. She was rich, possessed other properties in the vicinity, and spent money like an empress. I recall the good woman distinctly. When I think about her—which rarely happens—I see a tall, thin, bony silhouette with paws and arms that never ended, endowed with a beautiful face illuminated by a pair of bloodshot eyes—it was said that she drank—and coiffed by a solid chignon like horsehair! At the age of fifty or thereabout, the whim took her to adopt—*hmm*, is that the right word?—to adopt a young man of twenty, blond and beardless, neither more nor less than an Adonis. A very amusing detail: he had the same paws as her, with long, bony hands, but very pale. She said that he must have belonged to the family because of that. You understand that no one demanded his titles; people avoided getting mixed up in their affairs. In any case, although well informed, I only observed him attentively once . . . and he was dead!"

Sellier shivered. "A singular idea, to adopt a dead man!" he said, mechanically.

"Wait! She had adopted him very much alive, the bitch! And she had herself served for warm work, I can guarantee it! He exhibited to you, while in good health, gleaming eyes, red lips and the figure of a young poplar, which made the mouths of all the local girls water; but he was locked up like a young cock and only had permission to sing from the old lady's roof. As she was always involved in litigation, I saw her arrive often at the study in her carriage, painted yellow and green. She came in like a hurricane, hat sideways, her clothes poorly fastened, reeking of liquor; she shoved everyone aside, howling when the boss, who detested her, didn't want to receive her. Then she sat down next to me and made me party to her chagrins, with shady glances that I didn't much like.

"Once she pinched my chin." Here the old man coughed. "Well, I was good-looking, wasn't I? I talked to her about the time when Madame your mother had just been born. Can you imagine that in those days—I was eighteen—I was as pink as a doll? I listened sympathetically go her misfortunes, indicated manners of procedure to her, but not for anything in the world did I want to go to dinner in her house, as she begged me to do from time to time, because rumor had it that she got ignobly drunk at dessert.

"When her last wheat-field had been sold—a superb lot, my dear doctor, an admirable plot of land that she sold in order to buy a rifle for her adoptive son, she admitted to me that she was going to decide to live sagely, retired in her house at the end of the village. She had got rid of all her surrounding properties, sometimes to buy weapons, sometimes to offer herself casks of fine wines; the whole mountain of rocks had passed that way! And she whined, protesting that she would be wise in future. Henceforth, she would devote her life to raising her son—God knows that the young orphan was already making his own way—and there would be no more partying. I took it all with a pinch of snuff; I had a desire to cry to her: 'Do you take me for an idiot, then?' I made such a fuss in the end that she didn't come back to the boss and I heard no more mention of her.

"You know our little town, doctor. She never changed. One doesn't occupy oneself with the neighbors, and its inhabitants are more like bears than humans. No one barked around the house. There was no gossip. The crafty blond fellow only went out in a carriage or on horseback. He didn't talk, saluted loftily, and looked at you to freeze the blood in your veins if anyone took it into his head to laugh at him behind his back. Furthermore, the old eccentric had taken it into her head to have herself served by deaf-mute domestics, poor devils that she extracted from the hospice next door, which the priests supplied to her, very regretfully, because they never lasted long in there before running away, their faces convulsed with terror.

"Sometimes, in summer, the adoptive son was seen walking on the terrace near the hazel trees. He was, it appears, frightfully pale, and he started getting drunk as well. There wasn't too much scandal about that, but one morning, the boss hurtled into the study thunderously, grabbed me by the collar of my waistcoat and shouted: 'Quickly, quickly! Let's go to Madame de la Messiale's house. She hasn't yet signed the deed of sale to the Bretaux, and if she passes before the justice the act will be null and void; the Bretaux will hold it against me for having missed the opportunity!'

"I knew that the deed wasn't signed, but I didn't understand why she had to go to court because of that. I asked the question in the way. 'Idiot!' exclaimed the boss. 'Don't you know, then, that the comtesse has just murdered her adoptive son? The entire street isn't talking about anything else!'

"In the house at the edge of the town, it was like going into a mill. Everything was all over the place. The mutes—a cook and a coachman—were weeping behind the door and uttering sighs that could split wood. There was even a priest in the drawing room. From the threshold of the drawing room I perceived the pale young man lying on a sofa. He seemed to be asleep, quite peacefully, his blond hair swept backwards as if by a gust of wind. His long hands were dangling to the ground and he was white, in the middle of those green hangings, as white as if he wanted to appear more dead . . . than a corpse. As for Comtesse Roberte de Messiale, Monsieur, she was so drunk that she could no longer stand up. No point in thinking about the deed, as you might think. The servants told us that he had been found there, completely stiff, and that the old lady was suspected of having poisoned him. An autopsy was carried out, and it was discovered that the poor fellow had eaten arsenic a week ago . . . what is it, Doctor?"

Sellier had just leapt up from his chair.

"Nothing!" he murmured. "Go on; your story is extremely interesting."

"On the other hand," the notary continued, "to the amazement of everyone, the old bitch exhibited a document in which the young man himself made his adieux, affirming that he would rather poison himself than live in perpetual intimacy with her! Why had she not offered that proof of her innocence right away? I don't know, but I believe that even more disagreeable things were probably revealed in that document. The priests refused to bury the suicide, which old Roberte went to the devil to bury, and then returned wearing mourning in great ceremony. She lived for a further seven years, perpetually drunk, and then died, glass in hand, singing an obscene song!

"I have reached, my dear doctor, the delicate part of my story. Nothing can give you any idea of my confusion when her testament was opened—a testament deposited with us—and it became known that she had bequeathed to me, your servant, her house on the edge of the town, all that remained of her former fortune, if we could not succeed in discovering a certain relative of her famous adoptive son—a cousin, I believe—living in England. I took all the necessary steps, I can assure you, for that legacy caused me more displeasure than satisfaction. The dead woman had had such strange mores! And I believe that I have never married because of my inheritance . . .

"In brief, in thirty years I have not caught wind of any serious trail. That cousin—a great lord, it appears—sometimes lived in America, sometimes in London, and had children. The truth is that he disappeared from circulation, with all his offspring. A fine family, if one can judge by the adoptive son! All in all, the scion, if there is one, would be no prouder of the adventure than I am.

"That doesn't prevent me, my dear Monsieur Sellier, from considering the house as belonging to me . . . without actually belonging to me. While I'm alive it will not be sold. When I die, I shall only bequeath it to the town to make an annex to the hospice. However, I'll sign a lease if you wish."

Sellier stood up, very pensive.

"That's all right," he said. "Let there be no more question of it. And I would be grateful to you, Monsieur Formel, if you didn't speak about all that to my fiancée, for she's very impressionable and is capable of forcing me to quit that old hovel, which pleases me. We'll arrange a lease, but you'll carry out repairs for me?"

"Oh, for that it's pointless to pester me!" sniggered the notary, putting his hand over his eyes by way of a shade. Damn it, you and your young wife will have nothing better to do during the honeymoon than install yourselves like two turtle-doves within it. You'll divine that if I were to exchange a green hanging for a blue one, Madame would want a pink one the next day. I don't want to take away the pleasure of playing owner. Do as you wish, as if you were in your own home and don't worry, as long as you don't send me any bills."

The old fox, thought Sellier, once he was outside the study. *He must be telling me a tall story, with his tales of suicide and poison. But in waiting for another anthem I'll have the famous green hangings cleaned from top to bottom. It's obvious that the arsenic comes from there and that what happened came about accidentally because of the ingredient used to fix the color . . . and no matter how little remains, the worthy Aunt Julia will always find enough if her sauces lack garlic one day!*

Very thoughtful, in spite of himself he headed idly in the direction at the old house at the edge of the town. Having not made Madeleine party to his step he did not have to render her accounts, fortunately. For almost a month, the black butterflies seemed to have been fleeing that sick mind one by one, thanks to the bandage of caresses that he deposited every evening in separating from his fiancée. Oh, *fiancée*, what a marvelous vocable! Yes, she was his. No one would take her away from him. And yet, as soon as he was away from her, she felt so alone, so lost in darkness, that he feared the slightest presage of sadness! What if someone were to tell her that legend about their nuptial dwelling? Too skeptical himself to occupy himself with it from any point of view other than the temporary interdiction of the sale, he became superstitious on the subject of Madeleine. The very next day, he would give orders for the hangings to be removed.

He hastened his steps and reached the rickety perron. In fact, its somber walls were crumbling and its guillotine windows were not very cheerful . . . however, was it not the paradise that contained his amour? He rang with a nervous hand.

Madeleine came to open the door.

"You're arriving appropriately," she said, a mocking smile on her lips. "My aunt is in the process of consulting Ludovic to learn whether my dress ought to be satin or muslin."

It was a matter of the wedding-dress.

She seized him by the arm, while putting her slender index finger over her mouth and leading him to the door of the drawing room.

"Look," she said, pointing at the keyhole, almost delighted by the prospect of proving to him that Madame Bordes was much more neurotic than she was.

He started to laugh too, for he had resolved always to show himself in a good mood, in order to react, no matter what it cost, against the melancholy ideas of the bizarre young woman; but he did not look, and let himself be drawn toward the garden,

"Perhaps it would be simpler to consult your taste first, Madeleine," he objected, and he added, swiftly: "Why penetrate again into the drawing room? I thought I had forbidden it."

"I'll remind you that it's Ludovic's sanctuary," Madeleine murmured. "He needs somewhere sheltered from my malice, and it's thought that . . . the arsenic will prevent me from going in."

"Bah! That will change. Tomorrow, workmen will rid the wall of those horrors, and we'll choose a pretty Pompadour paper to replace them . . . won't we, Madeleine?"

"At your orders, my dear doctor."

She lowered her head, playing with a little pebble with the pointed tip of her shoe.

"What are you thinking about?" he asked, passing his arm around her waist in order to bring her closer to him.

"I'm thinking about something very curious, Edmond. My aunt can't be in her normal state, because she's consulting Ludovic in my father's absence, and once she didn't bother him when she was alone. Do you understand that?"

"I confess, my dear, that I don't understand anything to do with spiritism in general, and your medium in particular. I'd rather talk about . . . the wedding-dress . . ."

She tapped her foot impatiently. "Well, doctor, I can guess; she's afraid that it will end up being realized."

"She'll play the comedy by herself? My God, we might all do as much. As long as she doesn't become her own dupe; that's the main thing. You have a cloud on your brow, Madeleine!"

"No, I assure you that I'm quite calm."

"Yes, give me that cloud right away, so that I can absorb it under a kiss; I want to drink in you everything that is somber bitterness, and only leave you rays of sunlight."

She extended her forehead to him passively, then looked over her shoulder, as was her habit.

The next day, Edmond had himself escorted by three workmen, whom he introduced into the drawing room. Aunt Julia had not had time to utter a cry before all the hangings were already on the floor.

"I hope you're not going to throw all that out?" roared Madame Bordes, as if they had wanted to rip out her entrails.

"My Aunt-in-law, said Sellier, who called her that to amuse Madeleine, "we'll certainly refrain from throwing them out. We're going to burn them!"

"Oh, that's too much! You're dreaming! Silk damask by the handful! Say, Madeleine, that you're not going to take it away . . ."

Madeleine was outside, leaning on the drawing room window-sill and contemplating the stripped walls, with long lustrous greenish tatters, which seemed viscous, like the scales of a dragon, scintillating with the reflections of the dawn. She uttered a great sigh.

"Indeed, it's a pity!"

"They don't make them like that any more," risked one of the workmen.

"Fortunately!" said Sellier.

"Come on, Edmond, you're not being reasonable," insisted the young woman. "It would be much better if I had a coverlet on my bed of the same kind, but if you fear that I might poison myself . . . !"

"On your bed! Imprudent child! Get away! I demand it absolutely!"

"Yes, I'll go . . . but I'll propose a deal to you; let's have that damask dyed . . . a color that will kill the other—and we'll put it back in place."

"Madeleine truly has an idea," approved the aunt, triumphantly.

"In red! That would be magnificent," declared Madeleine.

They argued. They got carried away, and Sellier yielded, naturally.

When the fabric came back from the dyer, Edmond had it replaced by night, in order to give his fiancée a surprise. He had bought a few trinkets and different furniture, and he wanted to dazzle her in the morning; but when they had crossed the threshold Madeleine, curious at first, expecting an agreeable spectacle, and Deslandes, rubbing his nose with satisfaction, recoiled, petrified.

The red cloth was black! In the space of one night, a mysterious chemical reaction had occurred, in combination with the damp secretion of the walls, and the fiancé received the fiancée in a drawing room hung with mourning.

XV

SHE locked the door with a key and ran to open the window. No! She could no longer breathe, either because the champagne really had overexcited her nerves, or because the emotion alone, even stronger than her intoxication, gave her the courage to flee. She decided to get away, straight ahead, without any precise intention of rejoining him—but her legs betrayed her, as they always do in bad dreams, and she collapsed on the window-sill, not daring to leap over, remaining there, dazed, twisting the pleats of her mantle around her, mechanically occupying herself with dissimulating her white dress and the strings of natural orange-blossom that were spreading their odorous petals everywhere. Again she heard the affectionate phrase of her husband, leaning toward her at dessert:

"You're wrong to drink like that, little fool, oh, you're wrong!"

Then the hectic hum of her father's sentimental ballad, the shrill voice of Aunt Julia abusing the dish-washers in the kitchen, the confused buzz of chairs shifting, as in church, the rustle of Madame Sellier's watered-silk shirts—for the widow, metamorphosed into a porcelain statue, had not addressed a single word to her—and, further away, much further away, a voice begging her fervently: "Madeleine! Madeleine!"

And he would come; he was already behind that closed door. Madeleine fell backwards on the bed sumptuously prepared to receive them. Was she asleep? Perhaps. Suddenly, she got up, draped herself in a dark cloak that would hide her from the gazes of passers-by, threw her black lace shawl over her head and leapt resolutely through the wide open window.

All her movements were accomplished without effort; she did not encounter any obstacle. Her dress, so heavy a little while ago, appeared to her veritably to have become two wings of vaporous plumage; a persistent odor of flowers exalted her; a triumphal march of perfume and whiteness was being played around her, and it was in a gala that she ascended toward divine ecstasy, to be at the same time the fiancée, the woman, the adulteress, the chimera and the queen! All her instincts of a perverted little girl revolting under the authority of an overly familiar master resumed their free course. She fled the tyrant who, at a given moment, would come to exercise the rights of his tyranny, and she would go to precipitate herself into the arms of the mystical beloved, beloved for the sole reason that he was no longer the master this evening and because he would remain the unknown.

"I love you like a mirror," she had often said to Hunter.

She would go to contemplate him, and their confounded breaths would not tarnish the mirror of their enchantments, for they would both remain pure.

It was raining. The weather, threatening since the morning of the wedding, had decided in the evening for mud. At a rapid, assured pace she headed for the meadow, pushed the gate and marched through the rain-soaked grass, sinking into it joyfully as into the down of an eiderdown. Oh, the glacial caress of the treacherous grass, the brutal cushion of a scratch along her leg shod in a transparent silk stocking, the bite of a blade of grass that saws your skin in a sly cruel fashion!

The meadow traversed, a kind of dementia gripped her, the involuntary desire to cry out, to roll, to bound, to appeal very loudly to the man who might not remember, whom she had not encountered for nearly a month, whom she had sought on the hills and in the forests. Inexplicably, her tightened throat could no longer let out any sound! During that solemn night, gestures dominated words, and would they not only be eloquent by virtue of being appropriately silent? She extended her arms, evocatively, leaping like a tracked beast on the slope of the rocky path. Ah! Finally she was finished with that enveloping, moist meadow, as elastic as the remorse circling her ankles like the coils of a snake. Finished, the hesitations of little girls who grope, not daring to launch themselves frankly on the road to perdition . . .

She summoned adultery to come and find her now, and to liberate her from her last anguishes of a woman blessed by the priest!

And now a shadow looms up, magnified; two arms respond to her arms, two arms seize her.

"I'm here; I was waiting for you! Oh, the terrible moment of expectation!"

"You! Hunter! Oh, I swore, I couldn't betray you. You're the man that no woman can betray, my beloved!"

She is swooning with joy, and despair too, and her delights are mingled with a terror that renders them more bitterly exquisite! How rapidly he is bearing her away! Their two cloaks, united in the wind, are flapping under the fatal, ironic rain, gradually transpiercing them and giving them, in spite of themselves, soft kisses, warm or cold, which flow and flow, insinuating themselves into their burning limbs.

Will Hunter burn himself? No! He is calm, conserving his beautiful phlegm of an adventurer; he still sees accurately, leaping ditches, avoiding brambles, charged with his heavy burden of human flesh and white satin. He bounds prodigiously, imitating Silence, who escorts them, ever faithful and mute.

"Where are you taking me?" she asks, anxiously.

Hunter holds her against him more tightly, and she suspends herself from his neck, her two slender hands serving as garlands.

"I'm taking you to the sabbat!" he sniggers.

"You're joking! Aren't you taking me home, to your house? I'll follow you, my lover, all the way to the end of the world!"

"Houses are banalities, the end of the world a banality! Me, I've discovered a cavern . . . or rather Silence has discovered it while scratching the earth. You'll see it; it's princely, worthy of you my doomed princess!"

"A cavern? Like brigands, then?"

"Yes, like the thieves that we are!"

The sound of their voices is muted. The fine and penetrating rain dissolves them, absorbs them. One would think that they were simply exchanging thoughts, heart to heart. Sometimes Silence draws nearer, sniffs them with his enormous muzzle and licks them with an expression of sinister bestiality. They arrive at the rock of the Chairs, gliding around the Shepherd's Table. There, behind the summit of the hill, at the place where there seems to be a fissure, the ravine of an ancient stream, Hunter parts the foliage; Silence extends like a phenomenal snake, scratches the earth, remembering, sniffing; a large stone goes to roll down the mossy slope in the direction of the little sacred wood. They penetrate into a sort of sticky funnel, which sucks them in; the rain stops falling, and can be heard pattering up above, on a plane surface.

"Do you know, Madeleine," murmurs Hunter, "that smooth rock known as the Shepherd's Table?"

"Yes. I remember that you appeared to me there one evening, like a god."

"Well, the Shepherd's Table turns; on turning, it brightens to light a corridor . . . I've carved steps myself in the friable terrain, and we're underneath it! We'll have light, because I've prepared a torch."

Breathlessly, Madeleine descends slowly, leaning on the shoulders of her beloved. It is a journey in traditional legend; after having floated in the confused dream of her imagination, she has reached the point of enthusiasm where, the stars being unhooked and the conquest of the sky being a mere game, one goes all the way to the inferno of pleasures to see where the pleasures of Satan are not worth more than those of the angels. A frisson shakes her, a frisson of pride and fortunate fear. She knows everything, but she wants to know even more. She is convinced that she will know more. Hunter asks her to duck down, not to raise her head like a proud bird. She might bump into the tenebrous vaults of his cavern, his realm, under which no one can exist without crawling . . .

The most difficult trajectory is finished; they have arrived on a bed of white sand, sand which one might think is made of pulverized skeletons. It resembles chalk and the dust is fine, pearly, and leaves no residue on the fingers; it has no smell except for a sweet odor of wheat when it is stirred, an insipid odor of gluten flour. Have generation lived there and died there, stifled by the indifference of centuries, along with the seeds or the debris of an immense family of humans stillborn to glory? The cavern is as narrow as a tomb. It is almost spherical, oblong in the form of an egg. Is it a hole dug by some antediluvian animal, round and colossally voluptuous, that has left behind, during its blind capers, its prismatic and snowy viscosities, in the soil and the roof? Or is it the sarcophagus of a king?

In a corner, a torch of yellow wax is burning, fixed upright. A heap of furs, a strange swarm of silky pelts, is rolled up in another corner. Hunter kneels down and spreads out the pelts with caressant, undulating gestures. Soon the cavern is lined, padded, thickened by a splendid variegated fleece. Here it is the back of a panther ocellated with golden poppies on a soot-black background. There it is the breast of a swan whose purity, in the gleam of the torch, takes on pink tints. There it is gray bearskin with blue reflections, yellow marten and silver fox, the skins of lions and the hides of lophophores, like rainbows, ostrich plumes, and even the tail of a peacock expensing in a bouquet of jewelry.

Hunter lifts up Madeleine's dark cloak. She emerges in all her candor of a virginal spouse, orange blossom scatters and her red hair is let down, going to lose itself in a lion's mane. She takes off her little white satin shoes. Her feet of a poor princess are damp through her fine silk stockings. Kneeling down, he kisses them and teases her.

"Oh, the light creature, the silly girl who has let her shoes fall on the path of evil!"

She blushes, collapses, ashamed, on the piled-up fleeces, and huddles there, her eyes shining with curiosity.

"Let's go to sleep," says Hunter, in an imperious but seductive voice, profoundly enamored.

"No! No, I don't want to sleep, I never want to sleep again!" cried Madeleine. "How can one sleep when one is where I am? Oh, dear enchanter that you are, my beloved! Isn't it charming, your realm, my magician? Now that I have visited the gulf where I have thrown myself into the power of your arms . . . I want to go even further! I want to descend even further, ever further, more delightfully low! I don't want either to rise again into the light or to close my eyes. On the contrary, I want to open them boldly to all the infernal marvels that your passion creates for me. If I love you as my mirror, I can't dread seeing myself entire in you! And I'll go as far as crushing my reflection, as far as devouring my person in order to find you behind it, in a limitless beyond where it will only exist any longer in us. No! No sleep! But to die in one another's arms, to enchant one another, in order to no longer know anyone but each other deified . . . !"

Hunter has lain down beside her, his head reposing on the young woman's breast; he has not budged, except that his meager and ivorine hands, his robust fingers, as strong as the death that she is evoking, have squeezed her supple satin-corseted waist. The fabric, suddenly split, has allowed the breasts to spring forth from their white sheath, even whiter because they are veined with azure and flowered with crimson. The strings break; the batiste tears; the skin itself is striped by fingernails. All is joy when he pronounces her name; all is dolor when he touches her. She yields and struggles with equal frenzy . . . but he has not yet had time to see her in all the splendor of her submissive perjury of vicious chaste beauty when a suffocating smoke invades the cavern.

Silence, sprawled in the middle of the corridor, gets up, alarmed, his eyes bulging from their orbits. He flees, abandoning them in a cowardly manner. Hunter has knocked over the torch without even noticing, his lips riveted to Madeleine's, and the fleeces, the furs, the feathers and the hides are ablaze, crackling, sizzling and throwing off sparks, spreading a sinister odor of burned flesh . . .

This time, Madeleine reaches the bottom of Hell; she will be immured, alive, in a furnace, and Hunger probably desires it thus. She writhes, utters a scream, and faints . . .

. . . Oh, dreamless sleep of mystery accomplished, repose of senses forever appeased, slumber of defunct vanities, slumber as sad as the road of death . . . !

When the young woman awoke, the first thing that astonished her was the curve of a curtain advancing over her bed. A wan half-light illuminated her room, her little former room of a demoiselle, become her sanctuary of a wife. A man, his back turned to the bed was sitting before a table, writing, his head supported by his hand. Clad in a light, brightly-colored morning garment, he appeared to be at home, his hair slightly untidy, his underwear crumpled.

Madeleine raised herself on her elbow, while the silk of her bedclothes made a silky song around her.

"Am I alive?" she said, in a curt tone

"Oh, it's not your fault, in any case," replied Edmond Sellier, turning round with a smile that unclenched his lips.

He was very pale, but retained a flame in the depths of his sensual brown eyes, velveted by amour. He came close to her, moved the curtain aside, and seized her hands, which he brought together with a grateful kiss.

"Oh, Madeleine, you're an alarming little woman!"

"Explain to me?" she stammered, hardly breathing, for they had doubtless been surprised out there, behind the hill, on emerging from their furnace . . . but for what could the husband be thanking her?

"I'll tell you later, since you've forgotten."

"No, right away, I beg you; I order you to. How am I here, lying down . . . in front of you?"

"Listen, my darling; you locked yourself in here yesterday evening, little fool, fearing I know not what brutality on my part—me, who loves you enough to break my head at your feet if that would be useful to you! Yes, you locked yourself in with a key; then, inflicting the

231

most revolting humiliation on me, on such an evening, you fled when I knocked discreetly on your door. You ran away from home—from *my* home—without waiting either for a prayer or a gesture of impatience. And you were found, after two hours of searching, lying on the path through the rocks, in a horrible state, soaked by rain, your hair streaming, your corsage open, torn by one of your abominable crises of nerves! Think, Madeleine! Two hours, two mortal hours of desperate searching, during which I daren't call anyone, out of respect for you and for me! Oh, Madeleine! I brought you back thinking that you were dead, imagining that you had been to throw yourself from the height of the rocks to the bottom of the mountain! And what was worse is that you recounted, in incoherent phrases, a story of a fire! You were burning! You were choking . . . you wanted to descend into Hell . . . ever further down, always further down. My little adored, look me in the face. Do you remember, at least, the story of the fire!"

Singularly, Edmond bit his lips as he reached the conclusion of his narration.

"And then?" cried Madeleine, putting up her scattered hair.

"And then . . . I undressed you, all the more gladly because you declared to me that you were too hot, in spite of the downpour you'd received. I put you to bed . . . and I hugged you for the rest of the night, as, I believe, one hugs naughty little children. Oh, Madeleine, will you always hate me?"

He knelt down beside the bed, still holding her feverish hands. Why, then, did he have that enigmatic smile of regret?

"I'm ill; I wanted you," she murmured, plunging back into the lace of her pillows.

He was silent. Their gazes collided, anguished by a pain they could not say, but the tenderness enclosed, involuntarily, in their senses, suddenly overflowed their eyelids and they started to weep. The physician, a calculator and philosopher, determined not only to cure her physical neurosis, stepped back in the presence of the abyss of mental neurosis revealed to him by the great drowned eyes of his wife; nothing remained of him but the lover, already not believing in the reality of the possession, jealous again of an *unknown* that he suspected in her . . . and which he had perhaps introduced himself.

Madeleine recovered first. "You haven't kept your promise," she said. "I'll avenge myself."

And that was the last word of their wedding night.

XVI

THEY were both sitting on the terrace. Dusk was falling and the clumps of box-trees ornamenting the paths of their garden along the flower-beds filled with blooms, took on the appearance of black snakes undulating around baskets full of jewels. Under the hazel trees a toad could be heard, whose lamentable *toue-toue* wearied Madeleine.

"Oh, make it shut up, I beg you!" she said, increasingly ill-at-ease.

"For that it would be necessary to flush it out," murmured Edmond, standing up and searching the shadows with his eyes.

"I beg you . . . truly."

"Me too—but it isn't an evil beast, a toad."

"You don't have to explain . . . just prevent it crying out, that's all."

Determined to crush it if he could find it, since it permitted itself to annoy his young wife, the doctor searched for the toad patiently, shifting the foliage and tapping the ground. The animal doubtless ran away, for there was a minute of bleak silence. Edmond came back to sit beside Madeleine, who drank in the breeze, panting.

"You ought to take off your corset, my dear," he said, caressing her hair. "It isn't reasonable to tighten it like that in your situation, when one thinks that before our marriage you never wore a corset, and that . . ."

She interrupted him harshly.

"I intend to keep my figure. Anyway, it isn't certain."

"For a little fool like you, of course, but for a doctor, it's another matter. I believe that in"—he counted on his fingers—"in, give me a little help, four or five months . . . Let's see, what shall we call him?"

She shrugged her shoulders. "We've only been married for a short time."

Edmond started to laugh wholeheartedly. "All right, let's talk about something else. Now your wretched toad is protesting."

The same *toue* resounded, more lamentably. One might have thought it the voice of a dying man moaning in the shadow.

"Oh!" exclaimed Madeleine. "I want to go inside."

"No, darling, a moment longer," sighed Sellier, drawing her to his bosom. "We're hardly ever alone at home, because of your family. Understand, then, my dear love of a cruel little wife, how painful it is for a husband who adores you perpetually to have witnesses. I can't speak ill of the joys of family life, since I desire to teach them to you and found one, but . . . I'm enraged! At dinner it's impossible to talk to you: Madame Bordes recites her eternal stories of spiritism, to which your father forces me to listen. In the afternoon I'm imprisoned out there with a surly society of invalids or with a mother who makes eyes at me, complaining that he gives the impression of condemning her to misery; and at night, under the pretext of a headache, you send me to sleep in a room other than yours. It's a heart-breaking regime!

He lamented very softy, laughing at the sad things he said, and the toad accompanied him dully with its monotonous note, like a tear falling into a fragile glass, already cracked, that might shatter into a thousand fragments at any second.

"My God," added Edmond, discouraged to see her face pale and hostile, "if we were richer, how far we could go!"

And he thought, his heart heavy, about their meager budget, equilibrated as best they could, of a maidservant who could replace Madame Bordes—although she had not offered—about the black curtains in the drawing room that had not been removed because of the expense, about the mourning and mediocrity that surrounded them everywhere, causing them to live in poor intelligence when he would have liked to take the young neurotic away from all the bustle and create an atmosphere of well-being for her in all regards. Instead of that, perhaps she was beginning to wonder where the realizations were of the happiness he had made her glimpse during the engagement.

"Why have you married me, being so poor?" she said, in an aggressive tone.

"Because you are yourself the true treasure . . . only, if you deprive me of yourself, what will I become?"

He sought her lips, which she tried to keep away from him.

"No, leave me alone, Edmond. I can hear someone. Someone's spying on us from behind the wall of the terrace."

"What an idea! You're always afraid that someone is watching us. Isn't it quite natural to see a husband kissing his wife? Anyway, I told Saturnin not to come this evening for the flowers; I'll water them myself tomorrow; it will amuse me."

"I repeat that I can hear someone walking."

"Bah! A passer-by. You're stifling, Madeleine! Would you like me to loosen your laces slightly?"

He tried to smile, and felt two little hands repelling him, as if quivering with a sudden disgust. Every time she testified aversion to him, she became more tender and milder almost immediately, seeking forgiveness for an impulse of hatred which was doubtless only involuntary. She ended up placing her head on his breast.

"I make you very unhappy, don't I, Edmond?"

She had great difficulty getting used to addressing him as *tu*, and they mingled *vous* and *tus* in a comical jargon of quarreling lovers, often much closer to one another when they said *vous*. The young man refreshed his burning lips in the golden waves of her hair.

Suddenly, a furious cry tore the air. It was so frenetic and so loud in the religious peace of an autumn evening that all the echoes of the valley roared, and the poor toad must have been pierced by it, killed, annihilated amid its clump of grass. Its plaintive *toue* expired, nothing wept any longer, and it was as if they found themselves again in the depths of a tomb brutally resealed.

Edmond stood up, sustaining Madeleine, whose teeth were chattering with terror.

"My God, what's that? One might think it were you're aunt's voice."

"Yes," she stammered, clinging to his shoulder. "I believe it's her."

Edmond expected anything at all since his introduction into the Deslandes family, but his multiple anxieties on the subject of Madeleine had not permitted him to study anything except the clouds wandering over her pale forehead, From time to time he had certainly perceived that Aunt Julia seemed more somber than usual. She dreamed for entire hours before her Ludovic, or talked to herself as she moved along the corridors, absorbed by an obsession. He put her manner of acting down to the old woman's irascible character, disturbed in her monomania of avarice, and scarcely paid any heed to it when he saw her direct a black look at him like those she launched at Madeleine.

"It's necessary to know what's up, though!" he murmured, clutching the young woman against him more tenderly.

"No, no, don't go, Edmond!" Madeleine exclaimed, prey to an indescribable terror. "There are things it's better not to know . . . never . . . never!"

Further cries, raucous and jerky, traversed the garden, reaching them through the wide open window of the funereal drawing room, in which the pretty trinkets, the modern furniture and the cheerful fabrics that had been added, thanks to the amorous husband, were extinguishing like vain lights in an overly dense night. In spite of his touching efforts it remained the sumptuous crypt that they had always known, even retaining a certain reek of its former odor of putrescence.

"You're going to stay here very sagely, and not budge until I come back to find you, my darling," Edmond said, quite emotional—for his presentiments as a physician warned him that a danger more frightful than death was lying in wait for them in their home.

"I want to go with you . . . don't leave me," stammered Madeleine.

"Oh, definitely not, especially in your condition. I forbid it."

He extracted himself from her arms and ran toward the house. On the way he encountered Jacques Deslandes, coming from the stable, where he went every evening to offer a sugar-lump to his son-in-law's horse—the distraction of an egotistical man whom humanity no longer interested.

"Did you hear?" he said, rolling his eyes.

"Is that Madame Bordes?" asked Sellier.

"You're joking! If we were in winter, I'd think it more likely that a wolf had got into the drawing room!" Prudently, he put himself behind his son-in-law, and the latter leaned through the window.

At first he could not see anything abnormal. Everything was black, as usual. The medium's table, ordinarily in the center of the room, was in its place, directly beneath the ceiling-rose, from which a little crystal chandelier hung, which Sellier had installed himself by hooking it on to the large copper ring that usually scintillated up there. But on examining the table more closely, it seemed to him that bright objects, like prisms, were heaped on top of it, covering it with a vague cloak of stars.

In a loud voice, he called: "Are you there, Madame Bordes?"

There was no reply. The howls had ceased, nothing was perceptible any longer but a low, tremulous breath. Suddenly, the form of a monstrous beast emerged from the shadow of the wall-hangings, and bounded on to the sofa, and then on to the armchairs, growling and whining in a strangled tone. Edmond shivered. Might Deslandes have been right, perchance, to mention a wolf?

The doctor seized his father-in-law's wrist

"Watch the windows while I make a tour in order to go in through the door. Above all, don't let Madeleine approach, I beg you."

Desolate at having to fulfill a suspect mission, Deslandes clung to the wall.

The door of the drawing room opened without any difficulty, and Sellier, armed with a lamp, penetrated into the vast black room. Then, by the raw light of his lamp, which he held up as far as possible, he recognized Madame Julia Bordes, his aunt, *who was walking on all fours!* As soon as she perceived him, she crouched down, parading her hands, violently clenched, over an armchair, seemingly unable to stand up again.

"Yes," she said, in a guttural accent that was not her own. "I tell you that *it moved . . . I saw it move*, and it planted its claws in my skull; it has claws like a bird, like an owl!"

Astounded, Edmond put his lamp down on an item of furniture and murmured: "Let's see, Madame Bordes, where is it, the thing that has claws?"

And involuntarily, he looked at the unfortunate woman's hands, now hooked, her fingernails, which one might have thought miraculously elongated by an occult power, an evil spirit having metamorphosed the old witch into a savage beast for having forgotten some rite during one of her conjurations. She ground her teeth.

"It moved, it moved! It turned!" she repeated, ready to pounce upon Sellier if he tried to belie her.

"Your table? But doesn't it always turn, my poor Madame Bordes, since you're a medium of the first order?" replied Edmond.

And while speaking in his most affectionate tone, the physician hurried in the direction of the windows, closed them solidly, detached the attachments of the curtains, and plunged the miserable creature into a salutary isolation, in the commencement of her eternal night.

Then he examined Ludovic and reconstituted the scene that had determined the fit of that abominable furious madness.

Sitting facing the table, imposing her hands on it with violent efforts of will, which, fatally, had caused an explosion in that brain of a naïve schemer, who had received full in the nape of the neck, at the moment when she had certainly least expected it, the little crystal chandelier, fallen from the ceiling. He picked up the large copper ring from the midst of the glass pendants, and was able to observe that it was corroded with verdigris.

The accident proved to be quite simple, although it had strangely complicated a situation that was already too tense.

Sellier went to Madame Bordes and tried to lift her up.

"My poor woman," he said, very gently. "It's necessary to calm you down. Tomorrow we'll take stock."

But she launched her right hand at him with the agility of a wild beast defending itself, and tore his sleeve from the shoulder to the elbow. Convinced henceforth, Edmond withdrew, carrying his lamp, fearing that he might feel that hand grip his back. He closed and locked the drawing room door and slid the key onto his pocket. Deslandes was prowling along the corridor, shivering with horror. He had seen the silhouette of his sister through the window, walking on all fours, and could not comprehend that that beast with hooked claws was the same woman with whom he had dined that evening.

"Is she mad, then? It's true madness?" he sobbed.

"Yes," said Sellier, harshly, exasperated to think that that monster was also Madeleine's aunt. "It's a matter of a very rare case; your sister is afflicted by lycanthropy, Monsieur Deslandes. You ought to have warned me."

"My God! My God! But it's the first time I've seen such a thing . . . it's just taken hold of her, my good Monsieur Sellier, Oh! Oh! Ly-can-thro-py! Don't abandon me my dear doctor . . . we're doomed! Ly-can-thro-py!"

And he collapsed on a chair, hiccupping the barbaric word, prostrate, as if he had been shown an entire legion of howling demons dancing in the bosom of the flames of Hell. The doctor took pity, however, on that poor solemn face inundated by tears.

"That means that the . . . invalid believes she has become . . . an animal . . . Anyway, we'll see, since you assure me that it's the first time . . ."

"What are we going to do?"

"Without hesitation, Monsieur Deslandes, lock her up tomorrow; I'll consult my colleagues in the town. We can't care for a dangerous lunatic here."

"Lock up my sister, my poor Julia! You can't think so! Can't she be saved any other way?"

"No! And then, I have my wife, who is pregnant, to save, which is quite sufficient for me. See! Do you hear? She's going to finish Madeleine!"

A raucous howl pierced the walls, quavering and heart-rending, alternately shrill and deep, seeming to rise from an abyss. Deslandes blocked his ears, almost mad with fear himself, while his son-in-law, atrociously upset, threw himself into the garden calling for his wife. He no longer found her on the terrace. She had fled, probably clawed by the superstitious vision of her famous *three-legged wolf*, the fantastic wolf that had haunted her as a little girl during her fevers of growth.

Yes, she had gone! A cold sweat moistened Edmond's temples. His formal intention to rid himself of the human beast that howled its song of death at him increased to such a point that he had a desire to retrace his steps in order to finish it immediately and strangle her in his robust healer's arms. He went back and searched the house from the cellar to the grain-loft. Madeleine was nowhere to be found.

The evening went by in frightful anxieties. He put Saturnin, their domestic, on sentry duty before the windows of the drawing room, which was carefully barricaded, recommending his father-in-law to put his bed across the door and leave, no longer being able to stay there. He ran through the streets of the town and went to find his mother, thinking that she might perhaps have thought of taking refuge there; but his mother received him sniggering.

"It doesn't astonish me," she said to him. "Madame Bordes has only got what she deserves. She offended me cruelly. God has punished her. God is just! No, my child, I haven't seen your wife, and I hope that she never comes here. I don't like madwomen or profligates. Go, go! You haven't yet told the entire chaplet! Providence has many others in reserve for you!"

Those sorts of consolations ordinarily left the young man indifferent, but in this circumstance, he too nearly howled all his despair. He departed again, half-drunk with rage, striking his fists against the walls. He escaped in the direction of the open country and traversed the meadows, sounding the bushes, the thickets and the bramble-patches, climbing up to the rocks, descending from the rocks to the little wood and stopping to call out her name, which the mocking echoes sent back to him. There was no moon; the night was obscure, and he turned in the path as the furious woman must be turning, down there, in the black gulf of that accursed drawing room. Momentarily, his soul of an honest skeptic weakening, he wondered if, truly, the beautiful hallucinated Madeleine had not been right to say to him, one day, that fear is the commencement of the supernatural—for, being afraid, atrociously afraid, of losing her, he ended up imagining that he saw her standing on the Shepherd's Table, her hair floating around her like a meteor.

Harassed by fatigue, he decided, however, to return. Dawn was blanching the hill when he opened the garden gate. Saturnin was asleep on the window-sill. He woke him up and the peasant rubbed his eyes confusedly.

"Have you seen Madame?"

"Who? The madwoman?"

"No! My wife."

"Oh, the other one," muttered the peasant, only half-awake and not embarrassed to give his intimate opinion. "Yes, I've seen her. She entered a little while ago through her own window."

Sellier did not waste time abusing him. He knew, in fact, that Madeleine conserved the deplorable mania of leaping through the casement of their bedroom. But since, this time, she had come back instead of fleeing . . . he ran to join her.

"You! You! My darling! My love! How desperate you made me. Where have you come from? Answer me!"

He found her in their sanctuary, next to their bed, leaning on the bedhead, her face confused, diaphanously pale.

"I believe I'm going to die!" she said, suffocating.

"Die? Why? Quickly, quickly! Get undressed and go to bed, I won't scold you. It's natural to be afraid. Me too, I've been afraid! We'll explain ourselves later. I adore you!"

He took off her clothes, kissed her hands, removed her ankle-boots, her stockings, and as he leaned over to kiss her feet he perceived that she was bleeding in long crimson streams.

"But you've had a miscarriage!" he cried, heartbroken.

"It's possible. I don't know. I don't like to occupy myself with dirty things!"

The sweet hope of paternity that he caressed was, above all, in his view, the redemption of the wife by the mother, and she called it *a dirty thing!*

"And . . . the . . . the . . . the child . . . our child?" stammered Sellier, bewildered.

"Oh," she said, in a tranquil tone, "*a dog has eaten it!*"

She could not admit to him, however, that on the terrace, at her aunt's howls of a wounded she-wolf, Hunter had appeared to her and had said to her, biting her neck in a sinister caress:

"Now I need your child for my dog."

XVII

EXHAUSTED, her eyes staring, her epidermis seemingly laid bare by the glacial air, sunk in a kind of somnolent unconsciousness, Madeleine clung to her window-sill. She could no longer go out, but she wanted to see him again, the handsome vagabond of amour incessantly prowling around their dwelling. Would he come this far? Had she not been too late in evoking him in the same place where she had seen him for the first time? The cold chased him away, that delicate being, and had he not already run far away from her, far from the criminal who had obeyed him in such a cowardly manner?

Her nerves, remaining, in spite of her weakness the dominators of her poor martyrized flesh, she ended up, by dint of thinking and dreaming, giving herself a violent fever. She wanted to see him again, so passionately that droplets of sweat pearled on her pale forehead. She did not doubt his fidelity, although she doubted her own. Only, since she was very ill, her husband's medical reflections tormented her because, as her body became increasingly anemiated, her brain became less powerful in conceiving the impossible.

Her fatigued hands fell back momentarily. She lay back in an armchair, closing her eyes. The bell of the neighboring hospice was ringing slowly, and she shivered.

A faint noise reached her from the terrace. Someone leapt over the wall. The branches of the hazel trees were shaking out there; the frail branches were stripped by the November wind, but it was not the wind, for the atmosphere was calm; the moon was shining with the serene limpidity of a bright eye. Madeleine draped herself in her black lace shawl in order to dissimulate the whiteness of her nightgown. It might also be the domestic, Saturnin, making a routine round. Doctor Sellier sometimes posted him in the garden when he feared a flight on the part of his poor fearful darling.

The image of her consternated husband softened her. Oh, he loved her with an immensely devoted amour! And when he was obliged to absent himself, under the threat, if he neglected his clients, of no longer being able to collect the money necessary to the satisfaction of her caprices, he always went away full of an anguish that caused him to be pitied. Yes, veritably that man loved her! And he was *not the other*. Or had she not had the courage to confess everything to him . . . ?

Madeleine opened her eyes again. He would no longer return, *the other!* It was over! Would she have the patience, the strength, to wait until next spring? She dragged herself to the door and listened, her heart oppressed. Nothing troubled the great silence of the corridor. Her father was asleep in his own room, as he slept every day, for since he had locked his sister away in an asylum of furious lunatics, the old man had not recovered from his confusion. He circled his room like a brute seeking a corner in which to brood his drunkenness.

Her mother-in-law must also be asleep—her mother-in-haw lived with them now, having deigned to forgive, insinuating herself into that tomb-like house in order to double her son's despair with a hypocritical and bleak resignation . . .

Everything was asleep. She went back to the window, leaning on the furniture, and then let down her hair with a rapid gesture that revived memories of former triumphs.

Hunter was there, standing before her, brightly illuminated by the moon and escorted by Silence, who was crawling behind him.

"Madeleine," he said in a curt voice, "the epoch of our adieux is getting closer, and for many evenings I have been waiting for you in vain on the mountain!"

"I nearly died," the young woman replied, a radiance of joy illuminating her drawn features nevertheless.

"Yes, I know," said Hunter. "The physician has forbidden you to go out—but the physician is your husband. What he orders or forbids you to do ought not to concern us."

She had a moment of stupor. It was odious to reproach her for missing a rendezvous when he risked killing her by demanding a simple stroll! A flame of anger wiped out the flash of joy. She looked at him like a queen encountering a wayward vassal. "You don't belong to me then as much as I belong to you?"

"I'm free; I want a free lover!"

Silence was sprawling on the path, hiding his muzzle between his enormous paws; Madeleine shivered in disgust.

"And you have the audacity to bring me that dog?" she added, leaning over. "You could have strangled him so that I would not see him again."

"Death is a sacred thing! It doesn't suit me to profane it in any fashion. And if you fear it so much for yourself, why talk about distributing it to others?"

"It's a matter of a dog, Hunter," she stammered, having understood that he was making allusion to the little soul in embryo that Silence's formidable jaw had crushed, offering it to himself as a last meal before immortalizing his hideousness.

"I love my dog; he's a faithful servant of whom I have need for work I find it repugnant to carry out myself." He had a strange smile. "Silence excuses my presence here, Madeleine."

She contemplated Hunter very attentively while he approached the window. Nothing appeared to have changed in him, and while she had suffered cruelly he had conserved his usual appearance of an impassive seducer. He wore the same dark costume, of the neutral tint that was simultaneously black and gray, almost shiny, as if worn away by a prolonged sojourn on marble, and where she could not recall ever having discovered previously the evidence of stitches. No line could be seen of his linen; his neck, of such rare flexibility, emerged from the dark collar of the garment as pure as a lily; the folds of his cloak wound very flexibly around his thin limbs, molding them with the surety of wet cloth. On touching that cloak one had the sensation of palpating thick silk, a kind of heavy, unctuous damask, which might have been woven in silk and avian down, perhaps in mud! His shoes were dusty, so dusty that they were confounded with the sand of the garden pathways, and thus, planted upright, without feet, one could have believed that he was undulating above the soil, emanating from the earth but not treading on it.

Madeleine surrounded his shoulders with her weakened arms; she kissed his forehead, still as smooth as the magic mirror in which she loved to reflect herself, body and heart, and immediately she was under the direct charm of his evil spell, identified herself with the baleful person that he was playing, no longer having any idea of finding him culpable, since he deigned to absolve her by returning.

"I assure you," Hunter said to her in a mocking tone, "that you're wrong to squander this hour in quarreling. I'm leaving . . ."

The young man's eye, whose inferior rings, blurred by bistre, went to join the arc of the brown eyebrows in a gentle curve, bruising them with voluptuousness; he smiled in the utmost depths of his eyes, and that happened as a ripple formed by a snake stirring in the depths arrives at the surface of the water.

She moaned: "I adore you! But you no longer love me"—making an echo of words that her husband gasped between the arms of his insensible wife.

She felt, however, quite well, almost happy, imagining that she was plunging into a cold bath after a terrible course during which she had walked on hot coals. He amused himself enlacing her fingers with his, one by one, flexing them, clenching them, trying to stick them together. He had not changed, for he must be thinking about something sinister.

"I've brought you flowers," he said in a whisper. "Look; there are heliotropes and vervain."

She sniffed the bouquet avidly and could not help looking, through the thin odorous branches, at Silence, who was licking her fingernails.

"My God! Where shall I put them in order that my husband doesn't find them in my room?"

"I'll take them away if you wish. I've been able, in one night, to efface the violets out there in the hollow of the blasted tree, in order not to awaken the suspicions of a jealous man."

"Or in order not to leave a single trace of your presence? Sooner or later, we might well be surprised, Hunter! And then, a bullet for you, a bullet for me, and that will be the apotheosis of this troubled life!"

"You'll receive both bullets," he replied, laconically.

"What a nasty pleasantry! You want me to die . . . You wouldn't try to defend me?"

"Yes! I'll place myself before you and you'll receive both bullets."

She burst into strident laughter. "Yes, yes! I'll receive both bullets. It's agreed!" Trembling, she added: "Stop this dog from licking my fingernails, then!"

"Nothing sticks to the fingernails better than dried blood, Madeleine."

He sat down on the window-sill, and she hid her face in his bosom.

"Don't weep, my fearful beauty! Look at these flowers instead. I've brought them to you from very far away, I picked them while they were asleep, in the dead of night. I separated them from their stems merely by pronouncing your name, and they came into my hands, climbed over me, madly enthused, full of dew or tears, sunlight or shadow, hearts swollen with the perfume of despair; they came in spite of their occupations of little slyboots, very attached to the thin filaments of their existence, piling up in my arms, which didn't desire so many, and they forced me—me, the sad sire—to serve them to you as a joyous offering, in order that you could help them exhale their souls to the stars, their souls of little beings dying of thirst! You always delight in a crime, being a woman! Aren't you glad to respire their last sigh?"

He cradled them with the sound of his musical voice, kissing her hair, cutting off her head under his caresses like the head of a flower, and crimsoning the superbly insolent mouth of her poor bloodless face of an invalid.

"Hunter! Take me away! I'm no longer afraid of your kisses. Take me away with the flowers that want to die. I'll follow you anywhere. Don't abandon me here, in the forgetfulness of winter. I'd become furious here and I'd imitate my Aunt Julia, who has gone to howl at death in the depths of a padded cell. I can no longer love anyone but you! I no longer want to share myself . . . it's too dangerous. Do you remember our wedding night? An evil spell weights upon us in this land. Let's go away! Why have you taken back the child, even if it was yours? Another horrible doubt that I daren't fathom! Well, answer me; must I die of regret?"

"Perhaps."

"Why, yes, why would you have taken back something you had given me . . . voluntarily, I suppose?"

"Libertine!"

She rebelled.

"Enough mockery, Hunter! You don't have any right to treat me so lightly, If I reason, one day, prophet of doom, or I compare, I'll finally be able to extract you from me as you have extracted the fruit that I carried. Let's recapitulate! You're a somewhat deceptive dream, after all. You've tamed me without my knowing with what end it was necessary for me to incline under your power. Your power!" She uttered a bitter laugh. "You've amused yourself cruelly, making me ride my chimeras, an egotistical philosopher who didn't enquire as to whether the freshness of the nocturnal path might eventually lead the poor wanderer to lose her appetite for the sweetness of life. Atheistic, you stole my sign of the cross from me, Blasé, you stole amour from me—that amour of which I only wanted to admit the chaste; you have, on the contrary, proved to me that it would be perverse. Senses, heart and brain, you have tripled everything in me, and you call that recreating the myth of primitive amour, the love of God, a single amour in three persons! You have declared to me that at one time. I think, when chaos reigned in the waves and the undivided mud, communicating under the species of seeds, the hearts of plants or the sexes of animals, lurked a being formed of three essences, which contemplated itself in noble admiration; it was this monster, you told me: you, me and my husband. You praised that absurd divinity as being the most real of all, and that toward which all the aspiration of woman go. You were making fun of me! You made me kill my child because I had to doubt the name of his father. You took away from me the sad joy of weeping with shame over the swaddling-clothes, when the vilest of prostitutes claims what consoles. You have made me measure the stupidity of my parents as if with compasses. Nothing remains to me of good on the earth. I am nothing more than an automaton devoid of entrails that one extends on furs or on flowers, according to the season, in order to exaggerate its puerility or its breakdown. You have shown me, in you, a man of stone who only loves himself, in passing via my admiration, and who reflects me as in an accursed prism, complaisantly detailing my faults and my qualities through the thousand facets of my pride! And now you come to cry 'Libertine!' at me. Nothing more of good remains to me on earth? Yes, truly, I still have vice, which is you . . . I forbid you to abandon me! And also the art of lying, which is my unique distraction! Of all my defunct ingenuousness, I retain the facility of betrayal. I want to use it, I lie ingenuously, as a lamb grazes. There are a thousand women in me. donning my dress by turns in order to salute, smile or weep, and truly, I cannot be happy without lying. But can't you guess that sometimes I lie to you as to the other? Tenebrous beau, who distances me from your lofty intellectual superiority, do you think sometimes about what I do in order to divide treason equitably between the two of you? Or have you finally married me off in order that another man can substitute for your . . . physical inferiority?"

Angrily, Madeleine suddenly met his eyes with her suddenly fulgurant gaze. He lowered his eyelids, appearing to collect himself in order to respond.

"Let's go! The hour has come to talk, Hunter. You want to internalize yourself in me by doubt. Now, I'm on the point of no longer doubting. Can the secret of your cerebral force also be that of your impotence? To whom did I belong on my wedding night: to you, my lover, or to him, my husband? You don't love me . . . my God!"—she added, twisting her arms—"I'm dying of it . . . I'm still so young, and I'd so like to live! No, it isn't sufficient for me to be loved like a sister or an idol . . . I simply want to be loved like a woman. I abdicate; I'm returning my crown of the Princess of Darkness!"

"Don't tempt me, Madeleine," he said, in a dull voice. "It's futile. Your love, whether it doubts or believes, is sufficient for me; the Prince of Darkness will never abdicate. I want your soul beyond death . . . and when you cease to doubt it will be too late for you to take it back. What does it matter to me that you accuse me of a human impotence, if I possess the superhuman power of Satan?"

"Man or demon, I desire you, Hunter, and I shall have you. I know you're jealous; well, if you still refuse yourself, go away, leave me entirely to the man who loves me enough to try to make me live."

Hunter tried to pull away.

"Ah!" cried Madeleine, enclosing him in a passionate embrace. "Am I not more beautiful, then, illness having entirely withered my body, and can my body not redeem my soul? Here! I'm drawing back *the limit*, so close your eyes if you aren't the one I love!"

The lace shawl fell, and with the black shawl the peignoir of white muslin. Madeleine surged forth, stark naked, svelte, suddenly magnified in her agonizing thinness, like a pale amorous phantom.

"Madeleine! Can't you hear the carriage? Shut up! Your husband has returned!" Hunter replied, whose eyes were shining singularly and whose long and livid hands were agitating anxiously on his cloak.

"Coward! Coward!" exclaimed the young woman, panicking. "Yes! Coward who is afraid of the other. Ah! Let him return, my husband, and let him kill you, if it's possible for him to kill a dead man! For I hate you, brain-stealer! I hate you, liar of amour! Let him come and let him take back my body with my soul. I don't want to play cadaver any longer, and my bed isn't made to be a cemetery! Yes, I prefer him to you!"

She had cried so loudly that the dog lifted his enormous head, examining his master as if awaiting an order.

"Silence!" growled Hunter, grinding his teeth, circling Madeleine's delicate neck with his long bony fingers.

Had he wanted to make her shut up? Had he wanted to kill her? She would never know; the final doubt subsisted eternally. It seemed to her that the ferocious eyes of the dog shone in the depths of Hunter's brilliant eyes, the charming and dreamy eyes of the elegant seducer, and that the heavy weight of a man's knee or an animal's skull pressed down on her breast of a poor invalid. Then she fell backwards, her neck almost wrung.

A carriage did indeed stop at the perron. Sellier, ever anxious when he left his wife in the care of his mother, came back, heart hammering and throat dry. It was midnight, and she was probably sleeping—badly—perhaps coughing?

He saw her lying on the ground, only veiled by her splendid red hair, facing the open window.

"That's how she's guarded!" he roared. "This is the state they put her for me! Oh, they've murdered her for me! Madeleine! My adored little wife! What have you done? My God! Why are you out of bed?"

He closed the window, fell upon the lovely body, too light, and laid it in their bed with the precautions of a nurse.

Madeleine unstick her eyelids and murmured in a hoarse voice, without being able to turn her head in his direction: "I'm well. Oh, I'm very well! Where's my bouquet?"

"What bouquet?"

"Someone must have taken my bouquet! But feel my hands! They're embalmed by heliotrope and vervain . . . it's proof . . ."

"Poor dear child! More odorous hallucinations! Your hands smell good—like your hands, that's all! Can you tell me why the window has been opened, on such a cold night?"

"You mustn't be annoyed," hiccupped Madeleine. "I sent your mother away because she was sleepy this evening. I was stifling . . . I had to have air . . . air."

He warmed her up with his kisses, weeping quietly, but not losing his head, not forgetting any of the necessary cares, massaging her gently over her entire body, which he wrapped in a shroud of caresses. She had been condemned for a long time, he knew full well, but truly, she had been finished off in that house where everyone agreed to find it natural that she was mad because of simple crises of hysteria. Oh, if she had not had the crises, if she had not had the miscarriage, if she had not shed all that blood on unknown roads!

Every time he came back, he sent her away sicker, for every time he clasped her against him he did not see her at all, dreamed that she was much better, that she was breathing and smiling more easily. He stayed for an hour, prostrate at the foot of the bed, praying to he knew not what God to render her, to work the miracle that he could not accomplish and that no one in the world could accomplish.

The moon, just then, passed the corner of the house. A complete obscurity invaded their room, the young woman's narrow bedroom become, by virtue of its caprice, a mysterious nuptial nest where one bumped into all sorts of soft and somber draperies. Sellier, abandoning her little clenched hands, which he moistened with tears, headed toward the table to search for the lamp, but did not have time to reach it. Madeleine sat up in the middle of her bed, throwing back the covers, seemingly illuminating the black background of the alcove with the reflection of the conflagration of her hair.

"There's someone behind the window, someone beckoning to me," she gasped, holding out her arms.

She turned her face over her shoulder and did not look at that window; however, there was such fear in her gesture that she leaned toward the panes.

"No, Madeleine, there's no one there!"

He listened for a second.

Suddenly, in the great silence, the faint howl of a dog resounded, coming from above, falling from the summit of the nearby mountain, and a hoarse cry responded from the depths of the alcove.

"The mute dog that howls! It knows that I'm going to die! Edmond, Edmond, save me!"

Putting her hands to her twisted neck, she fell back, strangling in furious hiccups that resembled barking. Sellier covered her with his body, as if to protect her against that imaginary animal howling *so really* through the mountains, and she stiffened in his arms. Much more rapidly than another man, he had the certainty that it was finished, because he was both the man who cared for her and the man who certified the death. Mechanically, he recoiled, separated himself from her immediately, in order no longer to see the still-phosphorescent stars of her terrible eyes, forever fixed; he huddled in a corner, repeating:

"And I'll remain alone, all alone . . . in the darkness!"

A PARTIAL LIST OF SNUGGLY BOOKS